Also by Adena Halpern

29
The Ten Best Days of My Life

pinch me

ADENA HALPERN

A TOUCHSTONE BOOK
Published by Simon & Schuster
New York London Toronto Sydney

Touchstone
A Division of Simon & Schuster, Inc.
1230 Avenue of the Americas
New York, NY 10020

First Touchstone trade paperback edition July 2011

TOUCHSTONE and colophon are registered trademarks of Simon & Schuster, Inc.

For information about special discounts for bulk purchases, please contact Simon & Schuster Special Sales at 1-866-506-1949 or business@simonandschuster.com.

The Simon & Schuster Speakers Bureau can bring authors to your live event. For more information or to book an event contact the Simon & Schuster Speakers Bureau at 1-866-248-3049 or visit our website at www.simonspeakers.com.

Designed by Renata Di Biase

Manufactured in the United States of America

10 9 8 7 6 5 4 3 2 1

Library of Congress Cataloging-in-Publication Data

Halpern, Adena.
  Pinch me / Adena Halpern.
    p. cm.
  "A Touchstone book."
1. Single women—Fiction. 2. Dreams—Fiction. I. Title.
  PS3608.A5487P56 2011
  813'.6—dc22   2010051369

ISBN 978-1-4391-7114-1
ISBN 978-1-4391-7115-8 (ebook)

In loving memory of my darling dad,
Dr. Barry Halpern (1928–2010)
I miss you every day.

pinch
me

1.

Never marry a man unless he's short, bald, fat, stupid, and treats you badly." In my head, I hear the words my grandmother, Dolly, has been saying for years. *"And above all else, if you find yourself in love with a good man, run for your life!"*

This what I'm thinking as Gogo gets down on one knee at the top of the Eiffel Tower in Paris and presents me with a three-karat emerald-cut ring.

Gogo.

Handsome with a full head of hair, treats me like a queen, summa cum laude Harvard Medical School graduate: Gogo.

Gogo.

The good man I'm madly in love with.

I can't really hear what Gogo is saying, but it sounds like something to the effect of *"You're the most beautiful person I've ever met, both inside and out . . . you're the woman of my dreams . . . Will you do me the honor of spending the rest of your life with me?"* I'm pretty sure that's what he's saying. My head is clouded with all those times my mother and grandmother sat me down and warned me that men are the enemy.

"The good ones are no good!" I hear my mother, Selma, shouting. *"Sure, they start out so nice and proper and they want to give you their hearts. Trust me, it's all a ruse!"*

"So will you marry me?" I hear Gogo say as I snap out of it.

"What?" I ask to stall for time.

"Lily." He smiles as he speaks with a nervous tone in his voice. "Lily Joan Burns. Will you marry me?"

"I'm sorry," I say, shaking my head, trying to get his words straight. "I didn't hear you clearly. Did you just propose?"

"I'm on one knee presenting you with a ring. Why else would I be doing this?"

"Oh, of course," I say, trying desperately to break a smile. All I can think of though are Selma and Dolly, back in Philadelphia, pleading with me as I packed my bags before I left.

"Just promise us you won't come back engaged," my grandmother begged.

"It would be the biggest mistake of your life," my mother added.

"So, will you marry me?" he asks again with a huge smile on his face. His voice is as joyful as I've ever heard it.

I stand there not knowing what to say. It feels like the longest few seconds I've ever spent in my life. Gogo's smile fades from his face.

"Don't you want to marry me?" he asks quietly, looking a little panicky. He's still down on one knee and he's got that ring in his hand. People all around us are pointing and smiling at the man proposing to his girlfriend on top of one of the most romantic spots in the world. One couple, an overweight woman in black wearing gobs of jewelry and her husband who is half the size of her, are holding on to each other and watching what should be the happiest moment of my life.

"That man is proposing!" I hear the overweight woman say, shaking her husband's arm in excitement. "Get the camera, Larry!"

"I've got it, Barb," he says, taking the camera out of his fanny pack.

"Why you're even going to Paris, I don't know," Selma complained. "It can only lead to bad news."

"Oh please, Mother," I said. "He wants to take me away. I've never been to Paris before. Don't worry, Mom. Gram, he's not going to ask me to marry him. I know Gogo. We're both career people. And we've only been dating for a year. No one in their right mind would ask a person to marry them when they've only known each other for a year."

"Look, I know we've only known each other for a year," Gogo says, still on his knee. That knee has got to be in pain by now, still leaning on the cement observation deck. "It's just that, well, when you know, you know."

I'm not going to lie to you. Even though I was telling my mother and grandmother that there was no way Gogo would propose, I had a feeling he would. No one with as perfect a relationship as we have would fly his girlfriend over 3,700 miles to the most romantic city in the world and drag them to the top of the most romantic monument in the world if they weren't going to propose. Deep down inside, this is what I knew when Gogo gave me the itinerary.

"A week in Paris. We'll stay at the George V. I'm going to take you to all of my favorite bistros. I can't wait to show you the *Mona Lisa*. I'm planning a whole day at Versailles. The first thing we'll do when we get there is go straight to the Eiffel Tower."

I could have said no to the trip. I could have told him that if this trip was all about proposing, I wasn't ready to get married. I didn't though. The truth is I want to marry Gogo. I've never wanted anything more in my life.

"I'm getting hungry. Are you hungry?" I ask, as I spy some kid eating a sandwich. I figure it's as good a diversion as any.

"That's your answer?" Gogo says, finally getting up while rubbing his knee.

"Well, kind of," I stammer, "but I do, I do want to marry you." I take Gogo in my arms. He looks embarrassed. He's looking down with a blank look on his face. The ring is still in his hand.

"I don't know, Lil," he says, sounding a little ticked. "I was looking for something more along the lines of 'I love you too, you're the greatest guy I've ever known, blah blah blah, yes, there's nothing I would want more than to spend the rest of my life with you . . .'" He looks at me with a combination of hurt and bewilderment in his eyes.

"I'm just . . . I'm just confused. Maybe we could wait a little bit."

"*Oh, thank God,*" I hear my grandmother and mother in my head say in unison.

"What the hell?" he asks confused. "Aren't you happy with me?"

"Honestly"—I sigh—"I've never been happier."

"So what's the problem?"

"Did she just say no?" I hear Barb, the overweight woman say to her skinny Larry. "Oh what a shame."

"I'm not saying no," I call out to her.

"So what are you waiting for?" Barb puts her hands on her hips as if she wants to scold me.

"So what are you saying?" Gogo says, taking a step back.

"Gogo, I'm crazy about you. I've never felt this way about any other man before in my life."

"So say yes!" Barb shouts.

"Say yeehaw!" another woman in her fifties shouts with a thick southern drawl.

"Right?" Barb says turning to her. "If a man as handsome as that proposed to my daughter, Lucy, I'd say yes before she could get the words out of her mouth. Wouldn't we, Larry?" she asks her husband.

"He seems like a nice guy." Larry shrugs.

"Look, can you give me a minute?" I holler out to the women.

Larry is still taking pictures of the whole scene.

"Larry," Gogo calls out exasperated, "can you put the camera away."

Both Gogo and I are getting annoyed at today's crowd of American yentas atop the Eiffel Tower, so Gogo takes my arm and opens the door leading me into the inside of the observation deck.

"I'm just confused right now," I say, walking over to the food counter.

"You had to know the relationship might be heading this way," he tells me. "I mean, falling in love, moving in together, never having a big blowout fight. It must have dawned on you that at some point we might want to make this relationship official."

"No, of course, of course I knew that we would get engaged one day. I don't know anyone who gets along as well as we do."

"So what's wrong?" he asks.

"It's not you," I utter, before I'm about to come out with the other half of the cliché. "It's me."

"So, what? You're not ready?"

"I still love you too," I tell him. "I love you like crazy."

"But . . . ?"

"I'm just not ready."

Gogo takes a deep breath and exhales. I don't know what else to do but look at him with sadness. My heart is just aching right now, for Gogo, for me. It's killing me.

Gogo walks up to the food service counter. I can only stare at him looking dejected among all the happy, hungry tourists at the counter. "*Deux sandwichs d'oeuf s'il vous plâit. Aucunes tomates sur le sien,*" Gogo orders as he turns to me. "I made sure there's no tomatoes on your sandwich," he tells me with disdain. The subject has changed, but the tone of incomprehension and resentment is still in his voice.

Gogo knows I hate tomatoes. He always remembers. Gogo always remembers how I order my food. God, I feel like crap. What is the matter with me? Why do I care what Selma and Dolly think anyway? I'm not five anymore. I'm a successful, smart woman who should think for herself already instead of listening to those two shrews.

Look at Gogo standing there watching the server make our sandwiches. He looks so forlorn. I feel like the worst person on the planet. What's the matter with me? I just turned down a marriage proposal in lieu of a sandwich.

Why do I listen to my mother and grandmother? Why am I so afraid of them? Just because they've had nothing but sadness and heartbreak in their lives with anything involving marriage doesn't mean that I will. It's not like I haven't told them that before.

"Why do you think that what happened to you will happen to me?" I complained to them as I finished packing my bags.

"Because we know!" My grandmother shuddered. "The Burns women are not meant for true love," she tells me. "Just listen to us. We don't want to see you get hurt like we were."

"Trust us," my mother added. "We're doing this for your own good."

"Look," I say, touching Gogo's back and standing to the side of him at the counter. "It's not like anything has changed. It's not like I don't still love you. It's not like I'm going to move out after we get home."

"You just don't want to marry me," Gogo says dismissively as he takes the sandwiches from the guy behind the counter.

"I just . . . I can't," I tell him as he hands me my sandwich. "I can't explain it. I just . . . I just can't. Now come on, let's go outside on the observation deck and you'll show me Paris. You said you'd point out Notre Dame."

"I don't want to go out there again," he tells me.

It kills me that I'm upsetting him. I've ruined everything.

"Well, we're here," I tell him softly. "Why don't we just see what we came to see and then we'll leave. Who knows when we'll be here again?"

I'm not quite sure if that was the right thing to say.

"I mean, I'm sure that we'll be here again. Together. I just mean who knows when that will be?"

Gogo relents and opens the door for me again as we head out to the observation area. We're both silent as we look out at the beautiful city. The thing is, I can't see anything. My head is swimming with thoughts. I can't concentrate on what's in front of me at all and I know Gogo is feeling the same way.

"So will you?" I hear a male voice behind me as Gogo and I turn around. "I mean I know it's only been three months, but when you know, you know. So will you?"

"Like you even have to ask!" I see the young woman with tears in her eyes staring down at the man proposing to her.

"You want to get out of here?" I ask Gogo.

"Yes," he says. "Let's take a walk or something."

We're sitting on a bench in the Champ de Mars eating our sandwiches out of cellophane wrapping. The park is packed with tourists taking pictures in front of the Eiffel Tower. Two adorable blond children speaking French are playing with a small poodle. An elderly couple sit on a blanket with a picnic basket full of cheeses, feeding each other parts of a baguette between kisses. Everyone is a part of the utopian scene here on this field except for the two of us.

"I'm sorry," I tell Gogo again. "I really am."

"Hey," he says, putting his arm around me. "It's okay."

"Does this ruin the trip?" I ask him.

"Well, it doesn't exactly make it any better." He laughs. "Do you still want to see Paris?"

"I'll make it up to you, I swear." Though I can't imagine how I could.

"Look, I'm upset. Can you blame me? Who wouldn't be?" he

says. "But maybe you're right. Maybe it is too early in our relation-ship to ask you to marry me. Maybe I'm being too quick about things. I just thought everything was going so well. I just thought, well, I'm crazy about you, Lil, and I've never felt this way about any-one before. I just thought to myself, well, if it's this good, it's always going to be this good."

I have nothing to say. He's right. So I take another bite of my sandwich as we sit in silence. It's something I can't believe myself. From the second we met, it was as if the stars aligned. I knew I had found my soul mate.

It was like a scene out of a movie.

Jonah had just ended things with me for the fifth time. He had asked me to meet him for lunch at Continental Mid-town. Short, bald, fat, and a big-time jerk, Jonah was my grandmother and mother's dream catch for me. I shouldn't have cared one iota about Jonah, only there was one thing that kept bringing me back to him. It wasn't his generosity. (Jonah is the kind of guy who yells at waiters and only leaves a 2 percent tip.) It wasn't his looks. (Jonah buys his suits in the husky man's department.) It wasn't his choice of music. (Jonah blasts John Mayer.) Still, my mother and grandmother were crazy about him and I had the one thing I wanted: I had someone. Truth? I was so lonely. Lonely and desperate. My internet dating profile might as well have read like the Statue of Liberty, "Give me your tired, your poor ..." I was sick and tired of being alone. Sure, I'd been asked out by a lot of good-looking, kind individuals. But Dolly and Selma's words always made me turn them down:

"It's the good ones who have something to hide. A bad egg can be your biggest blessing."

This message had been hammered into my head for as long as I could remember. When you hear it enough, no matter how smart you are, you start to believe it.

"Look, babe," Jonah said as he bit into his tuna sandwich, leaving a hunk of it on his left cheek. "I'm not going to beat around the bush. It's not me, it's you."

"But things were going so well," I cried. "Didn't you tell me the other week when you came back after breaking up with me that you were in this for the long haul?"

"Depends on what your definition of *long haul* is," he chuckled.

"Tell me what I did," I cried.

"You work a lot," he said putting his chubby fingers on my shoulder.

"I'm successful," I reason. "I'm the youngest vice president of current advertising that Sacki and Sacki has ever had."

"And that's a big part of the problem," he said. "I'll start to depend on you to bring home the money and then right after the *I do's*, the next thing I know you'll be quitting your job to become a lady who lunches and where will that leave me?"

"You do well."

"Of course I do well, but a person can get used to living on two salaries."

"So I won't quit my job."

"And then what?" he continues. "You pop out a couple of kids and that gorgeous body of yours goes to sag city and what am I left with? A couple of screaming brats and a wife I'd be embarrassed to show in public? I'm sorry, Lily," he said, standing up. "You're a nice girl and all, but that's not the kind of life I want for myself. See you around," he said, walking out of the restaurant.

I put my head down. I was so upset, so torn. It wasn't like I even wanted a guy with absolutely no redeeming qualities to him, it was just that, well, Selma and Dolly insisted. My elders should know what's best for me, right? That's what I always figured. You have to understand. It's not like I didn't know that a guy like Jonah wasn't worth an ounce of my time. After all Selma and Dolly had said to me, I just didn't know who was right.

"Excuse me," I heard a voice say at the next table as I buried my head in my napkin. "I didn't mean to overhear that conversation, but did that guy just break up with you?"

"Yes," I sobbed.

"And you're crying because . . ."

"Because I've had it with men," I said. "That guy was the best thing I had going for me. What am I going to tell my mother?"

"You'll tell her that you deserved better than that."

For the first time since he started speaking to me, I looked over at him.

In a word: breathtaking.

If Hugh Jackman and George Clooney had a baby together, it would be this guy. The way his dark hair just flowed. Later, I would laugh whenever elderly women approached him on the street just to run their fingers through it, and he let them! And those eyes. Gogo's eyes are literally like pools of sparkling blue water. Perfect nose, perfect chin.

Bottom line: He was perfect. My grandmother and mother would hate him.

"I don't normally get involved in other people's problems, but come on, that guy was the worst," he continued.

"I know, I know he was, but you don't understand."

"Understand what?" he said, looking out the window at Jonah getting into his bright fluorescent yellow Hummer and shrugging off the parking attendant with his hand out asking for a tip. "Oh that's perfect." He added, "Am I on some hidden camera show?"

"No." I laughed. "It's a long story."

"I've got the time," he said. "My name is Gogo, by the way."

"Gogo?" I laughed again. "Is that your real name?"

"Kind of," he said.

"What's your real name?" I asked.

"Oh, that's too personal," he said. "I don't usually tell a woman my real name until we've been dating for a couple of months. For me giving it up is telling a woman my real name. That's when I know the relationship is meant to be."

"And how many special women have there been?" I ask, I admit, flirting a little bit.

"Up until now?" he asks.

"Yep."

"Two," he answers, melancholy. "One in the fifth grade. She left me for Rob Appleby, who had just moved to New York from London. Accents. The other was Rhonda, just after college. She broke my heart. She left me for my roommate, or rather, she climbed down from the top bunk to the bottom bunk."

"Bummer." I tried to see this guy through Dolly and Selma's eyes. He looked to be in his midthirties. *Why hasn't he been in a serious relationship since Rhonda?* I thought. He looked like the kind of guy women would drop their greatest loves for. *He must be a player*, I thought. *He's after my bank account. Maybe he is worth a chance . . . No, not now. I need a break.*

"Well"—I held out my hand—"it was nice meeting you, but I have to be back at work."

"It's a really good name," he said. "It's worth spending the time to find out."

"Thank you," I said getting my keys from my purse, "you're very sweet. I'm just not looking to date right now. You know, I just got out of a relationship. I think it's only right that I spend a little time by myself before I start dating someone new, you know, why bring that baggage?" I excuse myself, trying to shrug him away.

"From what I saw of the girth of that guy, that's way too much baggage for anyone to bear."

"So how much time do you think a person should spend mourning a relationship?"

"With a guy like that?"

"Yeah."

"Five minutes ago would have been too much time."

This made me laugh.

"Come on, how about I join you for lunch?" he asked. "I can't leave a woman crying into her salad."

"No," I say, "I don't think so. I'm really not hungry anymore, to tell you the truth. I think I'm just going to go back to my office and bury my head in some work."

"You know what always makes me feel better when I'm down?" he asks as he motions the waiter. The waiter promptly comes over to him.

"Two hot fudge sundaes, please," he orders.

"Oh, no," I tell him as I shake my head at the waiter, "that won't be necessary."

"Trust me." He nods to the waiter.

Five minutes later Gogo had joined me at my table and we were gorging on the sugary delight.

We haven't spent a day apart since.

Three months into our relationship, Gogo and I were lying in bed after yet another round of the best sex I've had in my life when Gogo turned to me.

"It's Stanley," he said.

"What?"

"My name is Stanley Goldblatt," he said.

I burst into hysterics.

"And that's why I never tell anyone my name."

"No, it's a good name," I said through my tears of laughter.

"It's an awful name. It was my grandfather's name, he died just before I was born, and my mother wanted to name me after him."

"So she couldn't have just used the *S* and named you something normal . . . uh, Steve, Stuart, even Sal, something more, uh, less awful?"

"Evidently he was a very good man. My mother said he was the perfect father. Always kind to her, he spoiled her with lots of love."

"Your mom was lucky." I sighed, thinking of the five men my mother married, the ones I called Dad, but only because I couldn't keep all their names straight since they came and went so quickly.

"Gogo is short for Goldblatt," he said. "I just couldn't change my name. I didn't want to hurt my mother's feelings. It makes her feel better to know I wouldn't change my name."

"What about using your middle name?" I asked.

Gogo winced. "Angus."

"Stanley Angus Goldblatt," I recited. "S. A. G.," I said, thinking maybe he could do something with the initials, but . . . "Sag. Wow." I took a deep breath. "You are a really good son."

"Speaking of mothers," he said, "when am I going to get to meet your mother and grandmother? You're always mentioning them, and I've never even heard their voices. Don't you think it's time you brought me home to them?"

"I can't do that yet. I'm not ready. They're funny about men."

"They must be if they wanted you to be with that Jonah guy."

"Well, they've been through a lot with men. They just don't want me to get my heart broken like they did. It's just a defense thing they have."

"You really think they'd hate me?" he asked.

"They're just cautious," I said. "It's like you respecting your mom's wishes and not changing your name. I respect my mother's wishes in not bringing home the perfect guy."

"So really, what you're saying is that bringing home the right guy would be the wrong thing to do."

"That's right, Stanley."

"You know your family is weird, right?"

"You don't even know the half of it." I sigh.

So I moved in with Gogo after we only knew each other for three months. I kept my house so Selma and Dolly wouldn't get suspicious. Gogo cracks that he almost broke up with me when he saw where I lived. Truth be told: I was a slob when I met Gogo, but to be fair to myself, I was always working, so home was just a place for me to change my clothes. I never liked living alone. Since Dolly was always cooking, I was at their home for nightly meals. My freezer was nothing but a solid block of ice. I never put anything in it, so there was no sense in defrosting it. But when I moved in with Gogo, I started spending more time at home. I wanted to be there, with him, in our home. And the relationship only got better. Gogo and I have the same taste in decorating. I like to sleep on the left side closest to the wall. Gogo likes the right. We're both early risers but late sleepers on the weekends. He likes to cook. I like to eat. I don't mind doing laundry. Folding is a Zen art for him. In all the time I've known Gogo, there's never been a harsh word between us. When Gogo decided we should go on a trip to Paris, I just knew.

"Look," he says, finishing the last of his sandwich. "Let's make a deal and forget about the proposal for the rest of the trip. Let's just enjoy our time in Paris. We're in one of the greatest cities in the world."

"Are you sure?" I ask him.

"No. But what other choice do I have?"

"What would you rather do?"

"I'd rather get really drunk right now and cry like a little girl," he tells me as if he's joking, but I know he's telling the truth.

"So let's go get plastered." I smile.

"I'd rather do it with a buddy. It's easier to curse your name if you're not there."

"So pretend I'm your buddy," I tell him as I lower my voice like a guy. "That Lily isn't even that hot. Why were you wasting your time?"

"Hey," he tells me, "that's my girl you're talking about."

I want to cry for him. I want to cry for me, but instead I just lean in and kiss Gogo. Luckily, he kisses me back as I take him in my arms. Then we head to the nearest bar, where we drink the day away.

It's two in the morning and my heavy-duty sleeping pill isn't working. My drunken stupor is long gone, but I still can't get the proposal out of my head. Whenever I get stressed like this in the middle of the night, I go to my source of calm. Some do yoga, some get massages. I stare at Gogo. Gogo sleeps like a corpse. He lies flat on his back with one pillow under his head and the covers pulled all the way up to his chin. He looks so childlike when he sleeps, not like the strong, confident man he is during the day. All he needs is the teddy bear. I love the way he rests his hands outside the covers by his sides (though sometimes in the real cold months, he keeps them by his side beneath the covers). Gogo never moves during the night. Whenever I wake up, tossing and turning, there's Gogo beside me in that same position he's always in. Nothing in the world has changed. The feeling of knowing that he's there and by my side and at peace with his world always makes me feel better.

Sometimes I can't help myself. I love Gogo so much, even though it might be four in the morning, I just have to tell him. So I wake him up, just like I'm about to do.

"Gogo?" I whisper to him.

"Yeah?" he whispers back immediately as if he's been up the whole time, but I know he hasn't. For someone who sleeps so peacefully, Gogo is a light sleeper.

Most people would get pissed if someone woke them up weekly (okay, maybe three times a week) for no real reason. All my old boyfriends would have said something like *"For Christ's sake, why did you wake me up? I have an important* (insert important activity, e.g., meeting, appointment, laser back-hair removal, etc.) *in the morning!"* Gogo never gets pissed off.

"I love you so much," I tell him.

And then he turns toward me and he swallows me in his arms as I rest my back up against him. This is the only time he ever changes position at night.

"I love you too, Lily," he whispers back.

As I lay in his arms staring out at the darkness I realize: this is the only place I ever want to be. Gogo's arms are the most secure place I've ever been in.

My mother and grandmother would just have to understand.

This was not one of their marriages. This is different. This is pure love. This is forever.

"Gogo," I whisper.

"Yeah?" He yawns.

"Will you marry me?"

Gogo sits up and looks down at me as he brushes the hair away from my face.

"Lily," he whispers.

"Yeah?"

"There's nothing in this world that I could want more."

And I kiss those lips, the only ones I ever want to kiss for the rest of my life.

2.

"*Why didn't we force her into lesbianism?*" my mother, Selma, shouts with tears in her eyes.

"That woman was perfect for you!" my grandmother, Dolly, cries, blowing her nose and wiping her tears. "And this backward state would never allow same sex marriage!"

"Look, I'm sorry, I'm not a lesbian. I tried for you, I did," I plead. "I'm just not interested in women."

"Where did we go wrong?" Selma dabs her eyes. "Did I not work three jobs to put you through Yale so you would become a work-horse and forget about men? I knew she should have taken a job in finance. They work those people to the bone."

"Advertising is a really hard field, especially in this economy. I work seventeen-hour days!"

"And who was taking care of you while your mother worked those three jobs?" Dolly adds. "It was those soap operas I let her watch when she was home sick from school. They only clouded her view of romance."

"You didn't do anything wrong. You were the best parents any girl could ever have. Look, if you just met Gogo, you'd understand why I want to marry him. Can't you just forget about all the heartbreak in your own lives for one second and give Gogo a chance?"

"And another thing, what kind of a name is Gogo?" Dolly scoffs and then tsks. "Would you look at that ring he gave her?" She grabs my hand, scrutinizing the diamond. "Would you look at how gorgeous this ring is? The cut, the color, the karat weight, that clarity! I'll bet this schnook paid retail too. No man is this good to give a ring like this if he doesn't have something to hide. Get away from him, Lily, trust me on this."

"*It's a nickname!*" I explode. "And this ring was given with his heart, it's beautiful, and so is Gogo. If you just gave him a chance, you'd see that!"

"We shouldn't have named her Lily," Dolly cries out. "It's too pretty. I told you to name her something less attractive. What was wrong with Ethel?"

"And we should have discouraged the way she eats," Selma continues. "Look at that gorgeous figure of hers. There's not an ounce of fat on her. We should have force-fed her fried foods morning, noon, and night." Selma bawls.

"Didn't I try?" Dolly says, taking her spoon to the bowl of mashed potatoes at the dining room table we're sitting at, trying to make me eat a spoonful.

"I already had two helpings," I say, pushing it away. "I'm full."

"And that's another thing, what rational human being only eats when they're hungry?" Selma protests. "With all the cooking your grandmother does, you'd think she'd be tempted to snack."

"Have another piece of chicken?" Dolly asks, putting the plate of chicken in front of me.

"Thank you, no," I say.

"Why I ever let her take cross-country running in high school, I have no idea," Dolly says as she puts the plate down and shoves it. "Who knew it would turn into a lifetime obsession? You know, you don't have to keep with the jogging," Dolly scolds me. "You graduated from high school over ten years ago. It wouldn't hurt you to spend a couple of hours in front of the television with a bag of chips." She turns to Selma. "She could have been as big as a house by now if I had only forbid her to join the cross-country running team."

"She's too smart. We shouldn't have let her get a library card," Dolly cries.

"She insisted on making her own money since she was fifteen," Selma says.

"She's the perfect woman!" Selma cries out. "Where did we go wrong?"

"Would you two listen to yourselves?" I scoff. "Even if I was overweight and didn't exercise and didn't have a good job and a good head on my shoulders, believe me, I'm still a good person inside. Someone would have seen that."

"Yes, but it would have been harder for them to see." Dolly sighs.

"*You're both crazy!*" I shout. "Now look. Ever since I could remember, the two of you have forbidden me to have any romance in my life. I have obeyed you and listened to you and what has it gotten me? Nothing but horrible men and a lifetime of loneliness. And then here comes this man, this sweet, wonderful, smart, successful, caring man who practically rides up on a white horse and saves me from a life I can only describe as the life you want for me: miserable. Why would you want me to be miserable? Me—the person you love most in this world. The person who has listened to you and obeyed everything single thing you asked of me."

"Not everything, obviously," Selma snaps.

"Well, we have tried to introduce you to some nice men," Dolly interrupts.

"Who? Jonah?"

"He wasn't so terrible, was he?" Dolly asks Selma.

"I like the one you met for her at the supermarket," Selma reminds Dolly.

"You mean outside the supermarket. Where he lived. By the trash bins," I hark back.

"Don't be such a snob," Selma scoffs.

"What about that entrepreneur?" Dolly adds. "He was really going places."

"He's not going anywhere until he completes his ten years without parole in state prison," I retort.

"Big deal, so he embezzled a few million out of some old widows?" Dolly sneers. "It was like he said at the trial. They had more than enough to live on."

"Do you even hear yourselves? And the craziest thing is that I've put up with it all these years. I've sacrificed my happiness for the sake of your happiness. But not anymore."

"I knew one day she'd revolt," Dolly says.

"You're right, I would," I cry angrily. "And that day is now. I am marrying Gogo Goldblatt whether you like it or not. You can skip the wedding and never see your grandchildren for all I care. I don't care if I never see you for the rest of my life. I'm through with the both of you. That's it. I've had it."

I plop myself down on the couch and start to sob.

"Maybe we have gone a little too far," Selma whispers to Dolly.

"It was only in her best interest," Dolly whispers back.

"Ma, I think it's time." Selma puts her hands up in defeat. "We have to tell her already."

"Tell me what?" I ask.

"Forget about your mother's craziness," Dolly shushes. "Selma, keep it to yourself."

"What?" I ask. "I knew it. All these years you've only wanted the worst for me when it comes to romance and when I finally find the man of my dreams—the man of any woman's dreams—you act like someone died! So what is it? What's the big secret you're keeping from me already?"

"Don't tell her!" Dolly shouts.

"She's twenty-nine years old!" Selma counters. "Let's tell her already and then she can make her own decisions. We'll lose her if we don't."

"Fine." Dolly backs down. "You want to tell her, let's tell her. She's old enough to know already."

"Lily, come here," my mother says, patting the seat next to her. "Ma, pour her a drink. She might need it after we confess the whole thing."

Dolly hesitates.

"Are you sure we're doing the right thing?" Dolly asks her.

"Yes. It's time. It's time for Lily to know already."

Dolly goes over to the living room cabinet and retrieves a bottle.

"Is peppermint schnapps okay?" she asks. "I also have that bottle of champagne to save for a celebration . . . Oh, I guess that's not appropriate."

"Forget the liquor," I plead. "Would you just spit it out already?"

"We thought we could keep it from you." Selma sighs.

"We thought if we just shielded you away from any good man, that you would just learn to believe that men were the devil."

"But that's crazy!" I balk. "Men are not the devil."

"They're not, of course they're not. Even we know that," Selma brushes off the idea. "But there's a reason for all of this. There's a very good reason we haven't wanted you to be happily married."

"Well, it better be a good reason," I say, folding my arms.

"Are you ready, Ma?" Selma asks. "Do you want to tell it or should I?"

"Let me do it." Dolly puts her hand on my mother's shoulder and then sits down next to me, putting me in the middle of these two women. "It's only right as the oldest Burns that I tell the story, just like my grandmother told me."

Dolly takes a deep breath.

"Look, how bad can it be?" I ask, starting to get a little anxious.

Dolly and Selma turn to each other and grimace.

"Lily," Dolly begins, "as you might know, your mother and I have both been very unlucky in love."

"I figured out after Selma's fourth marriage that it wasn't all rosy." I laugh.

"Well, it took your mother some time to understand things and you've always been much smarter than us, so maybe it's better that you hear the whole story and understand why your mother's marriages have been the way they were. Maybe you'll understand why I only married once and never as much as looked at another man again."

Dolly sighs.

Selma motions her to continue.

"Well? I'm waiting," I say irritably.

And then they proceed to tell me the story . . .

The Curse of the Burns Women:
A Tragic Tale
As told by Dolly and Selma Burns

"The year was 1907," Dolly starts. "Or was it 1909?"

"What's the difference?" Selma asks.

"It's family history," Dolly explains. "I don't want to start the story of our family history by getting it wrong. Then it will be wrong from here on out for generations to come."

"It was 1907. I'm positive."

"Are you sure?"

"She's sure," I say, already exasperated.

"Okay, so the year was 1907. The place: the small town of Lokwunden, Austria. Did you know that that's where you're from?"

I actually didn't know and I find this fact very interesting, but I don't let on.

"Of course." I nod.

"Well," Dolly continues, "as the story goes, Great-Great-Grand-aunt Emmalina had caught the eye of Hermann Burnswurst, the baker."

"Everyone who was anyone shopped at Burnswurst Bakery," Selma adds.

"Oh yes, it was *the* place for breads and cakes."

"Hermann was a rich man."

"Now, word on the *straße* had it that Hermann was thinking of making the big move: America. Hermann had big plans. Hermann wanted to open up a chain of bakeries and he knew that America was the place to do it. Hermann had purchased two tickets on the midnight train to Holland, scheduled to leave a week from the day he bought the tickets. From there, Emmalina and Hermann would take the Noordam ship to America. The gossip was that he had already asked Emmalina's father, Krumpke, for her hand in marriage and Krumpke had eagerly accepted."

"So what's this got to do with me?" I interrupt.

"Please, Lily, would you stop interrupting?" Selma admonishes. "You're ruining the flow of the story."

"Thank you, Selma." Dolly nods. "Now, Emmalina was head over heels with Hermann. What woman wouldn't be? Handsome, smart, and successful, Hermann was equally smitten with his Emmalina. The two of them made a dashing couple. Everyone said so—"

"All except Emmalina's older sister," Selma interjects.

"Astrid."

"And Astrid was my . . ."

"Great-great-grandmother, yes," Selma replies. "Astrid was the girl that everyone had but no one wanted."

"Astrid was already twenty years old, an old maid in most eyes," Dolly clarifies. "It was said it was easy for Astrid to lure a man. Oh, she was stunning—full, voluptuous figure, smoldering eyes, and gift for dressing right. Astrid was by far the prettiest girl in all of Lokwunden and everyone knew it. The problem wasn't her looks. The problem was her personality."

"Such a shame." Selma grimaces. "If it weren't for . . ."

"See, Astrid had been a difficult birth and Krumpke prayed that if she would be healthy, he would shower her with all the material objects she could ever want. As a result, Krumpke had spoiled his oldest daughter and Emmalina was always second fiddle. While Astrid was wearing the latest styles, Emmalina would get the hand-me-downs a year later. Astrid slept on a bed of goose-feather blankets a foot high. Emmalina slept on a bed of straw. Men were always calling on Astrid, and she always accepted dates, but when the men realized how spoiled she was, they never called again."

"Who makes someone sleep on a bed of straw and the other gets goose feathers? They were child abusers!"

"When you have children of your own, you'll understand," Selma interjects.

"Emmalina, on the other hand, was always the quiet one. Emmalina never complained about the treatment she got compared to her older sister. She never complained about the clothes. She never complained that her bed was too uncomfortable. She didn't have to. All of that stuff didn't matter. Emmalina had what Astrid didn't: a man. Not just any man, a man with big dreams."

"Obviously, Astrid was viciously jealous," Selma continues. "Hermann was the one man in all of Lokwunden who hadn't made a play for her. He was too infatuated with his Emmalina to see beauty in any other woman. And for that, Astrid was secretly head over heels for him too."

"I still don't see what this has got to do with me."

"We're getting to that," Dolly says, bothered.

"Continue, Ma," Selma calms her.

"Thank you." Dolly takes a breath. "Now, one day before the train was set to leave Austria, Emmalina was in the kitchen of her home working on her future husband's wedding gift. Emmalina was a fine baker in her own right. She had been working on an idea she had for a chocolate cookie. So after realizing she had run out of baker's chocolate, she took some semisweet chocolates that Hermann had given her as a gift and began breaking the chocolate into the batter. What came out of the oven was something she'd never seen before. Instead of the chocolate melting in the batter, the chocolate stayed intact."

"Can you believe that?" Selma exclaims. "Your great-great-grand-aunt invented the chocolate chip cookie!"

"But you hate chocolate chip cookies! You never let me have them in the house! I had to smuggle Mrs. Fields in and keep them under my bed when I was younger."

"If I had known you brought chocolate chip cookies into this house, you would have been grounded," Selma says, perturbed.

"But our aunt invented them! Did she ever take out a patent? If there's proof that she really did invent them, we could be trillionaires!"

"Well . . ." Selma sighs.

"As it turns out, no one would ever know it," Dolly adds.

"With the aroma of butter, brown sugar, and chocolate wafting through the house, Astrid entered the kitchen to find her sister standing over her latest concoction," Selma reports.

"Now I'm hungry." Dolly turns to Selma, licking her lips. "Do we have any sweets in the house?"

"I'll check," Selma says, getting up and walking into the kitchen.

"Oh, this story always makes us hungry, my apologies," Dolly says to me. "Anyway, Emmalina handed a cookie to Astrid. 'Tell me if you think it's good,' she asked her. Astrid hid her anticipation for the warm treat. There was no doubt in her mind that Emmalina had stuck semisweet gold. When she bit into it, she knew that cookie would make her sister and Hermann richer beyond their wildest dreams. It was so unlike a plain chocolate cookie, which masked the taste of the brown buttery goodness. This was a delight to the senses, a true work of art."

"Here, Ma, there was some frozen Sara Lee in the freezer. Do you want me to nuke it in the microwave? It only takes ten seconds." Selma hands her the frozen piece of pound cake.

"That's okay, I'm too hungry to wait that long. I'll just suck on it until it gets softer." Dolly puts some in her mouth. "Sof, du storphy condinues . . ."

"What? I can't understand you with that cake in your mouth."

"Sorry." She swallows. "So as the story continues, you get it, Astrid was going to do her best to put a stop to it. Astrid, after all, was a very difficult birth and why should Emmalina get the best when Astrid always got the best?"

"So she seduced Hermann!" Selma dramatically waves her arms in the air.

Dolly stands up and throws her arms back. "Seduced him like no woman has ever seduced a man before."

"How did she do it?" I ask, wide-eyed.

"You know the phrase, 'The way to win a man's heart is through his stomach?'" Selma asks as Dolly tries to bite into the cake.

"Yeah."

"Coined by Astrid," Dolly mutters through the hard cake.

"Chocolate chip cookies *and* a proverb." Selma smiles proudly. "Can you believe how influential this family has been to the world?"

"Wait." I pause, trying to figure it out. "You're telling me that

Astrid went over to Hermann's house and told him that she made the cookies and Hermann believed her?"

"Imagine tasting a chocolate chip cookie for the first time," Dolly explains.

"It's the most popular cookie in the world. Imagine the first person, a smart successful baker with his mind on the future, tastes it, and what do you think happened?" Selma takes a magazine off the coffee table and fans herself.

"Not to mention the fact that Astrid was so pretty," Dolly adds.

"The prettiest girl in all of Lokwunden." Selma nods.

"So he had no choice," Dolly tells me.

"And he went for it," I conclude.

"Hook, line, and sinker." Dolly nods.

"Is that where that expression comes from?" Selma asks.

"It might as well have," Dolly figures.

"So then what happened?" I ask, taking a piece of the partly thawed cake and stuffing it in my mouth.

"That night"—Dolly looks into my eyes—"with just the clothes on her back, Astrid left with Hermann on the train to Holland."

"They changed Emmalina's name on the tickets into Astrid's," Selma explains.

"And then they went on to America." Dolly looks at Selma as if they have rehearsed this part.

"Or did they?" Selma holds up one finger and widens her eyes.

"And that's where the curse comes in," Dolly whispers dramatically.

"Oh, come on," I say.

"This is the part you've been waiting for," Dolly says, taking my hand. "Emmalina awoke earlier than usual with the biggest smile on her face and a wealth of anticipation in her heart. It wasn't about going to Holland on the train. It wasn't about the trip aboard ship to America. It was that she was going to do it with Hermann by her side. So many women in her town had only gotten married as an arrangement: a cow for an engagement, a chicken coop for dowry. She was marrying for love. With all the luck the stars had bestowed on her, it wouldn't matter how poor they got, or how hungry they got, at least she and Hermann would do it together and that made her feel like the richest woman in the world. Who could sleep with thoughts like that?"

"Emmalina slowly got out of her bed . . . ," Selma continues.

"So as not to wake the rest of the family with the straw-crunching sounds coming from her mattress," Dolly adds.

"She crept to the kitchen figuring she would make her family one last big breakfast. Instead of finding herself alone though, she found her parents sitting at the table. In front of them was a piece of paper," Selma continues.

"'Emmalina, dear, please, sit with us.' Krumpke pulled out a chair for her."

"'Is everything all right?'" Selma recites in a voice Emmalina might have had.

"Krumpke and her mother, Fannie, looked at each other with heavy hearts," Dolly says, putting her head down.

"'Emmalina,' Krumpke began," Selma repeated in a deep voice, "'What might seem like bad news now will eventually be the best thing that's ever happened to you.'"

"'Please, please tell me,'" Dolly says, acting as Emmalina.

"Krumpke and Fannie handed her the piece of paper they had found on the door that morning. It was from Hermann:

"*Emmalina:*
    "*I have chosen to go to America with Astrid and share her chocolate chip cookie recipe with the new world.*
    "*No one makes a fool out of Hermann Burnswurst.*
    "*X*"

"She told Hermann that it was her recipe?" I question. "This is why you won't let me have chocolate chip cookies in the house?"

"Astrid was a ruthless woman." Dolly shakes her head.

"Astrid told Hermann that Emmalina never loved him. She was just using him to go to America," Selma cries.

"And the worst lie of all . . . ," Dolly prompts Selma.

"Astrid told Hermann that Emmalina hated baked goods!"

"And then what happened?" I ask on the edge of my seat.

"Well, by this point, the new Mr. and Mrs. Burnswurst are on the ship headed towards America. The captain of the ship married them at twilight," Dolly adds.

"Astrid had her man," Selma reiterates.

"That night they made mad passionate love," Dolly says, taking the magazine and fanning herself.

"The marriage was consummated," Selma concludes.

"The next morning, Astrid was in all her glory. She was headed to America to start a new life with Hermann. All was going fine for her."

"Only there was one thing she didn't know about Emmalina," Selma adds.

"Yes." Dolly nods. "When Astrid stole Hermann, Emmalina became bitter."

"Her parents tried giving her Astrid's bed of goose feathers. They gave her all of Astrid's beautiful clothes."

"None of it worked," Dolly interjects. "Emmalina had had enough."

"Enough," Selma repeats for drama as she waves her arms.

Selma and Dolly sit down on either side of me. Dolly takes my hand.

"A week later, aboard ship, while Astrid and Hermann were eating their breakfast, a telegram arrived for Astrid." Dolly sighs as she turned to Selma and nods. "Go ahead, Selma."

"Excuse me for just a moment," Selma says to me as she walks out of the living room. Dolly takes my hand again.

"Astrid knew who it was from."

"It was from Emmalina," I conclude.

"That it was." Dolly nods. "Astrid laughed when she saw the telegram, she actually laughed."

"And you know she laughed because . . . ?" I ask.

"Oh, this story is well documented," Dolly affirms. "So she laughed and excused herself from the table to see what Emmalina had to say. Out on the deck, Astrid opened the telegram."

"I've got it, Ma," Selma says, appearing in the living room with an envelope.

"And Lily"—Dolly presents—"here is the actual telegram."

Selma, who has put on white gloves, slowly takes the paper out of the envelope and hands it to me. It is old and yellowed and the original creases where Emmalina had folded the telegram are so flimsy I have to hold it gently in my hand.

WESTERN UNION

MY SISTER ASTRID STOP

YOU MAY THINK YOU ARE GETTING AWAY WITH
EVERYTHING STOP YOU MAY THINK THAT ALL YOUR
DREAMS ARE ABOUT TO COME TRUE STOP THIS IS NOT
TO BE STOP

ASTRID I HAVE CURSED YOU STOP

LET IT BE KNOWN FROM THIS DAY FORWARD THAT IF
YOU MARRY ANY MAN OUT OF LOVE THE TWO OF YOU
WILL SUFFER UNIMAGINABLE CONSEQUENCES STOP THE

```
ONLY MAN WHO WILL STAY WITH YOU IS A MAN YOU
DESPISE STOP

THE ONLY WAY YOU WILL AVOID MY TERRIBLE CURSE
IS IF YOU WED AN IGNORANT SLOVENLY MAN WHO WILL
MAKE YOUR LIFE MISERABLE STOP SHOULD YOU FOLLOW
YOUR HEART YOU WILL BOTH FIND YOURSELVES IN A
HELL OF YOUR OWN MAKING STOP

I HAVE ALSO TAKEN THE LIBERTY OF CURSING YOUR
BLOODLINE FOR GENERATIONS TO COME STOP SHOULD
YOU BEAR A DAUGHTER SHE AND HER SPOUSE WILL
SUFFER THE SAME FATE IF SHE IS FOOLISH ENOUGH TO
MARRY FOR LOVE STOP THE SAME HOLDS TRUE FOR THE
GENERATION AFTER THAT AND THE GENERATION AFTER
THAT AND SO ON STOP

YOUR SISTER EMMALINA STOP
```

"Oh come on!" I shout. "This is crazy! Emmalina had gone crazy! And by the way, that was an expensive telegram."

"It must have cost her over a dollar! That's how crazy with anger she was," Selma adds.

"And Astrid thought it was crazy too!" Dolly continues. "Witnesses said she laughed and laughed at this crazy telegram, for five minutes she couldn't catch her breath she was laughing so hard."

"And then, it happened," Selma pronounces.

"Suddenly, she heard a crowd screaming inside in the dining room. The door swung open and a woman appeared," Dolly describes.

"'A doctor!'" Selma shouts, acting out the scene. "'Is there a doctor out here? We have a man choking inside on a cookie!'"

"Astrid's cookie?" I ask.

"What?" Dolly answers.

"Was it the cookies that Astrid made?" I ask again.

"Astrid didn't make any cookies. She stole them from Emmalina."

"I mean Emmalina's chocolate chip cookie? Was that what choked him?"

"Oh, no it was just a cookie that was made on the ship." Selma laughs. "How ironic was it that it was a cookie?" Selma poses. "I never even thought about that before."

"Isn't that something?" Dolly nods, "the parallel never occurred to me either." Dolly clutches her heart.

"So what happened next?" I ask.

"So Astrid jumped up and ran toward the door." Dolly gets up, reenacting the scene, and so does Selma, who plays Hermann, clutching her neck with her hands as if she is unable to breathe.

"There she saw Hermann, his face was bright red. He was clenching his throat. He looked her right in the eye as his face turned a shade of blue." Selma dramatizes this by coughing as she gives herself a mock Heimlich maneuver.

"In the next second, Hermann collapsed," Dolly explains as Selma drops to the floor.

"Astrid headed over to his side," Selma says, getting up and taking my hand beside me.

"He was dead," Dolly says taking the other.

"So when the ship arrived at Ellis Island, Astrid had a dead husband to bury. With no money to get back to Vienna, she had no choice but to stay in New York," Selma explains.

"That night of passion?" Selma reminds me. "It produced a daughter."

"Of course it was a girl," Dolly explains. "Your great-grandmother, Hilde Burnswurst."

"Who had a daughter . . ." Selma adds.

". . . And her husband, what a shame." Dolly sits back down.

". . . And so on and so on and so on." Then Selma sits back in the sofa.

"And now you know," Dolly tells me.

"And now she knows." Selma exhales.

We sit in silence for a moment.

"Any more of that Sara Lee?" Dolly turns to Selma.

"Nah, that was it," Selma answers.

"Oh, what a shame."

"A big shame." Selma nods.

I was the only one still on the edge of my seat, the telegram still in my hand.

3

I've been sitting in the same position for the last five minutes. Selma and Dolly have since gotten up and started clearing the dining room table. I've been turning the story over and over in my head and I can only come to one conclusion:

"*THAT IS THE BIGGEST CROCK OF CRAP I'VE EVER HEARD!*" I explode. "All these years you've kept me from any kind of pure romance because of that story? It doesn't even make sense!"

"It makes perfect sense," Selma insists. "If you marry for love, it's bad news for you and the groom—especially the poor groom."

"How do you know the curse is real?"

"Let's look at the evidence," Selma pleads.

"First there was your great-grandmother, Hilde, the product of Astrid and Hermann," Dolly begins.

"She married her great love, J. J. Gainsboro, in June of 1928. J. J. was a star on Wall Street, a real titan. They lived in a spacious home on Long Island." Selma has a look of longing.

"A forty-room English castle with ten acres of manicured gardens."

"In 1929, Hilde gave birth to a girl they named Dolly."

"You," I remark.

"Yes, it was me." Dolly beams, picturing her young life.

"And then . . ." Selma looks over at Dolly.

"The crash of 'twenty-nine."

"He was the one who started it."

"Told all of his clients to invest in silent pictures. 'The talkies will never make it,' he said."

"And then of course . . ."

"*The Jazz Singer*," they say at the same time.

"It was like a set of dominos: one bank fell, then the other, then the other, and pretty soon the whole country was left in dire straits. Hilde and I were left with nothing," Dolly reminisces. "He had to move to a remote island off Fiji. Mother and I couldn't go; you know, she freckled."

"So Hilde and Ma made their way to Philadelphia," Selma explains.

"We couldn't stay in New York anymore. There was too much sadness. Philadephia was where Hilde met Gerard, my stepfather." Dolly smiles.

"Gerard . . . the second great love of her life. They were so happy. Until he became addicted to Coke."

"Drugs?" I ask, shocked.

"Drugs?" Dolly laughs. "Not cocaine, Coca-Cola! He drank it by the gallons."

"Got big as a house," Selma adds.

"Couldn't fit through the door after a year," Dolly explains. "It became his life. The addiction became too much. He would steal money out of her purse and head to the soda shop. She couldn't trust him anymore and finally had to leave him. If only they had Diet Coke back then. Or Tab."

"Then she married Leon."

"Which would have been fine except he was already married to another woman and had a family with her."

"There was no clue that he was married. Leon and Hilde owned a business together. They were together twenty-four hours a day! And then, poof, he has this second family. That's the way the curse works. When did he even have the time to make the other family? He didn't! The curse!"

"Next was Franklin," Dolly continues.

"Struck by lightning."

"Did he die?" I ask.

"Die?" Dolly replies, as if I just asked her the most inane question. "No, he didn't die. He became a human flycatcher. The flies would land on him and he'd light up and electrocute them. He kept us up all night with the buzzing and flashes of light coming from his body every time a fly would come near him. We had to keep the windows permanently closed, but those flies just kept finding their way in. Mother said it was like sleeping in a bed with a neon light, flashing, flashing . . ." She blinks her hands in my face.

"After that, Hilde gave up." Selma sighs.

"She got grumpy from the lack of sleep. They turned on each other, fought all the time. It was over. But that's when I met Sherman."

"My father," Selma explains.

"But that was an accident." I remind her of his near drowning.

"Why we decided to vacation at Niagara Falls, I'll never know." Dolly shook her head. "Who survives Niagara Falls?" she asks rhetorically.

"He became a huge sensation. The papers were filled with stories about the indestructible Sherman. The fame just got to his head."

"And yet he couldn't open a jar of jelly," Dolly says, folding her arms in disgust. "He was so kind and loving before the Niagara *fall*, and then he was too good to open a jar of jelly for me. I couldn't take it anymore. You know how I feel about the spotlight. Sherman, he went and joined the carnival circuit. He married the woman with two heads. Shame. I loved him so."

"I was three years old," Selma says sadly.

"And then of course, August Reinhart came into the picture." Dolly sighs.

"Who?" I ask.

"August Reinhart not only went down Niagara Falls, but he did it while reciting Shakespeare."

"Act one, scene one, from *Richard the Third*," Selma adds. "'Now is the winter of our discontent . . .' People say it was an incredible performance."

"So August killed Sherman's career. The two-headed woman left him for the tattooed man and we never saw him again." Dolly sighs. "By the time Selma became of age to marry, I begged her not to."

"She told me the stories of the women in past generations."

"She didn't believe me, just like you don't."

"It took me five husbands to figure out that she was right."

"One husband got it worse than the next." Dolly sighs.

"And I guess that brings us up to date."

"I still don't believe it," I say, getting up and walking around the room. "They were all just coincidences, Mom's first husband—"

"Paul."

"Hirsutism," Selma mumbles.

"What?" I ask.

"Excessive hair growth. It's a disease."

"He could have joined her father in the carnival," Dolly surmises.

"No, he joined the circus, which was fine. He was clogging up all my drains."

"And the second one, my father," I say.

"A Macy's Thanksgiving Day parade carried him away," Selma recalls.

"He got sucked into the Mighty Mouse float."

"Well, that's what we told you." Selma sighs. "It was actually a marching band from Louisville. He just got swallowed up in between the first and second tuba and that was the last I saw of him."

"Did you try to look for him?"

"Of course I tried. No one knew what I was talking about. How crazy does that sound? A tuba from Louisville ate my husband. Who would believe me?"

"I did," Dolly says.

"Thanks, Ma. Now what happened to the next one?"

"The third one got the hiccups," Dolly reminds her.

"Oh, you're right. The poor thing. It started one day and he just couldn't stop. I tried everything, scaring him—"

"You scared me," Dolly adds.

"I scared myself. Never got a hiccup since."

"And what happened to him?" I ask.

"He had gone to Atlantic City for the weekend without me, and while he was there, the hiccups stopped. When he got home and saw me, they started again. I knew there was no hope," Selma recalls.

Dolly looks down shaking her head.

"The fourth one just ran off one day. No one knew where he went. He just started running and never came back. What happened to the fifth one, I can't remember anymore." Selma turns to me for the answer.

"Mafia."

"Oh yes." Selma laughs. "The mob hit."

"A mob hit and he wasn't even in the mafia. He was a pastor!" Dolly explains.

"He didn't even know where he got the gun from. He just found it in his hand and shot a man."

"Did he kill him?" I ask.

"No, shot him in the foot. The mafia was so happy about what he'd done, they made him a made man. Evidently, the man he shot owed money. So he joined the mafia. Lives in Arizona under an assumed name now."

"But that still doesn't mean that it's all because of the curse put on by Emmalina!" I tell them. "There is no proof!"

"Proof?" Dolly cries. "You want proof?"

"Yes, I want proof," I demand.

"How much more proof do you need?" Selma implores.

"For crying out loud, four generations of women have watched the men they love face the most unimaginable fates!" Dolly cries out.

"I bet if you could ask all of our husbands if there's a curse, you know what they would say?" Selma asks me.

"Except the one who got his tongue caught on the pole that snowy day."

"Which one was that?" Selma tries to think.

"My third dad," I say sorrowfully. "We were catching snowflakes on our tongues. I thought it would help with the hiccups. He wasn't looking where he was going."

"Now do you believe us?" Dolly asks. "Now, do you see why we've tried to dissuade you from any and all romance in your life? Do you see why you've been forbidden to eat chocolate chip cookies?"

"Do us a favor, Lily, please, don't get married. For Gogo's sake, for your heart, please, we can't bear to see another Burns woman hurt. We can't see another man who loves us get hurt!"

"Well, I still don't believe it," I say, getting up.

"She's just like I was." Dolly turns to Selma. "I told you it wouldn't make a difference if we told her. She's got that hard head just like you."

"Lily," Selma tries to reason, "you're a smart girl. Look at all the evidence."

"I'm sorry, but I just can't take any of this seriously. It's the twenty-first century. Everything that happened, they were flukes!"

"Flukes?" Dolly cries out. "Parades that carry men away, a man who doesn't die going down Niagara Falls, mob hits—Lily, these were no flukes. One bad accident, one time, okay, I'd think it was a fluke, maybe one or two of the husbands run off with some other woman, or someone dies of a heart attack, but Lily, be reasonable, be smart about this. I ask you: are you in love with Gogo?"

"Of course I'm in love with Gogo."

"Is Gogo in love with you?"

"He's madly in love with me."

"So you cannot get married."

"But what you're telling me is that they don't die," I try to rationalize.

"No, they don't die; worse, they live with terrible consequences, so terrible, we can't even be around them! At least with death, that's final, but with this curse, you don't know what's going to happen. Think of poor Gogo." Dolly shakes her head.

"Ma, look at that gorgeous ring he gave her," Selma says, taking my hand and sticking it in Dolly's face.

"I've never seen anything more beautiful," Dolly cries.

"You said it was too perfect. He had to be hiding something!" I say.

"That was just to throw you off the track." Dolly sighs. "You can tell from this ring that this is a very thoughtful man."

"And to take her to Paris and propose on the top of the Eiffel Tower," Selma sighs. "It's something I could only dream about."

"The romance of it all." Dolly begins to tear up.

"Tell us, Lily"—Selma takes my hand—"was it as romantic as I picture in my head?"

"Who are you people?" I draw back. "All of a sudden you've both gone gushy on me? All these years you've had hearts of stone and now that you've told me this cockamamie story, it's like the floodgates have opened."

"Do you have any idea what it's been like for us all these years?" Selma pleads. "You had to have known we were secret romantics."

I ponder this notion. "Well, I always noticed that when we're watching *The Way We Were*, you always want to turn it off when Katie and Hubbell move to Los Angeles."

"Oh, don't even get me started." Selma starts tearing.

"Why did they have to break up, why?" Dolly shakes her head. "Why did he have to sleep with Beekman Place, of all people?"

Dolly heads toward the end of the room and looks out the window, taking a moment to herself.

"When I think of what our lives could have been if Emmalina hadn't cursed our bloodline, if Astrid wasn't so spoiled. I'd have had Bert Poolson across the street." Dolly sighs. "If we could only be together. He's my Hubbell Gardner."

"Old Man Poolson?" I laugh. "The angry guy across the street who you're always fighting with?"

"He loves your grandmother." Selma sighs sweetly.

"And I love him." Dolly sighs back. "Why do you think he's so angry? Why do you think I fight with him all the time? It's a complicated relationship."

"He must have asked your grandmother for her hand in marriage, oh, how many times, Ma?"

"Seventeen," Dolly answers, still looking out the window.

"I didn't even know you had feelings for him," I say.

"There's a lot you don't know." Dolly exhales.

"You think men weren't chasing after me?" Selma whimpers. "Look at my figure," she says, standing up and presenting herself. "I'm fifty-five years old with the body of a thirty-five-year-old."

"That's pushing it a little, Selma," Dolly interjects.

"Okay, fine, forty."

"Forty-five, I'll give you that," Dolly counters.

"It's all that pent-up sexual frustration," Selma explains.

"Is that why you're always going to the gym?" I question.

"Can you think of a better reason?"

"They line up for her by the treadmills." Dolly smiles proudly.

"And I have no choice but to cut them off. You should see this gorgeous trainer always lurking around me, twenty-five years old and he's begging me for dates. For the sake of his own life, I tell this young, gorgeous Adonis, 'No, go away.'" Selma starts to bawl as Dolly hands her a tissue.

"And why do you think I cook and cook? We have two refrigerators full of enough food to feed an army here."

"I just thought you liked to cook," I say.

"And yet we have no dessert in the house," Selma says to her.

"Baking has never really been my forte, you know, because of the story and everything," Dolly explains. "Anything to keep my mind off of that wonderful man just across the street. That's why I cook so much, so I can forget about that dreamboat. So close, so very, very close, and yet so, so far away." She shakes her head as if to get the thought out of her system. "That reminds me, how about some steaks tomorrow night? I can marinate them and grill them—what do you think?"

"So all these years, I thought that you thought that men were the enemy, and really, all this time you've been frightened by this curse." I put my arm around Selma.

"Don't you see already?" Selma dabs her eyes and blows her nose. "We're telling you for your own good. You can't marry Gogo. You can't marry anyone you have any feelings for. If you marry the man of your dreams, it's only going to turn into a nightmare."

I have to admit, what they're saying is really starting to make sense. If you had seen all those husbands come and go, you'd start to believe it too.

"So maybe I watch Gogo's every move. We won't go to Niagara Falls. I'll cover him in bug repellent."

"Been there," Dolly answers.

"Done that," Selma adds.

"We've tried that. It doesn't work," Dolly declares.

"And really, is your life so bad?" Dolly poses. "You've got a great job, a family who loves you. So what if you never have romance in your life? So what if you live the rest of your life alone?"

"I'll tell you what's going to happen," I answer. "It's going to mean that my life will never be complete. I will be lonely for the rest of my life. I will never know what it's like to experience pure love, romance, someone by my side to go through life with, for better or for worse."

"I'm afraid that's the curse, darling," Dolly answers as she pats my shoulder. "And there's nothing that can be done about it."

"Are you okay?" Selma asks, putting her arm around me.

"I don't know," I say, trying to come to terms with everything.

But I can't let it rest. There is no way that some curse from over a hundred years ago is going to affect my life.

"Look, I'm a smart woman. You sent me to school, I studied hard, and I've learned a lot in life. I'm going to figure this out for us one way or another."

"I wish you could, sweetheart"—Dolly sighs—"but we've tried everything."

"Just give me a little time. I'll think of something," I tell them.

"Just make sure that you don't do anything crazy," Selma warns me. "The curse is too powerful to mess with."

"And above all," Dolly adds, "don't marry Gogo. You promise?"

My head is swimming. The thought of having to leave Gogo, to never see him again. How would I explain it to him? How could I begin to leave the one thing in my life that's ever made me happy?

"You promise?" Selma repeats.

"Fine," I answer with my fingers crossed behind my back.

4.

It's not easy to date the perfect man when you've never dated one before.

When Gogo called me the morning after our first meeting, I couldn't understand what he wanted.

"Dinner, Saturday night. A date. The thing where I pick you up and we go to a restaurant and share a meal with a bottle of wine," he repeated a few times until I finally understood what he was asking.

He arrived at my home on time. I was so used to my dates arriving an hour late or not showing up at all that he woke me up from a nap. Can you imagine? This was how low my expectations were.

"I just assumed you wouldn't show up," I said, taking the flowers from him.

"Don't you remember I called this morning to firm up the plans?" he asked.

"Sure, but I figured something would have come up for you."

"Like what?" he asked.

"I don't know," I said recalling past excuses, "maybe houseguests suddenly showed up. You caught a bad cold. Your baby mama showed up at your door handing you the child you never knew you had."

"That's what I said to the other girls I had dates with tonight," he joked. "Come on," he said, marching me to my bedroom and stopping at the door. The gentleman that he is wouldn't walk in. "I'll call the restaurant and tell them we'll be a little late so you can get ready."

When I think of that night at the restaurant, staring at him as he talked about his career as a pediatrician, it was like he was playing some kind of part: the gorgeous smart guy with a heart of gold. Who knew that he actually existed in real life?

"Are you interested in having kids?" he asked me.

"Sure," I said.

"You'd be a great mom," he said.

"Why would you say that?" I asked.

"The way you talk about your mother and your grandmother. You really care about them," he said.

And when he dropped me off at my door without slobbering all over me and grabbing my breasts, I thought he just wasn't interested.

And then he called the next morning and asked me out again. And again.

One Saturday night, two weeks after we'd met, he cooked dinner at his house. It was chicken cacciatore, my favorite, and afterward we sat on the couch, where he said the following words, the most romantic words anyone has ever said to me: "I DVR'd that show you like, the one you said was your favorite."

"You mean the one you said you hated?" I looked at him cock-eyed.

"That's right."

That's when I knew I wanted to kiss him. I wanted to grab and smother him with kisses all over his face. Only I didn't.

"That was really sweet of you." I smiled, sitting back on the couch with my arms folded. "I'll watch it sometime when you want to do something else."

"Well, maybe I'll get into it," he said, turning it on. "I mean, if you like it, maybe I'm missing something."

Somehow during the show, I fell asleep. A few hours later, I woke up to find Gogo sitting across from me reading the newspaper. A blanket was over me.

"I'm so sorry," I said, pulling the covers off.

"No big deal. You must have been pretty tired," he said, moving some disheveled hair from my face.

"I guess I was," I said, wiping my eyes and getting up. "Well, I guess it's too late for you to take me home. I'll just call a cab."

"Don't call a cab." He laughed. "I'll take you home. You could also stay here if you want."

"Oh no," I said, "I've taken too much of your time already."

And then he leaned in and kissed me. All I could think about was the bad taste in my mouth from all the garlic from the chicken cacciatore. *He must be desperate if he's making a move on someone with bad breath.* The thing is, though, he didn't seem to care and all I wanted to do was kiss him back.

Gogo took me in his arms and we continued to kiss for I don't know how long and I didn't care. The feeling of his lips on mine, it was a feeling I'd never felt before. It was the most perfect kiss in the world. My heart was beating like crazy and all I wanted to do was rip his clothes off, but if I did, I knew that would be the end of it. When he started to unbutton my blouse, though, I just let him. The whole thing had gotten so steamy; I've got to unbutton my collar even as I tell the story.

Gogo took my hand and we ran into the bedroom, where I had the greatest sex of my life. My God, I never knew what it was like for someone to want to please me like that. I'll spare you the details, but if you've ever found yourself with the perfect man like I had, you know exactly what that sex was like.

I woke up early the next morning. It must have been around five or six. Gogo was sleeping silently next to me, that kind of sleep I still love to watch.

I knew in my heart that this was it. Something this good could never last. Everything in the world at that moment was perfect. If he woke up, everything would change. So I just lay there silently watching him, wishing that every morning could be like this, waking up to such a kind person. We had only been on a few dates, but I knew I was in love with him, what woman wouldn't be? The problem, though, was that I knew what happened to guys once you slept with them.

I had the choice to get out of that bed and leave while everything was good, or wait until he woke up and suffer through "I'm really busy at work right now, but I'll call you" or "I'm not in the right place right now to start a relationship." I decided to leave.

I looked over at Gogo one more time and then I slowly got out of bed as quietly as I could so I wouldn't wake him. What I didn't count on was the hardwood floor that creaked the second I put my foot down.

"Where ya going?" he asked sleepily as he reached over for me.

"I have to be someplace early today," I told him. "Sorry to wake you. Go back to sleep."

"Where do you have to be early on a Sunday morning?" He laughed.

"Church," I uttered.

"I thought you were Jewish," he said.

"Temple?" I asked, hoping that would work.

"I'm sure the rabbi will understand," he said, pulling me back toward the bed.

"No," I said, pulling back, "he won't. I can't," I said sadly, putting on my clothes.

"Is everything okay?" he asked me.

"Sure it is," I said.

"Are you sure?" he asked again.

"I'm positive," I said. "It's so early, go back to sleep."

I finished getting dressed, left the house, and used my cell phone to call a cab. As soon as I hung up, I heard Gogo's door open.

"Is it someone else?" he asked from the door.

"What?" I asked, turning to him.

"Are you seeing someone else?" he asked me.

"I didn't want to disturb you any more than I have," I told him. "I just called a cab."

"Why?" he asked. "I would have taken you home."

"I'm fine," I told him. "Just go back to sleep."

"Lily, what is this? What's going on here?" he asked, walking out of his house in his boxers. "You don't have work to do, do you?"

"Well," I stammered, "to be honest, no. I just, I just had a really great time last night and I didn't want hear those words."

"What words?" he asked.

"You know, the ones a guy says once he's slept with you, 'I'll call you sometime,' or 'I'm moving to Alaska.'"

"I know you dated that moron, but are you that damaged that you can't tell if a guy likes you or not?"

"I'm not damaged," I told him, offended.

"So what's your problem? Lily, I'm not moving to Alaska. I'm not going to stop calling you just because we slept together. Jeez, you'd think you never dated a guy who ever treated you right before."

"Well, maybe I haven't," I told him. "Maybe there are no good men in this world."

"And who told you that? Your mother? Your grandmother?"

"No," I told him. "Experience."

"Well, then I'm here to change things. It's time you had a good guy. Now come on, come back in the house and let's make you some breakfast, okay?"

"I don't know."

"What's the worst that can happen?" he asked. "So if I turn out to be a bad guy, you'll know that I'm like all the rest. If I turn out to be one of the good ones, well . . . you never know until you give me a chance."

Gogo smiled at me, this warm, inviting smile, as he took my hand.

"Are you sure?" I asked him. "Because I don't know if I could take it if you suddenly turned into one of the bad guys."

"I promise you I won't," he said. "At least for now," he said, taking my hand. "I don't start being an asshole until at least six months into the relationship."

"I thought you haven't really been in a serious relationship since college?" I smiled.

"That's the only one I admit to," he joked. "Come on back inside," he said, leading the way.

When the cab came a little later, Gogo ran outside and gave him a tip, and then sent him on his way.

In the last year, I've learned to trust this person who makes sure there are socks on my bedside table just in case my feet get cold during the night. I've learned to love the person who doesn't mind when he's the only guy at the chick movie or who allows me to keep the thermostat at a warm 77 degrees while he's sweating bullets. Most of all, though, I've gotten used to loving it when I arrive at work each morning and find that my first email of the day is from Gogo. Most times it's just a little note:

I'm missing you already.
G

Sometimes it's a goofy picture, like the one of the monkey holding a box of chocolates in his hand and pursing his lips like he's blowing a kiss.

Other times, though, it's words of love I just can't believe some-one would feel so free to say:

> *Thank you for making me the happiest man alive. I plan on spending the rest of my life making sure you feel the same way.*
> *All my love,*
> G

And this is what I have to break up with.

All because of some curse made by a great-great-grand-aunt who got shafted by my great-great-grandmother.

Bitch.

I left work early today. There was no way I was going to get any work done, so I faked a cold coming on and hightailed it out of there. I called Gogo's secretary, Bernice Zankower, a sixty-some-thing heavyset woman who was always bubbly and bright when I called, and asked her to schedule some time for me in between little Jeremy Taylor's tetanus shot and Morgan Carson's sore throat with-out telling Gogo I was coming by.

"That's so romantic, you're surprising him." She sighs.

Ouch.

"You're the best thing I've seen all day," Gogo says when he sees me in the waiting room.

"Hey." I sigh. "I needed to come and see you."

"Sure," he says, kissing me on the forehead. "Let's go back to my office. I've got some things I want to show you."

As we head into Gogo's office, the first thing I see on his desk are some ivory invitations and some lace samples.

"Dr. Hunter's daughter just got married and he had some of these samples left over. I like the ivory invitations, don't you?" he says, picking up the card.

I take it in my hand, but I just can't bear to think about other people who got to spend the rest of their lives in wedded bliss.

"Gogo," I say with a sigh, "let's have a seat."

"Sure," he says, taking a seat on one of the visitor chairs and pulling the other out for me. "What's up? Are you okay? You don't look very good."

"Gogo, you know I'm crazy about you, right? You know that you're the only man for me. You know that you're the only person I want to spend the rest of my life with, right?"

"Okay . . ."

"Well"—I breathed in—"I . . . I . . ."

"But you're nervous," he finishes for me.

I don't know why I don't tell him the truth. I don't know why I don't just tell him I need to end it. It's just that he's sitting there in his white doctor's coat looking so handsome.

"Yes, I'm nervous." I exhale.

"It's just jitters," he says, extending his hand and rubbing my shoulders. "You have so much tension here," he says, getting up and massaging my shoulders.

"No, I know what jitters are, but you just don't understand. If I could just explain things to you, you'll understand everything."

"You're scared, Lil, of course you are. No one could fault you for that."

"No, but you don't understand."

Gogo stops massaging my shoulders and bends down in front of me.

"Lil, do you know why I love you so much?" he sort of whispers.

"Why?"

"Because in the time that I've known you, you've been so caring toward me that you never stop to think about yourself."

"But there's a reason—" I say, trying to interrupt, but he's on a roll.

"And when I do something for you, you take the smallest gesture and appreciate it more than anyone I've ever known. Sometimes I look at you and I feel like I've been put here to make you happy. I'm so excited to do that for you, Lil."

I jump up and pull my chair away. I can't take it anymore.

"I CAN'T MARRY YOU BECAUSE THERE'S A CURSE PUT ON THE WOMEN IN MY FAMILY. IF I MARRY YOU OR SPEND ANY MORE TIME WITH YOU, SOME-THING REALLY BAD WILL HAPPEN TO YOU," I blurt out.

Gogo sits there looking at me in shock.

"That's why I went out with all those men who treated me like crap. That's why my mother and grandmother insisted I never fall in love with a good man. Gogo, I'm telling you, for your own good, we need to break up and never see each other again. My great-great-grandaunt Emmalina put a curse on the women in my family that says if you marry for love, something really bad will happen. I've seen my mother have to divorce five men under mysterious cir-cumstances—excessive hair growth, one got kidnapped by a tuba, the hiccups—and I just can't do that to you."

Gogo sits there, still staring at me.

"I think you've snapped," he finally says. "I'm going to write you a prescription for some Ativan."

"No, I haven't. Look, let's go to see Dolly and Selma; they'll ex-plain everything to you. I'm telling you, once you understand it, it will all make sense. Look, I'm sorry we fell in love. I'm sorry I have to do this, but the reason I'm breaking up with you is because I love you like I've never loved anyone else in my entire life."

"But this is crazy," he says, starting to get angry. "If this is the best excuse that you could come up with to end this whole thing, then I don't want to be with you."

"But I love you, I do," I say, taking his hand. "I just can't see you for the rest of my life. It's the curse."

"A curse?" He laughs.

"A curse, I swear." I insist, "I'm calling Dolly and Selma; they'll explain it to you. They explained it to me. It makes sense, Gogo, just trust me, I'm not doing this for any other reason than love."

"And what will happen to you?" he asks. "Where will you go?"

"I'll move back into my house. I'll go on with my life. You will meet someone else."

"And won't you meet someone else?"

"No, I'll go on and live my life alone. That's the curse. There's nothing I can do about it."

"I think I'm going to have to call the cops on your mother and grandmother. What kind of people would convince you that this is possible?"

"They're wonderful people."

"It's like Stockholm syndrome, except your mother and grandmother are convincing you to spend your life alone."

"Look, what do you want me to say? How can I prove it to you?"

"Let's get married tonight," he proclaims.

"I just told you—"

"What did you say could happen to me, I could die? So I'll watch out for falling branches."

"No, you don't die, it's worse. A branch will fall on you and it will get stuck in your arm and they can't surgically take it out, so you'll have a branch in your arm for the rest of your life."

He bursts out laughing.

"You think I'm kidding. I'm telling you, it's the curse!"

"I'll wrap myself in bubble wrap."

"I thought of that, of just watching every move you make, but this curse is really strong."

"So I'll take my chance."

"I can't do that to you."

"Lily," he says angrily, "I've had it. I'm done with all of this. I don't know what else I can do to show you that I'm a good guy. If you don't want to marry me, just say it, just say it."

"I want to marry you, Gogo, I keep telling you that. How many more times do I have to keep telling you? I want to marry you, I just can't."

"So then marry me tonight. Let me worry about those problems, or walk out that door and we'll never see each other again. It's your choice, Lil."

I want to walk out that door. I want to do what I have set out to do, but you have to understand, this is love. He is willing to take the consequences. He is willing to do anything it takes to be with me.

"So what's your answer?" he asks.

"Do you promise to watch yourself?"

"I promise. I'll watch every move I make."

"You're telling me that you'd be prepared to do this."

"Like I said, let me worry about it."

"Fine," I say, folding my arms.

"Fine," he says, folding his arms.

"So we're getting married right now."

"I'll cancel my appointments for the rest of the day."

"And you won't come crying to me if you're pinned under a five-ton semi," I tell him.

"How could I? I'm pinned under a five-ton semi."

For the first time all day, I laugh. I look at Gogo and just know. Gogo is strong, he's smart. If any man can get by the curse, it's Gogo.

"Then let's go," I say, walking toward the door.

Gogo runs ahead of me to open the door, but I stop him in his tracks.

"And from now on, I open the doors," I say sternly, pointing my finger at him. "You never know if someone's got an anvil rigged up to fall on your head."

"Yeah, because it's so often that we find ourselves stuck in a Bugs Bunny cartoon."

We jump on the next plane to Las Vegas, quickly get our marriage license, and settle on a little chapel just east of the main strip.

As the Elvis impersonator reads the vows and Gogo repeats them, and then I follow, my heart is overflowing with happiness. We are a team and we are going to take this on together.

"I now pronounce you man and wife," Elvis announces, as our witnesses, the other people in line to get married, throw rice.

This is the happiest moment of my life.

It's dawn by the time Gogo and I get back to our hotel room.

"How you doin', Mrs. Goldblatt?" he whispers as he takes me in his arms.

"Mrs. *Stanley* Goldblatt is just fine." I smile as I kiss him.

"And do you see? I haven't choked on anything. No anvils came out of the sky and struck me down."

"I keep trying to tell you, it's not that kind of curse. It doesn't kill you. It just makes your life miserable."

"I know you'll take care of me," he says, kissing my head.

"Gogo?" I smile.

"Yeah."

"Pinch me."

"Why?" He laughs.

"I'm just so happy. This feels like a dream. I just want to make sure that all of this is real."

"Okay," he says, sitting up laughing. "Now, where would you like to be pinched?"

"Oh, I don't care, on the arm is fine," I say, leaning on his chest as I hold out my arm.

Through the morning sun, I see Gogo's hand go toward my arm. I watch as he puts his hand on me, sticking out his index finger and thumb and taking my skin in between them.

I feel the pinch; it isn't painful or anything, just a tug to my arm.

"This is real." I smile at him. "It's all real . . ."

The next thing I know I'm in my old house. I am lying in my old bed. Clothes are strewn everywhere, just like they were before I moved in with Gogo.

I sit up and look around me. I look down and see that I'm still clothed in my jeans and tank top I was wearing seconds ago in Vegas. I feel like I fell asleep in my clothes, but I grab my arm, still feeling the pressure of Gogo's pinch.

"*What the—?*" I shout, turning over in my bed. "*Where? How?*"

I jump out of bed and run into the living room. Two seconds ago I was in a gaudy hotel in Las Vegas!

I run to the kitchen, I don't know why. I think I'm just trying to see where I am, what's different, have I been dreaming? I open the refrigerator. I had unplugged it a year ago to defrost the ice and never plugged it back in. When I open it, though, there's that block of ice built up in the freezer. The only thing in the refrigerator is a moldy half a sandwich. I slam the door shut. Frankly, the smell emanating from that sandwich is a little too much for me anyway, even in my current state.

But no, I'm not dreaming. I was just in Las Vegas. I look down at my hand, but there is no engagement ring, no wedding ring.

I run back into the bedroom and grab the phone and dial.

"Please, God, let him be all right. Please let him be alive!" I cry out.

The phone rings once, twice.

"Hello?" the angry voice says on the other end.

I exhale.

"Oh thank God. Gogo, it's me, are you okay?"

"Who the hell is this and why are you calling so early in the morning?"

"It's me, it's Lily!"

"I don't know who you are. Please don't call this number ever again."

"But it's *me! Lily! Your wife!*"

"I don't know who put you up to this, but my wife is sleeping next to me. Now I'm turning my phone off. Please don't call here again."

The phone clicks.

I hang up in shock, my mouth gaping open as I'm unable to move. All I can do is sit and stare into space.

5.

I can't believe I didn't listen to them. I can't believe that I allowed this to happen. How could I have let this happen? Thank God I spoke to him, though. Thank God he seems fine. Angry but fine, and I'll just explain things and we'll go from here." I've said these words over and over for the last hour as I waited until I knew Gogo would be in his office. The clock has finally struck 7:30 a.m. and I'm on my way. "Gogo, I am your real wife," I rehearse over and over as I leave my house and get into my car. "We got married two hours ago in Las Vegas and you're under a spell." Oh God. I hope it works. I start the car and floor the gas on the way out of my driveway as I head over to see what's become of him.

Of course Gogo will take me at my word and we'll straighten out this whole mess. Whoever he is married to, she will just have to understand that Gogo and I are meant to be. The whole thing sounded logical as I finally arrive at Gogo's office. Crisis and curse averted.

But something is funny about Gogo's office. Gogo always had framed pictures of the Peanuts characters on his wall, and I notice they aren't there now. Maybe they took them down for cleaning. Also, four kids are in here screaming bloody murder at the top of their lungs. This isn't something one usually finds in Gogo's office. While most pediatrician's offices have screaming kids in their waiting rooms, Gogo's doesn't. The kids know they are going to see Dr. Gogo. This is one of the many things I love about him. Gogo's patients are never afraid of him. When they sit in his waiting room, they only anticipate kindness. Today, though, there must be a bad earache going around. I had never heard it this loud before.

"Hi, Bernice." I sigh with relief when I see Gogo's secretary sitting at her desk.

"What?" she shouts through the screams of crying children.

"Crazy day here, huh?" I shout back.

"It's a day like all the others," she deadpans. "Now what's your child's name?" she asks, looking down at her appointment book. "The doctor is running late, as usual."

"Gogo? Late?" I shout above the ruckus.

"Excuse me?" she bellows. "I didn't catch your son's name. Did you say his name was Gogo?"

"No." I laugh. "Gogo. The doctor. Dr. Goldblatt," I say.

"Who? I'm sorry, there's no Dr. Goldblatt here," she says. "You're in the wrong place."

I turn around and look at the office door to make sure I'm actually in the right place. Gogo's nameplate, outlined in balloon shapes, is usually posted on the door. It's not there. Instead, a formal nameplate in brass says Dr. Winston Hamilton.

"Is this the third floor?" I ask.

"Yes," she says.

"Excuse me," a mother with a crying child shouts, "I've been waiting here for over an hour. Can you tell me how much longer?"

"The doctor has a heavy load today," Bernice shouts back, uncaring.

I look over at the woman whose poor child is crying as if he's in a great deal of pain.

"Don't you think you should let the doctor know what's going on out here?" I ask.

"You've obviously never been to a pediatrician's office before." Bernice laughs.

"Of course I have!" I say to her. "And Gogo would never let these kids cry like this."

"Well, maybe they should go see this wonder doctor," she smartly remarks.

"Did you say you know a better pediatrician?" the mother asks me.

"Yes, I do, he's wonderful," I say, turning to her.

"Can I get the number?" she asks as the other mothers lean in.

"Can I get the number?" another asks, taking out her phone.

"Well, he's . . ." I walk out of the office and look down the hall. This is it, office number 311. There's no way Gogo's office could be anywhere else. Maybe he moved his office. That is all I can figure at this point.

"Can he get me in for a ten o'clock appointment?" another mother asks.

"I'll . . . I'll find him for you and let you know," I tell them.

I get back into my car and pull out my BlackBerry. I have ninety-two emails from work, but there is no way that I'll be going in and I literally haven't missed a day of work in the ten years I've worked at Sacki and Sacki.

"Hello, Rebecca?" I call my secretary in a groggy voice.

"You sound awful," she says, "but you have to get in here immediately, the Best Buy people are going to be here this afternoon. Do you have your presentation ready?"

"Oh crap," I exclaim. "The Best Buy account, I totally forgot!"

"You must be sick," she says. "You've been working on that pitch for the last two months. You've made me stay here past midnight every night and now you can't remember? Did you fall down or something?"

"No." I cough. "I have a really bad virus. I'm lying in bed. I can't even lift my head," I say, cleaning some lint out of my car's console unit.

"Well, I'll tell Gerry you're sick, but she's not going to like it."

Gerry is the president of our division and normally we get along, but I knew this was no good.

"Look, patch Gerry through and I'll explain things to her." I cough again.

"Get your ass in here by noon or you're fired." These are the only words that Gerry says to me. I try to get a word in, but she hangs up before I can get my first fake cough out.

But I can't think about that now. Let her fire me. Something that's been the center of my life for the past ten years has suddenly become unimportant.

I have no choice. I have to go over to Gogo's house and find Gogo. I have no idea what I'm going to say. I just hope that Gogo's wife, whoever she is, isn't there. I keep praying to myself, *Please don't let Gogo's wife be there. Please don't let Gogo's wife be there.*

I pull up to Gogo's home, the one that until yesterday was also mine. Truthfully, it looks better than it looked when Gogo and I were there. Lining the walkway are rosebushes, blooming in pinks and white. Personally, I would have gone for oranges and reds, but who has time to garden like this?

I walk up to the door and ring the doorbell, still praying, *Please don't let Gogo's wife be there*, when I hear a female voice shout through the door, "Who is it?"

Who is it? Who am I? I think as the female voice repeats, "Who is it?"

"Uh, um," I say as I hear the locks to the door unfasten. Bottom lock goes to the right, top one to the left.

And as the door opens, I see in front of me a woman who looks to be about my age in a pink leotard with a sweatshirt over it. She has red hair, which is tied in a bun on top of her head. She looks like she just stepped out of an eighties Jane Fonda workout tape.

"Can I help you?" she asks.

The thing is, she doesn't look mean or bitchy. She looks like a normal down-to-earth person in bad workout gear. What could I tell her?

"Yes, does Gogo Goldblatt live here?" I stammer.

"He does, but he's at work right now," she tells me. "Is there anything I can help you with?"

I look into the home that only yesterday was mine but today looks like it fits squarely in the alternative universe I'm now living in. Our modern caramel suede couch is replaced with a pink floral couch. The walls, normally white and bare with black-and-white photographs, are now robin's egg blue. A doily is sitting on a birch coffee table where our streamlined glass and metal coffee table used to be. Frankly, it looks like the Easter Bunny has vomited all over what was once my living room.

"Would you mind telling me where his office is?" I ask, hoping I can get in and out of there.

"Would you mind telling me what this is about?" she asks, looking confused.

"Well," I say, trying to come up with a good excuse, "my son . . . daughter . . . my twins are patients of Dr. Goldblatt's and I was driving by hoping to get a prescription for some . . . Tylenol."

"Oh." She laughs. "I'm sorry, you have the wrong house. My husband isn't a doctor."

"Gogo Goldblatt?" I ask. "The pediatrician? But I've been here before and Dr. Goldblatt is always kind enough to give my kids a prescription when I can't get to the office."

"You've got the name right, but my husband works with drainage systems."

"Drainage systems?" I ask incredulously. "You mean like ear, nose, and throat? He's an ear, nose, and throat doctor?"

"No." She laughs again. "For homes. My husband works in my

father's downspout company. That's so funny to think of Gogo as a doctor."

"It's not that funny," I say, defending my husband.

"You're not supposed to think it's funny. You don't know him," she says, referring to her husband. "You know," she says, starting to get annoyed, "I wish I could help your children, but I'm sorry, you have the wrong house." She starts to shut the door.

"No, wait!" I shout. "Can you just tell me what a downspout is?"

"This is getting to be a little much for me," she says. "I'd like to shut my door now."

"No, wait, please," I beg, pushing the door back open. "I swear to you, I'm a normal human being. I'm not a crazy person. I just need to find your husband."

"And why on earth would you need to find my husband?" she asks, sounding really pissed.

"I . . . I . . ."

"Are you having an affair with my husband?" she asks. "Did he tell you he was a doctor?" She looks out the door and toward my car. "Are your children in the car? Are they Gogo's children?"

"What?" I ask. "No. I don't have children. I lied. I just said that so you would tell me where Gogo was. To be honest with you, we used to date and there are some things I need to say to him. I just, well . . . You understand as a woman, I need . . . I need some closure."

The woman grabs the door.

"I find it hard to believe that you're not having an affair with my husband. My husband and I have been married for twelve years. We were married one month after we graduated from college. Maybe the two of us should go down to Gogo's office and the three of us can figure this out."

"Since college?" I ask, backing away from the door, trying to get myself out of this. "You know what? I think," I said, trying to get out a fake laugh, "I think I have the wrong Gogo Goldblatt, oh well, la dee da," I sort of sing. "Well, I guess I'll be seeing you around," I say, creeping off the stoop.

"Wait a minute." She stops me. "Are you the one who called here at the crack of dawn? My husband answered the phone? You said he was your husband?"

"What?" I say, trying to look surprised. "No, that wasn't me. I sleep twelve hours a night, like a rock. I never use the phone before ten a.m."

"It was. It had to be," she says, interrupting me. "I believed him when he said it was some crazy woman. Now I'm not so sure."

"Okay," I say, backing away from the door and heading down the walkway. "I've made a terrible mistake here. I obviously have the wrong Gogo Goldblatt. I'm sorry I've wasted your time, Mrs. . . . ."

"It's Rhonda," she says angrily. "And if you'd like to sort this out with my husband, you can find him at Carverman Downspouts, corner of Fifty-Fourth and City Line Avenue. You'll find my father there as well. He'll want to hear about this too. You can't miss him. He's the big burly guy who works out every day."

"No"—I wave my arms, smiling and waving, walking swiftly toward my car—"that won't be necessary. There's been a big mistake here." I push the unlock button on my car key incessantly to make sure it will be open by the time I get to it.

"And by the way," she shouts from her door, "if you were going to steal someone's husband, why would you pick my husband? You should have picked someone cuter with a little more going for him."

Then she slams her door shut.

I start my car and floor the gas, screeching out of there as quickly as I can.

I drive a few blocks, and when I feel that I'm safe, I pull over and rest my head on the steering wheel.

How am I going to get out of this one? How am I going to convince my husband that he is really married to me? What did I do? What did I do?

The clock in my car says 10:30. I know I have to be getting to the Best Buy meeting to give whatever pitch I'm going to give, but I just have to get to Gogo. I just have to make sure he's okay. I still don't know how I'm going to explain everything to him, or how I can save him from his wife thinking he had an affair.

I think, *I'll just get to Gogo. I'll just see if he's all right. I'll just take a look at him and feel out the situation and if it feels right, I'll explain everything to him.*

Gogo's office isn't so far away from where I am, and soon I pull into one of the vacant spots in front, my head still spinning. I can't cause any more trouble than I already have, but thinking about it, I wonder if maybe this is the best thing, maybe Gogo would divorce Rhonda and we could be together and stay married . . . or remarried, whichever.

And suddenly I see him. There he is! My heart is dropping. There he is.

He looks thin. Why does he look so thin? Poor thing looks tired too. He looks awful. His hair isn't as full and shiny as it normally is. No elderly women would want to run their hands through it now. And he's pale, so pale. Doesn't he go out in the sun anymore? He looks like he hasn't seen sun . . . ever. Is it possible that he's shorter? I don't care, though. There he is, my Gogo!

"*Gogo!*" I shout, getting out of the car.

He looks at me, perplexed.

"*It's Lily!*" I shout. I don't care if he knows me or not. It's my Gogo, my soul mate and only love.

"Are you the crazy person who just came over to my house?" he shouts in my face.

"Yes!" I smile ecstatically. "It's me! Lily! Don't you remember me at all? Look at me? Don't I look a little familiar?" I can tell from his face that he has no recollection of me, but I'm just so excited to see him. He has to remember, he just has to!

"Look," he says heatedly, "I don't know who you are or why you're screwing with my life. I have been married to the same woman for the past twelve years. I don't know who put you up to this or why you picked me, but I'm going to ask you to leave me alone. You've caused enough problems for me today. My wife thinks I'm having an affair. If my father-in-law gets wind of this, I'm in even bigger trouble. Please, I'm asking you, whoever put you up to this, for me, please leave me alone."

"But Gogo," I say, trying to reason, "I know this sounds crazy. I know I sound like a lunatic."

"Yes, you do, and in a minute I'm going to call a cop. Now please, leave me alone."

The look in his eyes—I've seen that look before. It's the look Gogo gives when he really wants something. The last time I saw that look, he was asking me to marry him. Now he has that look for the opposite reason.

"I'm sorry," I say, brokenhearted. "I am sorry if I caused you any trouble today."

"Now please stop bothering me."

"I will," I say, realizing I'm getting nowhere. At least I can see that he is all right, tired and old-looking, but all right. That's the most that I hope for at this point, and I'm not sure where to go from here. I turn around and head back toward my car.

And then it occurs to me. "Your name is Stanley!" I say calmly.

"What?" he asks.

"Your real name is Stanley," I say, hoping for some glint of recognition.

"How did you know that?" he asks.

"Because I'm telling you the truth. In some other dimension or something, something I can't explain to you in a parking lot, we were married and I know that your real name is Stanley. Your name is Stanley Angus Goldblatt."

He stands there incredulous. "But no one knows that."

"I know that no one knows that," I tell him. "But I do. I know you. You're Stanley Golblatt, named after your grandfather on your mother's side."

"I can't imagine how you'd know that," he says. "No one knows that. Is this a part of the joke? Who told you that?"

"You did!" I rattled off his social security number.

"Anyone would know that."

"You had a mole removed on your stomach and you love the scar from it because you say it makes you look rugged."

Gogo lifts up his shirt, exposing the scar. Then he puts his shirt back down again.

"Look," he says, "I still don't know if this is some kind of joke."

"Here," I say, opening my car door and grabbing an old receipt. "I'm going to give you my phone number. If you want to call and let me explain sometime, I will. I'll leave that up to you."

I scribble my number on the back of the receipt and hand it to him.

"Just, just think about it," I say, starting to cry as I get in my car. I don't know why I'm starting to cry, maybe it's seeing Gogo and him not knowing me. Maybe it's how awful he looks. Either way, the tears are coming.

I leave Gogo standing there as I pull out of the parking lot.

I drive a few blocks, and when I can't take it anymore, for the second time today, I pull over to the side and rest my head on the steering wheel.

Then I reach into my bag, take out my phone, and dial. My hands are trembling.

"Burns residence," I hear Dolly's friendly voice answer.

"Grandma?" I barely get out through my tears.

"Lily, sweetheart, what is it?" She panics.

"I . . . I . . . ," I say, starting to bawl. "I've screwed up. Big-time!"

6.

So you're saying he works making drainpipes?" Dolly says, repeating everything I just told her as she fills my plate with pancakes, bacon, and sausage.

"No, he makes downspouts," I correct her as I push the plate away.

"What the heck is a downspout?" she asks as she pushes it back toward me.

"I'm not sure," I say, blowing my nose.

"They're the gutters outside the house. You know, when we call the man each year to get the leaves out of the gutter? That's a downspout," Selma explains as she looks into the mirror, straightening a sweatband around her head.

"Oh that's just sad," Dolly says.

"Well, whatever it is, it's not a pediatrician," I cry.

"There, there." Dolly sighs, putting her arms around me.

"So you say he's thin and tired-looking," Selma adds, as she gets down on the floor and starts stretching her legs.

"He's a shell of the man I knew yesterday." I cry as I add, "Mom, what are you doing?"

"I'm stretching before I go to the gym. I like to be ready to get on the elliptical machine right when I get there. Carter, he's that twenty-five-year-old trainer I was telling you about? If I'm not on that machine he'll start talking to me and the next thing you know we'll start dating and we'll get married and then a barbell will fall on him."

"At least he knows who you are," I sob.

"And the trainer isn't married to a witch of a woman," Dolly adds, repeating what I told her.

"Well, I'm sure anyone would turn into a witch if someone showed up at their door and it looked like they were having an affair with their husband."

"So let me get this straight. He's tired, thin, he's got a bad job and a witch of a wife. Is that it in a nutshell?" Dolly sums up the situation.

I watch them sneak a smile at each other.

"Don't you dare say that he's perfect for me now. Don't you dare feed me any more of that!" I howl.

"We're sorry," Selma says, putting her arm around my shoulder. "It's just that, well, it's not like you weren't warned."

"But what was I supposed to do? He gave me no choice. He said he understood all about the curse and he'd watch himself, you know, in case a tree fell on him or something."

"But who would have expected something like this?" Dolly wondered.

"The curse just keeps us guessing and guessing, doesn't it? What's going to happen to the next guy?" Selma ponders as she stretches her hands over her head and thrusts her hips from side to side. "It's just so bizarre. You're telling us that you got married and then—"

"Wait a second. Before we go any further we should at least hear about the wedding." Dolly claps her hands with excitement. "Did you wear a veil?"

"Oh yes, I'm getting ahead of myself. Lily, you must sit and tell us all about the wedding. Oh, to have walked you down the aisle, you know it's always been my dream. So tell us, was it beautiful?" Selma begs.

"It was beautiful. It happened in Vegas and an Elvis impersonator presided and I wore jeans and a T-shirt and carried plastic flowers and Gogo wore jeans and flip-flops"—I start tearing up again—"and it was the most romantic wedding I've ever been to." I start howling.

"An Elvis impersonator?" Selma balks.

"You carried plastic flowers?" Dolly sighs.

"It wasn't about the stuff, it was about the marriage, the love," I bawl.

"Oh sweetheart," Selma says, grabbing the tissue box. "Cry to Mama, cry to Mama." She hands me another tissue.

"The thing that hurts the most is he doesn't even remember me. He doesn't remember that I exist. I thought that maybe if he saw me, you know, not just heard my voice on the phone but saw me in the flesh, that he would remember me and our love for each other."

"Nothing, not even love is as strong as the curse," Dolly warns me.

"But you remember me telling you all about him. You remember the ring I showed you?" I ask.

"Honestly?" Selma turns to Dolly. "I remember telling you all about the curse," Selma says to me.

"I remember sitting here and eating that Sara Lee and telling you all about our family history. Do you remember her mentioning this man?" Dolly asks Selma.

"What did you say his name is?" Selma tries to think as she sits down on the floor with her legs in front of her and touches her toes.

"Gogo, Gogo Goldblatt."

"Nope." Dolly shakes her head. "Doesn't ring a bell."

"You mean to tell me you don't remember why you told me about the curse, but you remember telling me about the curse? Don't you remember I had this big gorgeous ring on my hand?"

"It's not that we don't believe you, sweetheart," Dolly explains. "We know how strong the curse can be."

"It's like the curse made everyone except you forget about this perfect dream man," Selma sums up, placing one leg in back of her neck.

"It sounds like even the dream man forgets he's a dream man," Dolly concludes.

"So what do you think I should do?" I ask them.

"What are you going to do?" Selma asks, placing the other leg around her neck. "You've done all you could do."

"I think you're at the end of your rope with this," Dolly tells me. "I mean, think about it. Let's just say for happily-ever-after's sake, let's say that he suddenly remembers you and he divorces his wife and he marries you and he gains some muscle back and he goes to medical school. Let's say all that turns out the way you want it to, then what?"

"Then what, what?"

"Then the curse will take another form. You and Gogo got off lucky this time. He didn't get swallowed up by a tuba or grow excessive hair," Dolly says, looking on the bright side.

"He didn't freeze his tongue to a pole," Selma reminds us, rolling onto her back and lifting her back into an arch.

"And a bolt of lightning didn't strike out of nowhere."

"And the stock market didn't collapse."

"Well," Dolly adds, "the economy *has* gone south."

"Yes, but that was before Lily and this Gogo got together, right, Lily?" Selma asks.

"Regardless, do you know how lucky you are that he's living some other life and doesn't remember you? You and Gogo got so lucky!" Dolly exclaims.

"How can you say this is lucky?" I stammer. "Gogo is miserable. I'm miserable!"

"At least he doesn't remember," Selma insists. "He doesn't

remember all the love he had in his life. He doesn't remember when it all went sour. Yep, you got off easy. If you get yourself back into it, there's no telling what could happen to Gary."

"Gogo," I tell her.

"What?"

"His name is Gogo."

"Was his mother a dancer or something?" Selma asks. "What kind of a name is Gogo?"

"We've been through this already," I sob. "I don't feel like explaining his name. All I know is that I want him back."

"Sweetheart"—Dolly puts her arm around me again—"you can look on the bright side."

"You mean there's a bright side in all of this?" I cry.

"There's the brightest side of them all." She sits beside me, takes my hands, and looks me right in the eyes. "Lily, you got to fall in love with a wonderful man. A kind, strong, handsome man who loved you so much that even when you warned him something like this could happen, he loved you enough to say, 'To hell with any curse, I don't care what happens to me, I want to be with you.'"

"And that makes you . . . ," Selma adds.

". . . the luckiest girl in the world. Some people live their whole lives and never find love like that." Dolly sighs.

"You had it. As short as it was, you experienced real love," Selma whispers soothingly.

"Then why do I feel so awful?" I weep.

"Because that's what real love does to you, but what you're experiencing now, all this sadness, it's not so terrible."

"How can you say that?" I ask.

"Because it proves that the love you have for Gogo is real," Dolly concludes.

"So I should try, I should try to get him back," I insist.

"What you should do is leave Gogo be. Don't hurt him any more than you already have. You have the memories inside of you; you have enough for the both of you," Selma tells me as she grabs her elbow with one hand and stretches her arm to the side.

"The best thing that you can do is accept that the curse is too powerful and you don't want to hurt anyone else," Dolly says.

"What you do is, you take these memories you have and you cherish them." Selma takes my hand. "They will be one of the most valuable things you will have in your life."

"You keep them safe in your heart," Dolly adds.

"And then you go on," Selma ends.

"And what do I do?" I ask.

"You live by the curse," Dolly concludes, as she looks out the window. "Oh, Bert Poolson, can you hear me now?" she shouts as if Old Man Poolson across the street could hear her. "I'm doing this for your own good, my darling." She walks over to the front door, opens it, and steps outside. "Hey, Poolson!" we hear her shout. "Your television was very loud last night. Either get your hearing checked or turn down the volume!"

"You're too sensitive!" Poolson shouts back angrily.

"If you have it that loud tonight, I'm going to call the police on you," Dolly says, slamming the door shut. "God, I love that man." She sighs dreamily.

"Do you really think I should give up?" I ask.

"It's the best thing for the both of you." Selma puts her arm around me. "Go on with your life," she tells me. "The only choice you have is dating a man you despise."

I know they're right. I know I should leave him be, but come on, what would you do? My mind is racing back and forth and every part of me just wants to run to him again, but what if I do get him back? What if something should happen to him? I would never forgive myself.

My phone rings and I see it's my office. I have a half hour to get to the pitch.

"Ugh." I sigh. "I have to go and pitch a prospective multimillion-dollar client."

"That's wonderful!" Selma starts jogging in place. "It will get your mind off of things."

"Thank goodness we taught her to work those ungodly hours," Dolly adds.

"I'll walk out with you," Selma says, putting some sweatbands around her wrists.

"Do you need me to drop you off at the gym?"

"Oh no, I'll run over there."

"Isn't that like fifteen miles away?"

"That's nothing!" She shrugs. "With all of my sexual frustration, I could run to Florida and back."

"TMI, Mom." I grimace.

Normally, I love coming into my office every morning. There's something about the hustle of all the people cramming themselves into the elevator and rising until we get to the top floor of Sacki and Sacki's East Coast headquarters. When I started out at the firm, I was ten floors below, and every couple of years I went up in floors until finally I was at the top. As the elevator opens every morning, I step out onto those beige marble tiles and say good morning to the receptionist behind the granite reception booth. The place is smart and sophisticated-looking with its beige leather sofas and Oriental rug in the waiting area. I even love how dressed up everyone always looks. Most people in the office hate that they have to wear suits and skirts, but I'm glad George Sacki, president of Sacki and Sacki worldwide, insists on it. This has been my home away from home for the past ten years. Normally, I love to hear the gossip of the day or who watched what on television last night. I love being able to tell everyone that I was in love and how wonderful he was. I love being a part of that team.

Today, I could give a shit.

Today I've got my shoulder sack in my hand and it's full of papers I once worked so hard on and now don't care about anymore. My hair, usually neatly combed, is hanging around my face. And then I remember: I'm wearing the jeans and T-shirt I was wearing last night—the night I got married.

"You have five minutes before the meeting!" Rebecca greets me in a crazed tone. "Gerry has been coming in here all morning asking if you've gotten in yet! What are you wearing?" she exclaims, looking down at my clothing.

"I'm ready," I tell her as she follows me into my office. "Just give me five minutes and I'll be ready. They're just going to have to deal with my attire this morning. I don't know, I'll work it into the pitch."

"What's the matter with you?" she asks. "You're not yourself. Did Jonah dump you again?"

"Who?" I ask, and then remember. "Oh yeah, Jonah. Has he been calling?"

"Lily," Gerry exclaims, exhaling as she comes into my office, "are you ready? What are you wearing?"

"Oh, this is for the pitch," I lie. "You'll see."

"Well, I hope so," she says. "You've got everything ready, right? The whole company is counting on you."

This is something that Gerry says that usually makes me feel good. I'm doing something for my family. Today, I don't feel like I'm doing something for my family. I'm doing something for my job.

"I'm ready," I tell her, trying to put a smile on my face.

"Good," she says. "Here we go."

I grab my papers as Rebecca grabs the poster boards we've been working on. I take a look at them just to make sure I've got everything straight that I want to say.

The pitch had come to me at one of those all-night sessions where everyone in the office tries to come up with the idea. The recession had hit us hard and we needed the Best Buy account. They wanted something new, something fresh. No one in the firm could come up with anything. And then it came to me. The idea had come from a conversation Gogo and I'd had. It was one of those innocent nothing conversations that a couple has. Gogo was going on and on about the graphics to his new video game. They really are amazing graphics.

"It looks so real," Gogo exclaimed, as he killed octopus-like robots with the click of his controller. "Remember Pong?" he asked, watching the screen as he pushed the buttons and flinched at the action in front of him. "When I was younger, all we had on the screen were two lines and a ball. What will our children's video games look like?"

Somehow, this little conversation got into my head. I started to think about it as other people in the agency gave their pitches. When I got it all laid out in my head, I just said it. The room went silent. Bruce Daniels, Gerry's boss, stared at me as if I'd just cured cancer. The whole room burst into applause:

We open on an elderly couple sitting in front of a beige backdrop, nothing fancy.

"In my day it was called email. You typed it out and pushed a button. It took over ten seconds to reach the person you were sending the letter to."

We cut to another elderly woman; this time it's a blue backdrop.

"The television was over two inches thick."

We cut to a series of elderly people now. The cuts get quicker and quicker.

"Sometimes the internet was slow."

"The iPhone was so big, you could hardly fit it in your pocket."

"It was called a scanner and it was a separate machine that downloaded pictures onto your computer."

And then we cut to black:

"What will you tell your grandchildren? Find it at Best Buy."

It's great, right? I'm sure they're going to love it. For the first time that day, I try to shake myself out of my depression and put on my work brain. If I can get through this pitch, I can tell them I'm taking the vacation I've never taken before. I can go home and figure out everything that's going on—the curse, coming to grips with what to do about Gogo. I just need some time to think.

"Here's our star!" Bruce Daniels announces as I head into the conference room. About ten people sit around the table; a few I've met in previous Best Buy meetings, but most are other members of the company I've never laid eyes on. I've always been good at this, though. This is the place I shine, the pitch session.

"Ladies and gentleman," Bruce announces, "I'd like to introduce you to our newest vice president and up-and-coming star at Sacki and Sacki, Ms. Lily Burns."

"Thank you," I say, wiping the hair away from my face as I help Rebecca set the poster boards on the stands.

"We open on an elderly couple sitting in front of a beige back-drop," I start, "nothing fancy." I point to the first board. That's when I notice.

There's no elderly couple on the board. Instead, it's a little boy holding a game console staring into a television screen. I look back at all the people looking at me.

"I'm sorry, we have the wrong board here," I say out loud, pointing at Rebecca.

Rebecca looks at the board and then looks at me, shrugging her shoulders.

That's when it occurs to me. There is no Gogo in my life. There-fore, the pitch that I came up with, the pitch that I know so well, is not the pitch on the poster board.

I'm standing here in front of a boardroom pitching a multi-million-dollar account I know nothing about.

"Uh, uh," I stammer, looking at the little boy in the picture again.

"Did you say this isn't right?" Thomas Difranco, head of Best Buy, asks. "Did she say she's got the wrong pitch there?"

"No!" I shout out, "I've got it right, I was just confused for a mo-ment. We open on a little boy playing with a game in front of his television," I stammer.

Rebecca points to the next board. In this one, it's a mother who looks like she's yelling at the boy.

"And the mother here"—I start sweating—"she's mad at the little boy because he's playing the game when he should be doing his homework."

Rebecca looks at me, wondering what the heck I'm talking about. I'm thinking the same exact thing. She points to the board. It's an older gentleman who looks like the kid's father on a computer.

"And the dad here—"

"You mean the grandfather," Rebecca whispers.

"I mean the grandfather. He's on his computer."

I look out at the boardroom again. Gerry's mouth is open. Bruce is eyeing me like he's about to forcibly throw me out of the building.

"See, what we're trying to get at here," I saying, clearing my throat to give me a couple of seconds to figure out what we're trying to get at here, "is that people need 'me time.' The boy just wants to play his game. He had a hard day at school. He doesn't need his grandmother yelling at him."

"Mother," Rebecca murmurs.

"Sorry, mother," I say. "And the grandfather. He just wants time away from the nurses at the old age home, so he goes onto his computer and he's got the world in front of him. And then we'll end with something like *Best Buy—Giving the World a Little Me Time*."

Rebecca changes the board to the actual slogan: *Best Buy—Reuniting Families Every Day*.

The room is completely silent. I've just given the worst pitch in the history of advertising. Why won't someone just speak up?

"I'm sorry," Gerry finally says, standing up and announcing to the room, "I thought this would be too much for her today. She's had a very bad virus."

"I have." I fake cough. "I only came in today because this was so important to us," I say.

"Would you like me to take over, Lily?" Gerry asks.

"Please," I tell her.

"What Lily is trying to say," Gerry continues as I sit down in her seat, shuddering as I put my head down, "is that this is all about families torn apart by electronics, computers, the internet. But what they don't realize is that the very thing that's pulling them apart can also bring them together again."

Rebecca pulls another board. It reveals the mother, child, and grandfather around a television together eating popcorn. A box on the right side of the television displays the image of a man who must be the child's father smiling at the family as they smile back.

"With new televisions that have internet capabilities, every family member is as good as there with the touch of a button. With internet capabilities on television, families are reunited once more. *Best Buy—Reuniting Families Every Day.*"

And then it hits me. The answer to everything.

"That's it!" I shout. "I'll find Emmalina's great-great-granddaughter! She'll reverse the curse!"

"Excuse me?" Bruce turns to me as the others look on.

"I'm really, really sick," I say to them, getting up. "I'm so sorry, I really have to go." I cough and heave as I rush out.

"Lily!" Gerry calls after me as I head down the hallway.

"I'm sorry," I tell her. "I'm so sorry. I know I just ruined everything, but I have something really important I have to get to."

"You know I have to fire you, right?" she asks, catching up to me. "I don't know who you are today. I can't understand why you would be acting like this."

"Gerry." I take her by the shoulders. "You're right, you should fire me. Now if you'll excuse me, I have to go."

Gerry stands there blank as I continue to walk away. "You're just going to give up like that?" she calls to me.

"Sometimes in life there are things more important than advertising." I turn to her as I continue to walk.

"Like what?" she shouts to me.

I don't bother to answer.

7

If your great-great-grandmother steals your great-great-grandaunt's man and your great-great-grandaunt puts a spell on your bloodline, not only are you blessed with the crappy fate of life without men, there's an added bonus: life without relatives.

All my life, holiday gatherings have consisted of just Mom and Dolly and me and one of the fathers I had at one time or another.

I can't say that holidays were all that terrible, but even at a young age, I knew there was something missing.

Yes, Dolly and Selma tried as hard as they could to make up for the fact that we had a small family, but still, I knew the other kids had something I didn't have: a large extended family.

It wasn't just holidays that were lonely. Even the pictures in our house looked scarce. Other kids had pictures of lots of family members. Mine only had pictures of the three of us.

"Why don't I have any cousins?" I asked Selma one day after I met my classmate Claudia's cousin Reza, who was visiting from Chicago. They looked so much alike, and I dreamed of having a cousin from a place as exotic as Chicago.

"Because Dolly didn't have any brothers or sisters and I didn't have any either," she told me.

"But why?" I asked her.

She bit her lip and told me to finish my homework. Now I know it was because of the curse.

I always thought that when I got married, I'd have five kids. I dreamed of having a large family seated at a big table at Thanksgiving with the big turkey and bowls of stuffing and mashed potatoes and homemade popovers instead of a four top with three place settings in the kitchen. When I met Gogo and found out that he wanted the same thing, I thought I was on my way to that Thanksgiving dinner of my dreams.

If I could find Emmalina's great-great-granddaughter, I could break the spell that has plagued my family for so many generations, and I could also be united with my large, happy extended family.

You cannot imagine how incredibly simple it is to find a long-lost relative these days with the help of the internet.

According to Selma and Dolly, Astrid and Hermann left Vienna in 1907. If Emmalina left Lokwunden and headed someplace else by ship, it had to be only a few years after that.

So I went to ancestry.com, and for no fee at all, I typed in the name Emmalina, the town of Lokwunden, and guess what came up?

EMMALINA LOCK

BORN ABT. 1888

DIED NEW YORK, NEW YORK 1958

So I paid for access to the website and found Emmalina's marriage certificate. She had married Charles Golden in 1912. According to a birth certificate found there, Emmalina and Charles had a son named Leon in 1914. Leon married Hettie in 1939. They had a son named Bernard in 1941. Bernard Golden is very proud of his alma mater, New York University. I know this because when I googled his name, most of what came up were events that Bernard and his wife, Annette, had attended and how much money they gave. According to the most recent alumni news events from New

York University, Bernard wrote to say that Golden Bakeries has been a profitable family business for the last one hundred years. Golden Bakeries. It made so much sense. Who on the East Coast doesn't know of Golden Bakeries with the best chocolate chip cookies in the world? He also wrote the following spring to say that his daughter Rose, NYU '03, has joined the time-honored family business. If Rose graduated in 2003, Rose is my age!

That's when I went to Facebook and I saw Rose's profile picture. It's Rose with her arms around a handsome, wholesome-looking guy who I'm assuming is her boyfriend. Rose has also graced me with the good fortune of not having to friend her, thus letting me see her entire page. (Though once I meet Rose, I'm going to tell her to change her privacy settings. It's just not safe; who knows what kind of crazy person is out there?) Rose Golden has 324 friends on Facebook. She is a fan of Golden Bakeries, Golden Chocolates, Michelle Obama, Gloria Steinem, the movie *Horrible Bosses*, and the character Cartman from *South Park*. I take from this that she's serious about work, admires powerful women, and also has a sick sense of humor. I see she is not married but is engaged to Leo Silver (Rose Golden Silver? Ha!), who I realize is the guy in the profile picture. Rose and Leo seem to have a happy relationship, according to her picture albums on Facebook. Rose sits on Leo's lap a lot for pictures. They kiss a lot when having their picture taken. Rose and Leo have been to London, New Zealand, and most recently, Mexico (hence the different photo albums entitled "London," "New Zealand," and "Mexico"). This past New Year's, Leo presented Rose with an engagement ring. In one picture, Rose is standing in a bikini and sarong on the beach, sobbing as Leo in long bathing shorts kneels down on one knee, presenting the ring to her. Leo looks longingly at his fiancée. A lot of Rose's friends have written congratulating them. Rose's friend Francis Daley sent a virtual bouquet. Allison Stubin wrote over and over, *"OMG!! OMG!!! You're engaged!!!"* Gina Hagy sent a virtual bouquet of flowers and signed it, *"can't wait to see the newly engaged couple this weekend."*

Another album on Rose's Facebook page is simply titled "Family." I'm assuming that's Bernard and Annette standing with Rose and Leo in one picture since Rose and Bernard have the same almond-shaped eyes. Rose is blond like me. Her hair is in a chignon. Rose is dressed in black ruffled shirt, Annette seems to be wearing a strapless gown, and the men are in tuxes. They must have been at a fancy event together and all of them look overjoyed as they drape their arms around each other. There's another photo with Rose and two men in suits who look to be around her age. The bottom of the photograph says Paul Golden, Chuck Golden, and they're outlined in blue, allowing me to click on those pictures. These must be her brothers, my cousins. They have those same eyes, the light hair.

A quick check of the Manhattan white pages tells me that Rose Golden lives on West End Avenue. Her phone number is right in front of my eyes.

I pick up the phone and immediately dial her number.

"Hey," the friendly voice says, "Rose and Leo can't get to the phone; leave a message."

When I hear the beep, I'm about to explain who I am, but then I stop and hang up. What kind of a message could I leave? *Hi, it's Lily Burns, your long-lost cousin. Hey, so your great-great-grandmother put a curse on my bloodline. I was calling to see if you wouldn't mind removing it for me, and then, hey, what are you and Leo doing for Thanksgiving? I really think Gogo and Leo will get along once Gogo remembers who I am.*

This is not the kind of thing you leave on a voice mail.

No, that would not be cool.

No, this is something that has to be done in person. So I scribble down Rose's address and phone number, grab my bag and head to 30th St. Station to take the train to New York.

Three hours later, I am in front of Rose's apartment building.

"Hi," I tell the doorman. "I'm here to see Rose Golden."

"Who should I say is calling?" he asks.

Again, this is a wrinkle in my game plan.

"You know what?" I say with a nervous laugh. "I think I'll just give her a call myself."

There's a Starbucks across the street from Rose's apartment. I decide to sit down with a latte to collect my thoughts.

Call? Write? Sneak past her doorman and get to her apartment? Whatever approach I used, springing this on her would be a shocker. I would just have to tell her plainly. I decide calling would be the best. That way if she thought I was crazy, a simple hang-up would be the least hurtful.

And then, oh my God, there she is.

I've studied her Facebook pictures enough to spot her in a crowd at a stadium.

There she is, my cousin, Rose, and she's holding hands with Leo, my future cousin-in-law. She's my height and I think we even look alike, though her clothing is a little more eclectic than my usual black suits. She has straight hair just like me and I wonder if she has problems making it look fuller like I do. Rose is wearing a short red skirt and black tights. Leo is in a suit. Rose looks very animated as she speaks to Leo. She almost has a skip in her step. My heart begins to sigh a little. I know that look. It is the look I had when I saw Gogo. I take a big gulp of my latte and rush out the door.

"Rose!" I call out to her.

Rose and Leo stop, still holding hands as Rose looks over at me from across the street. She squints her eyes, looking at me curiously, wondering who I am. As soon as the traffic slows, I make my move toward her.

"Do I know you?" she asks me.

"Not really," I tell her, "but I'm kind of a long-lost cousin."

"How do you know who I am?" she asks.

"Well . . ." I don't want to get into the whole thing. "It's a long story, but I'm Lily Burns," I say, sticking out my hand.

"Rose," she says, taking my hand. "And this is Leo."

"Hi," he says, a little bewildered.

"Listen," I start, "I know this must seem really weird, me stopping you on the street like this, but I'm in kind of a bind and I think you're the only person that can help me. Do you think we could maybe go back to Starbucks and have a talk? There's something I really need to ask of you."

"Who did you say you were?" Leo asks out of concern. Who could blame him?

"Look, I know this sounds crazy, but I really need your help. It concerns our family tree."

"No," she says, taking a step back, "I don't think so. We have something we have to get to."

"Wait, please," I start to beg. "Look at me, I'm a totally normal person. I swear, I'm not trying to rob you or scam you into something. I swear to you, we're long-lost cousins. My great-great-grandmother and your great-great-grandmother were sisters. My great-great-grandmother stole your great-great-grandmother's man and her chocolate chip cookies and—"

"Wait a minute!" Rose shouts. "Are you a part of the family that got cursed?"

"*Yes!*" I exclaim, taking a deep breath. "Thank you. I didn't know how I was going to tell you about the whole thing."

"What are you talking about?" Leo asks.

"It's a long story," Rose tells him.

"Yes," I say, starting to get choked up. "It was my great-great-grandmother, who must have been this horrific spoiled person and I really want to apologize for what she did. I don't know why she did it. I'm ashamed of what she did and I assure you that the women in my family did not take on her selfishness."

"Get out of here!" she shouts with a huge smile on her face. "You mean to tell me that the curse really exists?" She looks at me wide-eyed. "My grandfather used to tell me the story when I was a kid. I just thought he was telling me a bedtime story."

"No!" I cry. "Your great-great-grandmother's curse was really powerful and we've all suffered since and I don't know how to reverse it."

"What the hell is going on here?" Leo asks again.

"Leo," Rose calmly tells him, "it's a family thing. This girl is telling the truth."

"I am. I swear I am and if you could just help me, if you could just hear about what's happened to the women in my family, maybe you could see your way to reversing the curse." I start to cry real tears this time, standing in front of these two people I've never met before. Rose looks around us and then at Leo.

"Okay, let's go up to our apartment and talk," she says.

"But we have our engagement party in an hour," Leo reminds her.

"He's right." She turns to me. "We do."

"A half hour," I beg her. "A half hour."

"Is this something that important?" Leo asks.

"So the curse really worked?" she asks again. "Like, it's really real, really totally real, and you've had bad luck with men all this time?"

"Doesn't everyone have a couple of bad eggs here and there?" Leo asks in an almost accusatory way.

"You don't even know the half of it." I sigh.

"I want to hear about it. Come on up," Rose says as she gestures me into her building.

The chocolate chip cookie business has been really good to Rose Golden. I see this from the size of her apartment. Rose takes me into the large living room facing south with a view of Manhattan I know must have cost over a million dollars. You can see everything from the Empire State Building to the Chrysler Building. The living room is decorated exactly how I might have decorated it—big, grand comfy couches, a large caramel-colored area rug over hardwood floors. And pictures everywhere of Bernard and Annette, Paul and Chuck and people who must be their wives and children.

"Would you like some mineral water or soda?" Leo asks as I take a seat on the big couch.

"Water is fine," I tell him.

"Hon?" he asks.

"Water is good for me too."

Rose sits down opposite me and we just look at each other for a moment. I don't know where to begin. I can't even believe I've gotten this far.

"You have a beautiful apartment," I tell her.

"Thank you." She smiles as if she's not exactly sure how to handle this situation. I mean, who could blame her? She's just invited a stranger who claims to be a cousin into her home because of a bedtime story her grandfather told her when she was a child.

"Here you go," Leo announces, coming in with the glasses. "I'll be in the study if you need me." He puts his hand on Rose's shoulder as she smiles up at him, lovingly touching his hand.

"He seems great," I tell her.

"He is. He's the perfect guy." She smiles.

"I have the perfect guy too." I sigh. "Had."

"Are you married?" she asks.

"Well," I stammer, "sort of. That's what I came to talk to you about."

I tell her all about Gogo and my dating history. It kind of just falls out of me and it feels so good to be able to gush for a moment. I tell her about Selma and Dolly and their marriage histories. I go on about that day in Paris when Gogo proposed and that night in Las Vegas when we got married. For a half hour, I spill my entire life and how it led up to finding her on Facebook, and Rose says nothing. She sits and listens to my entire story from beginning to end.

"So you mean to tell me that Gogo has no idea that you exist?" She looks at me cockeyed.

"And he looks just awful. And he's married to a woman that I know he doesn't love and who doesn't love him, but Gogo, being who he is, I know he's only staying in that marriage to be honorable. That's Gogo."

"So how do you think I could help?" she asks me as if she's really intrigued.

"I'm hoping that you can reverse the curse," I blurt. "I'm hoping that in some way you can do some kind of spell on me that will make Gogo remember me again. I just don't know what else to do," I say as I throw my hands in the air.

Rose gets up out of her seat and walks over to my couch. She sits down next to me and just stares at me for a moment.

"I forgive your great-great-grandmother," she says in a mystical voice. Then she waves her arms in front of me as if she is performing a magic trick.

I look back at her trying to feel a change in my body, goose bumps or something that would cause me to believe that her words worked.

"Do you think that did it?" she asks in her normal voice.

"How do I know?" I ask her.

"Call Gogo!" she says, picking up her phone and handing it to me.

But before I can call Gogo, my cell phone rings. I look down at it and see that it's Dolly.

"Gram!" I say, answering the phone as I look at Rose.

"Hi, sweets," she announces. "Are you coming over for dinner tonight? If you are, do you think you could bring me a head of lettuce? I'm all out."

Rose begins waving her hands at me as she bounces up and down on the couch. "Ask her if she knows who Gogo is. Ask her if she remembers him," Rose whispers excitedly.

"Gram," I ask her, "do you know who Gogo is?"

"Who?" she asks.

"Gogo."

"You mean the guy you told us about?"

"Yes!" I shout as I jump up and down in my seat. Rose takes my hand and continues to bounce with me.

"The one you said you married and now he's married to someone else and he has no idea who you are and now he sells downspouts?"

My smile drops from my face. I stop bouncing. Rose stops bouncing.

"That's the one," I tell her.

"So did you say you were coming for dinner?" she asks.

"No," I tell her somberly. "I'm in New York. I'll come by tomorrow."

"What are you doing in New York?" she asks.

"I'm trying to reverse the curse. I'll let you know if it works."

"Oh, you poor girl." She sighs. "I know exactly how you feel. I tried that once too. Is it working?"

"No," I answer glumly.

"Well, if anyone can get the curse reversed, you can, sweetheart. Let me know how it goes."

I hang up the phone.

"I'm sorry," Rose tells me sadly.

"Well"—I try to smile through my sadness—"it was worth a try. Thank you for believing me, though. Thank you for understanding. This really means a lot to me. I knew it would be a long shot, but I'm just at my wits' end here."

"I'm sorry," Rose tells me sadly. "I look at my Leo and when I think . . . I can't imagine my life without him. If the tables were turned, I would be knocking at your door too."

"And I would be helping you as you've tried to help me. Thank you." I smile.

"You know," Rose ponders, "as long as you're here, why don't you come with us to my engagement party?"

"Oh no," I tell her, "I've bothered you enough already." I look around the room for my bag.

"No," she says, taking my hand, "I think it would be nice if you met the family. That's the least that I could do for you. Maybe someone else in the family has an idea."

"Did you say your grandfather was still alive?" I ask her.

"No," she tells me sadly. "Both of my grandparents are gone. You know, it was my grandfather's side of the family. He was the one who was the descendant of Emmalina."

"I know," I said, "ancestry.com."

"So come with us anyway," she repeats in a kind voice. "I know my family. They'd welcome you in."

"They sound nice."

"They are. The Goldens have lived good lives. We've had happy marriages. There's never been a divorce in my family tree. That's what's making me feel so awful. We've all been so happy, and I've been thinking about that a lot since I got engaged. I can't imagine what your family has been through. Is it possible that Emmalina gave my family tree some kind of reverse curse? Like a blessing or a wish of some kind? I'd hate to think that, but how did we get so lucky? It makes me feel awful for you."

"Please," I tell her, "don't feel awful. I saw Emmalina's note to Astrid, and trust me, it said nothing about making her family tree full of happiness. Your family just had a great bit of luck. You have nothing to be sorry for. You only have to rejoice." I smile.

"But I'm angry with Emmalina," she exclaims. "Emmalina is just as much at fault as Astrid. Look at what she's done to you."

"I can't think of who's at fault anymore." I sigh. "I just want to fix it. I just want my Gogo back; that's all I want. That's all I care about. I just want my life to go back to the way it was."

"You're coming with us tonight." She puts her arm around me. "You need some cheering up. I'll loan you one of my outfits. We're about the same size. I think we kind of look alike," she says, looking at my face.

"I thought the same thing!" I exclaim.

Rose grabs my hand and takes me back to her bedroom. Her closet is the size of my bedroom. We decide on a basic black shift dress. When I try on her shoes, we laugh at how remarkable it is that we've even got the same size feet. Pretty soon it's as if we've known each other forever. I tell her I hate the color eye shadow she's putting on. I know we're friends forever when she tells me to go fuck myself. Only a true friend could say something like that and get away with it.

On the way to the party, Leo keeps saying to us, "I just don't get it, you're really related?"

"We're related," she tells him as she smiles at me.

The party is being held at a restaurant in Soho. Rose introduces me to Bernard and Annette, who take me in their arms once Rose explains who I am, that the curse, a story told by an old grandfather was actually real. I meet my cousins Paul and Chuck and their families. And then I meet dozens of other cousins that I didn't know existed. I am dizzy with new relatives and I almost forget why I came there in the first place. It is only when Bernard gets up to toast his daughter that I remember.

"My darling Rose," Bernard starts as the room quiets down, "we are here not just to toast two people who love each other enough to commit to living the rest of their lives together, but we are welcoming in a new generation in our family. Pretty soon you'll have kids of your own and you'll want to shower them with as much love as you have for each other. That's what marriage is. It's taking that love you share for one another and sending it on to future generations. Rose, if you and Leo are as happy as your mother and I have been, then you will succeed in life. You will know because you are going through life together. Together. You will go through many ups and downs, but you will always have someone by your side. Your children will learn from that, and they will continue to follow that tradition."

I start to tear up.

"Rose," he continues, "for your mother and me, what a joy it has been raising you. Your kindness and love for your family have no bounds. Your joyful exuberance has always made our lives so much brighter. It's not easy for a father to see his daughter fall in love and start a new chapter in her life. You want the best for her. As a parent, you would go to any lengths to make sure your child is never hurt. There comes a day, though, when you just have to trust that you've brought her up well and she's able to take care of herself. And when I see the smile on your face when you look at Leo, there is no doubt in my mind that you've made the right decision.

If I could have picked your husband for you, I couldn't have picked someone who is more generous, more loving, and more understanding of you. Leo lets you be who you are. You were perfect to begin with, but Leo fills a void I never saw. He completes an already perfect daughter."

I'm so overcome with emotion at this point that I'm on the verge of a crazy cry, but I keep it in. Bernard sounds like Dolly and Selma. All they wanted to do was make sure I never got hurt. All they wanted for me was what Bernard wanted for Rose—happiness.

"So if we can all just raise our glasses. Here's to happiness, love, and the start of a new branch in our family tree."

"Hear, hear!" people shout. "To Rose and Leo!"

"To Rose and Leo," I say softly through my tears.

As we sit in a cab on the way to Penn Station, I thank Rose and Leo for allowing me to take part in such a beautiful evening.

"You know something, Lily?" she says. "You need to go win Gogo back."

"But how can I? He's married. He doesn't even know I exist."

"I was listening to my dad tonight. His words were so true. There just has to be some part of him that remembers you. After all, you said he wasn't happy."

"He's not," I explain, "but that doesn't mean I can just go and claim him. I mean, I already tried and he just didn't listen. I can't bother him again. I gave him my phone number. All I can do is hope for the best."

"Just remember," Leo chimes in, "he's not happy in his life. He's not happy with his wife."

"He's right," Rose repeats.

As we get to Penn Station, I hug my cousins and thank them again for listening and for being so unbelievably gracious.

"I'll keep thinking of a way to reverse the curse," Rose whispers to me.

"Thank you," I whisper, hugging her again. "Thank you."

On the way back to Philadelphia, I think about family—Rose's family and my family and how much they really do have in common.

Families protect the ones they love. Dolly and Selma spent my entire life trying to make sure I wouldn't get hurt emotionally. They did everything in their power to make sure my life wouldn't be affected as theirs were. They tried to protect their child and shower her with as much love as they could so I wouldn't be completely broken.

Bernard and Annette showered their child with love, so much so that she would help a strange cousin who just showed up at her door.

That is the power of family.

I wish Gogo could meet Rose. As I rest my head on the window of the train, I wish that one day the Burns family and the Golden family could have holidays together and our children would know each other.

I still have no idea how to accomplish that.

And as I fall asleep on the train, I dream that we are all together, Rose and Leo, Annette and Bernard, Dolly and Selma, Gogo and me, a happy large family, sitting around a Thanksgiving table with so many family members we practically spill out the door.

8.

Before I go any further, I want to point out something really important.

It's not like Gogo is always so perfect.

No one is totally perfect. Gogo is a normal good guy, but like anyone else in a relationship, he does things that grate on my nerves. I don't want you to start thinking that maybe I'm making more of Gogo than he really is. He's wonderful and kind and handsome, but frankly, he can also be a pain in the ass.

First of all, Gogo never throws anything out. He's on the verge of being a hoarder. It's always "Maybe I'll need this in the future." Even though we have fine plush cotton white terry-cloth towels, which match the bathroom so perfectly that I had to fight a woman at a Macy's sale to get them, Gogo refuses to throw away towels he's had since 1993. "I'll use them for rags," he'll tell me. So then I tell him to throw away the towels he's been using for rags and he'll say, "They're still good rags." So we've got a linen closet full of old cruddy towels and sometimes I can't even close the damn thing.

It's not just towels either. I had to throw away sheets from the twin bed he had growing up. We don't even have a twin bed in the house! He has sweaters and button-down shirts stored up in the attic that are so out of style, I was watching an old episode of *The Cosby Show* and actually saw Bill Cosby wearing one of the sweaters Gogo has stored up there.

Our shelves are crammed with books that he'll never open again: "Who knows if I might want to reread *The Canterbury Tales* one day?" he'll tell me.

"But you also downloaded it on your iPad, your Kindle, your Nook, and your Sony Reader," I remind him. Did I mention he's a tech whore too? He has to buy every gadget that comes on the market.

And it would a little more okay for Gogo to keep his old college mini refrigerator that doesn't work, or the tag-sale-bought blue Berber fleece chair he had from his first apartment with the macramé doily he made in the seventh grade that rests on the head of the chair so "the top of the chair doesn't get worn out"—all of that would be kind of fine if he didn't throw away all of my stuff!

And hoarding is not the only thing that bothers me about Gogo. Gogo is one of those people who still doesn't get that you don't need to shout into a cell phone. You try and tell him that he can talk in a normal voice, but he continues to be one of those annoying twits who speaks at volume ten in a restaurant, elevator, supermarket, or other public place. People come up to him all the time and complain, but he always apologizes and says, "These damn cell phones, no one can hear you." I swear he's going to break my eardrum: "I'M GOING TO BE LATE, DARREN GREENWOOD DISLOCATED HIS SHOULDER AT LITTLE LEAGUE."

Speaking of deafening noises coming from Gogo, the way he blows his nose each morning could wake the dead. I'll be asleep and he'll wake up before me, but of course he can't walk into another room and blow his nose. He's got to do it where it seems like he's blowing right into my ear. This is how I wake up almost every morning, with Gogo blowing what sounds like half his brain into a tissue. He might as well put a leaf blower to my ear; I think it would be quieter.

And I know that women have this thing about putting the seat down in the bathroom, and I do appreciate Gogo's effort in that he never fails to put the seat down. It's just that he also puts down the lid. I can't tell you how many times I've gone into the bathroom in the middle of the night and sat down on that cold lid. I don't know what's worse, no seat or that lid. I've told him how much I appreciate his effort in putting that seat down, but could he just leave the lid up?

"That's gross," he tells me.

Is that gross? What is so gross? I don't think it's gross, but you tell me.

Speaking of the bathroom, why does he always tell me when he's going into the bathroom? "I'm going to take a shower," he'll call out when I'm in the other room. And if I don't answer him, he'll call my name over and over, "Lil? I'm going to take a shower," until I finally say it's okay. Like, what does he think? Does he think I'll think he got abducted if I call his name and he doesn't answer? Does he think that if I hear the shower running and the bathroom door is shut, I'll think the kidnappers are trying to throw me off the track for an extra ten minutes?

And another thing—sorry, I'm on a roll here—Gogo can't fix anything. "Why call a plumber when I can just pour some liquid Drano down the pipe?" he'll tell me. I know my hair and how it gets caught in the pipes and how it's only $100 to get the guy to come and clear the clog with that snake thing. When I was growing up, there were three women clogging the pipes with our hair. We had the plumber on speed dial. Hair clogs are something I know very, very well. "Nah," he says, pouring the entire bottle in the drain. The clog got so bad that the pipe burst and we had plumbers here for three days fixing the mess.

Gogo can't tell a joke to save his life. I've seen him bore a dinner party enough for everyone to clear out by 8:30.

Gogo drives too fast in parking lots and he always misses the good spaces. We'll drive around and around at forty miles an hour and I'll see a perfectly good spot and say, "Right there, there's a spot right in front," but he'll just go right by it. I'll see another spot where someone is just loading their groceries or their kid in a car seat or something, it will take two minutes of waiting, but Gogo can't waste that time, so we're off looking for another spot. As always, we're left walking from the furthest spot in the lot, usually when I'm in heels.

And one last thing: this one is the kicker. Gogo can never admit when he's wrong. One time he took the spare key and forgot to put it back in our hiding spot. I had gone out to get the mail dressed only in my robe (Gogo was waiting for an important document and he asked me to check if it had arrived) and the door accidentally locked. Did I mention it was raining? I ran to where we keep our extra key and it was gone. I had no phone with me and none of the neighbors around us were home. There I was walking up to each door in my drenched bathrobe and bare feet. When he finally drove up and saw me sitting there, he said, "Why didn't you unlock the safety lock when you went to get the mail? How was I supposed to know you locked yourself out? You should have called me." I could have shot him right then and there. No "I'm sorry, Lil, it won't happen again" or "I feel terrible," nothing like that.

Maybe I'll feel scorn for an hour or two (or three), but then he'll do something that always makes me forget any annoying thing he's done. He'll notice when I'm sitting on the couch that maybe I could be cold, so he'll come with a throw and place it over me. I'll go to pee in the middle of the night and the lid is up. I'll find some old books of his in the trash. I'll call out Gogo's name, and when he doesn't answer, so I'll go into the bedroom and hear the shower running with the bathroom door shut and wonder why he didn't mention that he was taking a shower. I'll catch him watching a comedian on YouTube and whispering to himself, "Okay, I see, so you pause *before* the punch line. That's what makes it funnier." And then I'll forget all about the crap that pissed me off in the first place, because that's what it is: insignificant crap. It's what makes a person normal instead of some storybook character of a man.

And now that he's gone, all those things I just mentioned? Those are the things I miss the most.

But this is helping, thinking of all those things about Gogo that grate on my nerves, thinking about all the little crap things he does that really get my goat.

Anything to ease this pain I have right now.

Anything to forget how much I miss him.

It's been three days since I got home from New York and I've spent them in bed. Rose calls all the time trying to lift my spirits and figure out how to get Gogo and me out of this mess. None of her ideas have rocked me, though "kidnap him and brainwash him back to reality" wasn't so bad.

My phone rings again. Thinking it's Rose again, I pick it up before checking to see who it is. "Baby!" the voice says. "Listen, I need a date tonight for this work thing and you'd be the perfect girl. I'd get one of my other girls, but this isn't the kind of function where it'd be cool to show up with a girl who looks like she popped right out of a *Penthouse* centerfold, so I thought why not call my old pal, Lily. This is a fancy affair, so wear one of those nice long dresses that you have. Wear the black one, it shows off your tits. Pick you up at seven thirty."

This is just the type of thing I need to take my mind off things. After all, Jonah isn't all bad. He's bad, but not completely awful. If I never get Gogo back, this is the best I have going for me, so I call him back later and accept.

I take a look at myself in the mirror. The person I see in front of me is so pathetic and pale and sad. Sprucing myself up a bit would make me feel better.

So I wash my hair, and then after that, I pour some lavender bath gel into the tub and proceed to sit there for the next hour as my body finally starts to relax. After I'm sufficiently pruned, I apply all the necessary moisturizing creams. I file and buff my own nails and give myself a good mani-pedi. I decide to wear my hair down. My hair has grown to record lengths since months ago when Gogo commented on how sexy it looked. It is now below the boobs, a huge accomplishment for me. I dry it without running a brush through it so it'll look a little more wild, with a seductive natural curl to it.

I call Rose in New York, who takes me through step-by-step instructions on how to give my makeup that smoky eye look.

I go into my closet and pull my sexiest black dress out and put it on, followed by my black Louboutin slingbacks. I'd gone back and forth on spending the money on them, and I was glad I did. When I look in the mirror, I see someone who is not only beautiful but strong. Seeing myself looking beautiful and together gives me the kind of confidence I need. It's funny how a bath and a change of clothing can do that to you.

By 7:30 I'm ready to go. Jonah hasn't called telling me he'd be a little late, but that's Jonah.

At 7:45 I contemplate perfume but decide against it.

At 8:00 I bend over, throw my hair in front of my face and spray some hairspray in it to make it fuller.

By 8:15 I'm watching a reality dating show about people who date while wearing masks so they can't base the relationship on looks. At 8:30 I'm pretty sure the guy in the horse mask is the guy to pick over the one in the Phantom of the Opera mask, but I can see where our bachelorette (wearing a peacock feather mask) is having trouble deciding. Horse mask guy wants to marry her right away and give her babies, and it doesn't matter what she looks like underneath her peacock mask. Phantom of the Opera wants to take it slow, see what life would be like in the real world without masks and extreme dates on hot air balloons.

At 8:30 peacock-masked bachelorette still needs some time to figure out which guy she should pick, so she boards an American Airlines plane, still wearing that cockamamie mask, and heads to her hometown of Beachwood, Ohio, to discuss the options with her family. By 8:45 she's back in Hollywood and has picked her man: horse mask guy. Before they even take off the masks, horse dude presents her with an engagement ring, which she happily accepts.

That's when I turn off the television. What kind of a girl accepts a marriage proposal from a guy she's never seen? Looks matter! Giving up the rest of your life to be with someone is not something that should be taken lightly just because the guy asked. Get to know someone, see how he treats you. And if he treats you badly, lose him. It's better to be alone and lonely than to be with someone and lonely.

At 9:00 I hear a car horn beep outside my house, but I'm already out of my dress and making myself a peanut butter and jelly sandwich. As I go to grab some milk out of the fridge, I hear the car horn again, this time with longer beeps. A moment later my doorbell rings.

"I've been waiting outside for five minutes," Jonah groans as I open the door holding my sandwich. "Hey, I like all that makeup you've got on. Now get that dress on and let's go."

"Yeah, I don't think so, Jonah," I tell him as I calmly take a bite.

"What do you mean, you don't think so?" he gripes. "So I was a little late. I've been late in the past and you've never cared. I had work I had to do."

"Jonah," I say, taking another bite, "I'm going to be brief here because frankly, I don't feel like spending one more minute of my time talking to you."

"Okay, here we go," he says, motioning his hand in a circle. "Give it to me, give me a little talking to, and then let's bolt."

"Jonah," I tell him, "do me a favor. Lose my number. You're just not the kind of guy I want to be with anymore."

"Oh yeah?" He smirks. "So what kind of a guy do you think you want to be with? Someone who calls when they're going to be late, or gives you flowers just because he was thinking of you. Hey, here's a sweet touch, how about a guy who holds out the chair for you in restaurants and keeps your picture on his desk at his office?"

"Well, yes, all of that, for starters, but it's more than that."

"And you think a guy like that exists? You think there's guys like that out there for you?"

"Yes, Jonah, yes. I know there are."

"Ha!" He laughs. "Good luck finding them, but come on, seriously, I need you to come with me tonight. I already told the clients I'd be bringing a date."

I start to laugh. "Jonah, you just don't get it, do you?"

"Well, why don't you try and fill me in?"

"Jonah, you're incredibly rude, you're obnoxious, and you have the worst manners of any human being that I've ever met. Jonah, you have treated me terribly, and up until now, I've allowed that. It's taken me a long time to figure it out, but the truth is, I deserve better. I deserve to be treated like a queen."

His eyes widen as his mouth gapes open. I'd feel sorry for him, but then I remember what an inconsiderate idiot he is. And then he breaks out into hysterical laughter.

"Good luck there, *Your Highness*," he says, bowing.

"And did I mention you're one of the more unfortunate-looking people I've ever met in my life?"

"You don't think I know that I'm ugly?" He laughs.

"No, I'm not sure you do," I said.

"You're serious about all this?" he asks me.

"Of course I'm serious!"

"Hey," he says, looking around from side to side for a quick moment, making sure no one else would hear him. When he sees no one, he turns to me, lowering his voice. "I know what I look like and I know I can be a cad, but what choice do I have? What do you think happens when I treat girls nicely? Who takes the short, fat, nice guy seriously in business? It's the assholes that people listen to. It's the assholes that women date. Look, I know you're hot, I know you're a better person than I am, but come on, if I was nice to you, you wouldn't have stayed with me. Gorgeous girls like you wouldn't even take my call."

"I'm different than most girls," I tell him. "Believe me, I'm much different than most girls."

"So look, now that we've had this talk all nice-nice, let's go. I'll be a little nicer to you. I'll be on time the next time we go out."

"Thanks, Jonah, but I think it's too late. I think this is the end of you and me," I say as my phone rings.

"But now I'm attracted to you!" he exclaims, stomping his foot. "No one has ever put me in my place before. It's like you know the real me."

"Good-bye, Jonah," I say dramatically, shutting the door as my phone rings again, but Jonah throws his foot in the doorway.

"Just give me one more chance!" he calls out from behind the door. "I think I'm falling in love with you!"

"Jesus, Jonah," I say, trying to kick his foot out the door as the phone rings again. "Take a hint!" I shout as he finally pulls his foot out and I'm able to shut the door.

I run to the phone just as it's on its fourth ring.

"Hello," I say out of breath.

"Lily, hi, this is Gogo Goldblatt."

My heart stops!

"Can I take you to dinner tomorrow night?" Jonah says through the door. "Just to make up for things? I'll get here a half hour before we're supposed to go out. I'll bring you flowers and candy and all that other stuff you like."

"Gogo, hi," I whisper, cupping my hand to the phone as I walk over to the door and open it. Jonah gets down on his knees, and I angrily motion to him to stop, and I slam the door again.

"Listen." Gogo takes a deep breath. "You've got me curious and I just can't get it out of my head. I just have to know, how did you know my real name?"

"Lily, can't we just talk this out?" Jonah whines as he knocks lightly on the door.

"I, uh, I told you, Gogo. I told you that, as crazy as it sounds, you and I were married and a curse that was placed on my family did this to you. In some other dimension, you're really married to me and we have a life together, a really happy life."

"Lily, how many more times can I tell you I'm sorry?" Jonah whines from the door.

"Look, can you just cut that stuff and tell me who's behind this? Can you just tell me once and for all who's playing this joke so that I can get them back?"

"*Lillllllyyyyyyy*," Jonah cries from behind the door.

"Hey, Gogo, can you hold on a second?"

"Uh, okay."

As I throw open the front door, Jonah falls on my feet.

"Jonah!" I mutter under my breath. "Would you please get the hell out of here?"

"Not until you say you'll give me another chance. Will you?" he asks, looking up at me with these sad eyes.

"Can't you take a hint?" I whisper angrily. "I'm married to someone else and that someone is on the phone right now!"

"You're married?" he exclaims. "You never said you were married . . . And *you've* been having an affair with *me*?" he asks, pointing to himself.

"Yes," I affirm, not wanting to give the true explanation, "and it's over now between you and me. You got that?" I whisper again as I grit my teeth. "Now go away!"

I shut the door again and go back to the phone.

"Gogo?" I say into the phone. "I'm sorry about that."

"Look, if this is a bad time—"

"Trust me, nothing is as important as this. I've got all the time in the world to explain things to you. I'm, I'm so happy that you called, Gogo; it's so great to hear your voice."

He pauses. "It's just that, you know, it's an odd thing for a woman to show up at my house like that and then show up at my work. I tried to think of any rational explanation as to how or why you'd know my name and my social security number and my scar on my stomach. I just couldn't come up with one. The only thing I can think of is that someone is playing a joke."

"Look, I know, I know, I know, I know that this all sounds unbelievably nuts and crazy and believe me, I'm a very together person. I'm not some lunatic here to blackmail you and collect all of your money or try to steal you away from your wife. It's just that what I'm saying is true. Look, is there someplace we could meet? If you start to get creeped out my me, you can leave, but is there any way that you would consider meeting with me so I could explain things to you?"

He sighs. "Okay, how about tomorrow?"

"Really?" I exclaim joyfully. "Okay, sure! What time? Where?"

"I'm going to be near Rittenhouse Square around two. Let's say that coffee place next to the Dorchester?"

"I'll see you there." I smile.

"And Lily," he adds, "I'm only meeting you to clear all of this up. Please understand that I have no intention of ever leaving my wife."

"I understand," I tell him. "Of course."

"See you at two," he says, hanging up.

"Yep! Everything is perfect!" I say to myself as I dial Rose's number.

"Rose! Amazing news!" I shout into the phone. "Gogo called! I'm meeting him at two tomorrow!"

"That's is the greatest news!" she yells. "I was just dialing your number! I think I've figured it out! I think I've figured out how to get him back."

"Tell me!"

"But I have to ask you this first. What were you doing before everything disappeared?"

"We had just gotten married."

"No, I mean, what were you doing physically? Did you kiss and then you were sent into this alternate reality?"

"I don't remember. Maybe we were kissing," I say, trying to think.

"Well, it might be kind of important that you remember, because whatever you were doing, maybe that's what sent you here."

"You mean a phrase, like 'Rumpelstiltskin', 'abracadabra', or 'If you build it, he will come'?"

"Exactly."

I try to think. "Well, we got back to the hotel room and we started to kiss and I was really happy . . ."

"And then?"

"And then . . . that's personal," I say in a hushed tone.

"What are you, fourteen?" she asks. "It was your honeymoon. Were you having sex?"

"We weren't having sex, yet," I tell her, starting to get worked up.

"I would tell you if we were having sex! It's just that we were talking and . . . it's personal."

"Well, what were the words?" she shouts.

"I don't have to tell you everything!" I shout back.

"I'm trying to help you!" she shouts.

"*Pinch me!*" I yell into the phone. "Okay? I was so freaking happy that we got married that I couldn't believe it was really happening. So I asked him to pinch me to make sure I wasn't dreaming. There. Are you satisfied?"

"That's so cute," Rose coos. "What's so embarrassing about that?"

"Nothing," I retort. "It's just . . . I was so happy and those were the last words I spoke to Gogo while we were man and wife and there's something sacred about that." I sniffle.

"But that could be it," she says.

"What could be it?" I ask.

"You said, 'Pinch me.' Gogo pinched you. And all of a sudden, he's gone. Maybe if you get him to pinch you again, you'll get back to where you were."

"Come on. You think it's that simple?" I ask. "It can't be that simple."

"Well, it's a theory."

"Okay, fine. When I go and see Gogo, a man who already thinks I'm crazy, I'll just ask him to pinch me. That'll show him how sane I am."

"Okay, maybe it's stupid. Maybe I'm just grasping at straws, but do you have any better ideas?"

"I guess not."

"Okay, so get him to pinch you and then give me a call and let me know if you're Mrs. Gogo again. We'll all have dinner."

"Thanks for the advice," I tell her. "Why do I feel like I'm just about to make things even worse?"

"How much worse could they really get?" she asks.

"Excellent point," I tell her, and we hang up.

I'm so exasperated. *Argh!* I clench my fists and shout to let the stress out of me.

"Lily?" I hear Jonah outside. "Is everything all right?"

"Bite me!" I yell back.

9

I'm meeting Gogo at two at the coffee place on Rittenhouse Square. I maybe slept twenty minutes last night until I finally got out of bed at seven to start getting ready. It's now ten thirty and I've tried on pretty much everything in my closet (which is now on the floor of my bedroom). I've tried three times to put my mascara on evenly, but it keeps clumping up, so I take it off and reapply it again. I don't even know why I'm trying to get it to be so perfect. I don't know why it took everything in my closet for me to decide on my tight jeans and a white top. I mean, after all, I'm going to see a man who has seen me hunched over a toilet at four in the morning after eating a bad oyster. He's seen me on a Sunday morning after a rowdy Saturday night of drinking and debauchery with friends and that time I got a bad cold sore on the side of my mouth. Each of those times, I asked Gogo to go away, but he kept coming back with water to rehydrate or tissues with lotion to ease the pain on my mouth.

Still, I want to look good for my man, even if he has no idea that he's really my man.

My living room is starting to look like a flower shop. There's roses and lilies and plants, and who had the time to make that flower sculpture of my face? What did Jonah find? An all-night flower shop?

After the fourth coat clumps under my lower lash, I decide it will have to do. I'll be late if I keep doing this, but oh, okay, one more time and then that's it.

After the fifth coat, it seems to be okay, and if there's no traffic on 76, it will take me only twenty minutes to get there. I take off my jeans and put on a pair of black slacks, contemplate the result for another half hour, and put back on the jeans. By the time that drama is over, I look at the clock and see that I've got a half hour to get downtown.

In one half hour I'll get to see Gogo. Though it won't be the same, the thought of sitting across from him makes me endlessly happy.

The only thing that worries me now is figuring out when to have Gogo pinch me. Do I just ask him, "Hey, would you mind pinching me on my arm?" Does that sound normal? Maybe I could work it into a story. "The funniest thing happened to me the other day. A man pinched me. Here, let me show you how I reacted. Now, you pinch me on my arm, right here," I'll say, pointing to the exact place Gogo pinched me before.

Argh.

When I get to the restaurant, he's already there and he looks as sad and pathetic as he did when I saw him at the downspout offices. He's reading the paper and I take a brief second to watch him.

I smile to myself and dream for a moment that we're meeting like we used to, a quick lunch in the afternoon to break up the monotony of the day. Whenever we'd meet for lunch, we'd exchange a big hug and kiss, bigger than when we'd get home at night. Having lunch together in the middle of the day was always a special treat. Sometimes we'd talk about what happened at work that morning, but mostly we just held hands for that brief hour, savoring a little bit of home in the middle of our hectic day.

"Oh, hello," he says when he sees me; he folds his paper in half and puts it beside him on the floor.

"Hi," I say as I sit down. The tight jeans I decided to wear today are the ones that tend to ride down my butt when I sit down, so I casually pull up the pants as I carefully take a seat. I probably shouldn't have worn them, but Gogo always said I looked sexy in them.

"Would you like some coffee or something?" he asks as he motions the waiter over.

"I'll just have what he's having," I tell the waiter. Gogo could have sludge in his cup and I wouldn't taste it anyway. The waiter could serve me stale bread with sliced calf's brain on top and I wouldn't taste it. That's how nervous I am right now.

"So," he says, taking a deep breath, "I guess you must be a little confused about me calling you after I told you never to call me again."

"Yes and no," I tell him, thinking maybe he's remembered something about me.

"It's just that it really caught me off guard when you knew my real name. I mean, no one, *no one* knows my real name. I started thinking about how you might know. It's on my tax forms, but how would you get my tax forms? It's on my marriage license, but I don't even know where that is. So I thought I'd just ask you."

"Gogo," I start, "it was like I was telling you the other day. I know it's really hard to believe, but in some other dimension or some other life—I don't know how else to explain it—we were actually together. We got married."

"Come on," he says, pushing back his chair. "Do you really expect me to believe that? Just tell me the truth. Why did you come to my house that day? Why did you come to my office?"

"Gogo," I begin, a little louder to get the point across. The waiter arrives with my coffee cup, so I lower my voice. "I know it sounds crazy, but it's absolutely true. We were married. There's a curse on my family tree. One second we're celebrating our nuptials, the next second you're married to another woman and our life together never took place."

"Okay, let's just say for the sake of argument that you are my *wife*." He smirks. "So tell me what you know about me. You must know more than my real name if we're actually married."

"Look, you want me to tell you about yourself, okay, I will. I know that you only take showers at night, never in the morning, because you like to sleep as late as you can."

"I take baths," he tells me.

"Since when?"

"Since years. Rhonda likes the shower really powerful and I don't. It feels like I'm being stuck with tiny needles."

"So why don't you change the setting on the showerhead when you get in the shower and then change it back for Rhonda?" I inquire.

"Well, I would," he says, sounding a little offended, "but the showerhead is on a dial and you can't just change it from one setting to another. Rhonda knows exactly the water power she likes and it takes forever to find it again."

"Okay." I stop him. "Forget that. What about your favorite foods? You love vegetables. You're the only person on the planet that I know who would rather eat brussels sprouts than french fries."

Gogo laughs. "Brussels sprouts? You think you're going to really make me believe all this because I might like brussels sprouts, which, incidentally, I don't, unless of course they're covered in cheese sauce."

"No," I insist, "you love brussels sprouts. When you were in college, you joined the co-op and you met a guy there who taught you how to make roasted brussels sprouts with balsamic vinegar and olive oil. It's your special side dish. You love to cook."

"Wait, that co-op supermarket around the corner from my

dorm?" he says, conjuring it up in his mind. "I never joined that co-op. Rhonda couldn't understand volunteering at a supermarket."

"What about this? You sleep on your back, facing up with your hands outside the blanket. You don't move at all during the night."

"I sleep on my side with a pillow between my legs. I've had a bad back since the Downspout Olympics."

"The what?" I ask.

"It's a sports thing my father-in-law created a few years ago. All the other downspout companies compete. I threw my back out in the high-jump competition."

"No," I tell him, "you always sleep on your back. You look so at peace when you're sleeping with your little hands sticking out of the covers and just the way your head rests on the pillow." I sigh.

"What did you do?" he accuses me. "Did you look into my bedroom window or something?"

"You think I'm that crazy?" I draw back.

"Yes, yes, I think you're crazy," he answers.

"Gogo, I'm telling you, I was married to you for six hours. We were together for a year. I tried to warn you before we got married. There's a curse put on the women in my family!" I say, exasperated. "Pinch me," I tell him, putting out my arm. "Pinch me right here." I point to the exact spot he once pinched. "That's what put us in this bind in the first place."

Gogo looks at me cockeyed. "I don't think I should be here anymore."

"You play video games," I say, trying to convince him. "It bothers me no end how much you love to play those video games, and you say the same thing to me every time, 'Look at the graphics on that thing.' I cringe every time a new video game comes in the mail. Our living room sometimes looks like a thirteen-year-old boy is living there."

"I haven't played a video game since I was thirteen," he answers accusingly.

"Well, I don't know how else I can prove it to you," I tell him, and frankly, I'm starting to get a little pissed off. "I'm telling you the truth. I swear to you. You always play video games, especially when you come home late from work if you had an emergency. That's when I never mind hearing machine guns coming from the television and watching you flailing around the couch with the controller in your hands zigzagging from side to side. When a kid gets really sick, sometimes, Gogo, I don't know how you handle it."

"So now you're telling me we've got kids in this other life?"

"No, in our life, you're a pediatrician."

"I'm a doctor?" He laughs.

"Yes, you're a fine, well-respected pediatrician. You're one of the best doctors I've ever seen," I say, starting to get upset.

"Okay, I see what's going on here. So you're someone from college. Did you live in my dorm?"

"I didn't go to your college," I tell him. "Why would you even think that?"

"Because I was premed in college. I was going to be a pediatrician until I started dating Rhonda and we got married young and I needed to make money, so I just dropped the premed and started working for her dad. But I guess you know that too."

"Well, in my reality, you didn't," I say, starting to get agitated. "You went to medical school and you became a doctor."

"So, let me get this straight. You're telling me, in some other world, I'm living out my biggest dream of being a doctor, and I'm married to you and I play video games and I love brussels sprouts."

"And you're a really nice person," I tell him, starting to tear up. "You're a loving, generous person and you treat me like a queen and if you just pinch me, maybe we can get back to that amazing life."

Gogo sighs and takes a sip of his coffee.

"Look," he says. "You seem like a pretty normal person other than the fact that you say we're actually married and living some other life somewhere."

"No, we're not living some other life somewhere," I tell him. "That's just it. We've been cursed and now you're living a life you don't want and I'm living a life I don't want and we're not together because—"

"Tell me a little more about this curse you keep mentioning," he says.

"Oh"—I throw up my hand—"it's not worth it anymore."

And it's right then when I realize that I should probably give up. This is not the man that I know. It's like Gogo has had some kind of lobotomy. This makes me incredibly sad. There's no point in trying to convince this person that he's really the love of my life. I'm realizing the sad fact that the person sitting in front of me is not the love of my life. My Gogo, he doesn't exist anymore, and tears start falling from my eyes as this realization hits me.

"Do I help a lot of kids?" he asks.

"Huh?"

"Do I help a lot of kids? You said I was a really good doctor."

"Yes." I sigh. "You're a great doctor. Everyone in Philadelphia sends their kids to you. When the holidays come, our house is filled with watercolor pictures and crayon drawings that kids make for you, thanking you for making them feel better when they've been sick or broken their arms falling off their bikes or when you've sat with them all night in the hospital because they're afraid about getting their tonsils out the next morning."

"Well," he says, smiling faintly, "that's nice to know."

"So tell me," I ask, "if you wanted to be a doctor so badly, you know, in this life, why aren't you?"

"It was like I said." He sighs. "Rhonda wanted to get married and I needed to provide for her. Medical school would have taken too many years. Plus, Rhonda wanted to have kids immediately and I wanted to be around."

"So you have kids?" I ask.

"Well, no. That part hasn't panned out yet. We've had some troubles with that."

"Oh," I say, "sorry to hear it," and then I wonder why I would be sorry for it.

"It's been tough on Rhonda. It's been tough on our marriage. We've thought about adopting, but with the money we've spent on fertility treatments, we're pretty much broke. That's why I'm hoping to get this promotion at work. I've been gunning for head of Northeast downspout operations," he says proudly as he reaches into his back pocket. "I've been looking to drum up some business around the Philadelphia tristate area, so if you know of any housing developments going up, please think of me." He hands me his business card. I look at it:

CARVERMAN DOWNSPOUTS

GOGO GOLDBLATT

GENERAL MANAGER—SALES

PHILADELPHIA TRISTATE AREA

215-555-2342

(CELL) 215-555-2959

"Well, I hope you get it." I try to sound upbeat, but it's coming out a bit melancholy. My tears have dried, but there's a lump in my throat and I know that anything I say will make my eyes water again. I don't know what I can do to get Gogo to realize we had a life together. And even if I did win Gogo back, how would we get our life back to the way it was? Would I have to start force-feeding him brussels sprouts? Would I have to go and buy a PlayStation 3 for him to play with? How would Gogo go back to being the man that I loved?

"Yeah, it's between me and the other guy I share Northeast sales with, Brad. Brad beats my ass in sales. He's my nemesis at work. It's a long shot, but if I could just get a couple of big projects, I think I could get the job. He even gets along better with my father-in-law. They're the same person." Gogo chuckles to himself. "Sometimes I think he wishes Brad were his son-in-law instead of me."

"I hope you get everything you want, Gogo, really I do," I say as I push away my coffee cup and get ready to leave. "Look," I add as the tears start again, "I'm sorry if I've wasted your time here. I realize now that this is crazy. There is no way I'll be able to get you to understand what's gone on here, and I don't want to disturb your life any more than I have already." I grab my bag and sit on the edge of my seat. I know my butt has become exposed, but that's not really bothering me at this point.

"Why are you crying?" he asks.

"Because this was crazy," I tell him. "It was crazy for me to bother you like this. It was crazy for me to think that I could just explain things to you. I didn't realize that it would be harder than that. You're married. You've lived a life that didn't include meeting me. All of the things I know about you, that's not who you are. That's the person I knew, and I guess he just doesn't exist." I stand up and pull my jeans to a comfortable position and decide I'm definitely going to throw them out once I get home.

"Well, I am sorry," he says sincerely.

"What would you be sorry for?" I laugh. "I should be thanking you for meeting with me at all. This was actually good for me. Now I can go on with my life. I guess when it really comes down to it, all

I really want to know is that you are okay. You seem okay. That's the best I could hope for, and that makes me feel at ease."

We walk outside onto Rittenhouse Square. The park is teeming with people on this sunny spring day. There's something really comforting about that. Even though I know now that my relationship with Gogo is over, the world hasn't stopped. People are going on with their days—people in business clothes sitting on park benches eating salads out of plastic containers, children playing on the grass as their parents look on thoughtfully. My life is just one story in this park. It's an odd story, but nonetheless, I bet other people here have their own odd stories to tell. Somehow, looking at all these people makes me feel like my life is not that strange. Marriages break up all the time. Mine is just one of them.

"Well," I say, wiping a tear from my eye, "it was good to see you. I promise I won't bother you again."

Gogo stands there staring at me, like he's trying to remember me, something, anything about me that might jog his memory. At least, that's what I think he's doing.

"This might sound weird," he says, "but I kind of feel bad leaving you like this. I hate to see a woman crying."

"Oh, I'll be all right," I say.

"Listen," he says, looking at his watch. "I've got some time to kill. Are you hungry for lunch? Maybe you'd like to get something to eat?"

"That's very sweet of you," I say, "but I'm not very hungry right now. I should be on my way."

"It's just that I'm looking at you and, I don't know, you really seem to believe all of this. There seems to be some truth in your eyes, and I think that if you were really insane, you'd probably try to convince me that what you're saying is really true."

"How does an insane person act?" I ask.

"I don't really know." He laughs.

"I'll be fine," I assure him. "Don't worry about me." I start to take a couple of steps away from him.

"Hey," he calls out to me. "When I'm feeling down, there's only one thing that makes me feel better." He smiles.

"I really don't want to take any more of your time," I say, looking back at him.

"It's no trouble, really," he says.

I continue to take a couple of steps, and then I realize what he's talking about. A wave of glee comes over me.

"A hot fudge sundae?" I say, even though I know I'm wrong. I'm sure he's about to recoil and say, "Chocolate chip cookies."

"Yeah," he says, looking at me quizzically.

I smile. "Well," I say, "I guess I've got the time if you do."

He thinks for a second and then says, "Continental Mid-town is around the corner."

And suddenly I catch a glimpse of Gogo, the old Gogo, the kind, sensitive Gogo I knew. The one I met that fateful day at Continental Mid-town over a year before.

"That sounds fun," I say shyly.

We continue to walk through the park, though we're not saying anything to each other. I don't know what to say. I'm afraid if I say the wrong thing, I'll offend him in some way and he'll leave. I've got all these emotions going through me right now. The right thing would have been to just let him be on his way. The right thing would have been to let this person I don't know just live his life the way he has for all these years and allow him to forget about the woman who knows he eats ice cream sundaes when he gets depressed. After all, that's not proof that he might be my husband. It's practically mandatory! Who doesn't eat ice cream when they're depressed?

Still, it feels like a little bit of home in the middle of an otherwise hectic day.

As we walk into the restaurant, I notice that our table is free, so I walk over to it and grab it, bypassing the hostess in case she wants us to sit someplace else.

"This one is good," I tell Gogo as he looks at the hostess for confirmation.

Gogo takes the chair facing the restaurant, but I make sure that I'm sitting in the same seat we were sitting in that afternoon, facing the wall. This was not something that normally happened when we went out. Gogo always gave me the good seat. That day in the restaurant, the first time we shared our hot fudge sundae, Gogo was already sitting at this table and I joined him. I don't know, maybe the seat will spark some memory for him. I'm grabbing at straws at this point.

"We'll have two hot fudge sundaes," Gogo tells the waiter when he comes over to take our order.

Hearing Gogo say these words, this also gives me a minor thrill. Again, grabbing at straws.

"So what do you do?" he asks me.

"For work?" I say and he nods. "I work in advertising, but I'm actually taking some time off right now."

"Advertising," he says, as if he's looking for words to fill up our conversation.

"Yeah," I say. "I've been working at Sacki and Sacki for the last eleven years."

"That's an ad agency?" he asks.

"Yep," I say without going into my usual spiel of its being one of the largest in the world, et cetera and so forth. "And you make downspouts?"

"Sell them," he tells me. "I guess that seems pretty boring to you. I'm sure most of the guys you date have exciting jobs."

"I don't date that much," I say without reminding him that I'm actually married to him. "And you've been married to Rhonda for how long?"

"Since college," he says, "twelve years."

"And that's been good?" I ask, not knowing how else to ask.

"The marriage?"

"Yes, you've been happy?"

"What's happy?" he asks. "Yeah, yes, I guess we've been happy, I don't know. The whole kid thing has been a big deal. Rhonda's been through a lot of rounds of hormone shots; we can't figure out why we can't get pregnant. It's taken a toll on the marriage through the years, especially now. She sees all of her friends having kids. Couples who haven't been married half as long as Rhonda and me are on their second or third kid and that pains her a lot. I try to make her feel better about things, but it can be hard sometimes. Do you want kids?"

"Do I want kids?" I repeat. "Uh, yes, of course I want kids someday, but I guess I haven't found the right person to have them with." Again, I want to tell him we had talked about it, but he doesn't seem to be bringing up the elephant in the room, so I won't either. This is a very delicate situation. After all, I've just started to give him the impression that I'm not a loon.

Moments later, two hot fudge sundaes dripping with chocolate sauce are served to us. I take my spoon and dig into the delight, but as I take a bite, I still can't taste anything. My adrenaline is still rushing. I'm not sure if I should bring up the reason we're here or let it lie. I don't know if this is the last time I'll ever be sitting across the table from Gogo again.

So I just don't bring up anything.

Gogo takes a bite of his sundae and we sit in silence eating for a moment. That's okay, though, because my thoughts are someplace else. I'm sitting with Gogo like we love to do in the middle of the day. He has to be back at work in a little bit because little Elvis Berstein is coming in. His mother thinks it's strep throat. I have the Watermark pen account's new ad campaign sitting on my desk that I'll get to once I clear my head.

"It's good," Gogo remarks, taking another bite of the sundae.

"How can it be bad?" I smile.

Gogo is going to mention that he'll be home early tonight and what should we have for dinner? I'm in the mood for chicken. We'll go back and forth before one of us gives in and agrees to pick up the chicken on the way home.

"Are you feeling any better?" he asks.

"I am," I tell him. "This was a great idea, thanks."

I would do anything to have to pick up that chicken after work. I would do anything to walk into that store and grab some chicken and then call Gogo and ask him if there's anything else I should pick up as long as I'm here. He'll say no, but then he'll call me when I'm in the car ten minutes later, asking me if we have orange juice in the house, and then I have to go back to the market.

Gogo takes his napkin and wipes some chocolate off the side of his mouth. I notice that he wipes his face with the folded napkin the same way he always wiped it. This might not seem like a big deal, but this was always something that irked Gogo about me. I crinkle my excess napkin into my hand and wipe my face. Whenever I used Gogo's napkin, he hated that I did that. This small, insignificant thing makes me smile.

"What?" he asks.

"Nothing," I tell him.

I wish I could tell him about the napkin, that this was a little thing from our relationship, but he wouldn't understand. There's no sense in bringing it up, though I really wish I could. I wish I could tell him I hate how neatly he always treats his napkin.

Halfway through the sundaes and we've barely said a word to

each other. I think about how tonight, after I make the chicken, there'll be that time where we don't know what to do. Should we make love? Is one of us too tired? Should we turn on a movie? It's my daydream, so we'll make love and then watch a movie.

"Can I get you anything else?" the waiter asks me as he comes over.

"I'm okay," I say, and the waiter poses the question to Gogo.

"No, we'll just take a check."

Tonight we'll make love and then curl up together and turn on a movie, some movie we've both seen a million times before that we just happen to catch coming on television.

"You ready?" Gogo asks.

"Yep," I say, grabbing my bag.

And I'll curl up in the crook of his arm and I'll put one leg over his as we watch the movie.

"Well, this was interesting," he says as we walk outside.

"It was," I say. "Thanks again." I put my hand out to shake his.

And then I'll fall asleep in that nook of Gogo's body. Maybe I'll wake up when Gogo moves and I'll turn to my side of the bed. Gogo will go into the other room and call Elvis Berstein's house to see how Elvis is feeling.

"Well, good luck," he tells me.

"You too," I say as I start to walk away.

And then at some point I'll wake up in the middle of the night. I'll look over at Gogo, sleeping on his back with his hands outside the blanket, and I'll think to myself, "I love this man. I love him so much."

"Gogo," I shout out to him as I see him walk in the other direction.

"Yeah?" he asks.

"One more thing," I shout, running back to him.

"Yeah?" He smiles.

"You already think I'm insane, so in case I never see you again, I'll just ask you. Would you mind pinching me?"

"Excuse me?" he asks.

"It can't hurt, I mean, literally, or figuratively, so if you could just pinch me to put my mind at ease, I'd really appreciate it, just so I know, you know, that I'm not dreaming now, or maybe I dreamed that I was married to you and now this is reality, or . . . oh, could you just pinch me?"

He gently takes my arm in his hand and looks down at it. I swear to you, I'm turned on by the fact that he just picked up my arm. I could attack him right here.

"Where did you want me to do it?" he asks.

"Right here." I point to the area on my arm.

I close my eyes. I feel as Gogo puts his fingers on my arm and grabs some skin. I can hear voices and cars all around me, but I try and block them out and just concentrate on the feeling of the pinch.

As I feel Gogo stop pinching me, I open my eyes and look into his. He smiles at me.

It takes everything I have to smile back as I shrug my shoulders.

"Well," I tell him, "it was worth the try. Thanks."

And as I head down Chestnut Street, I am once again a part of the world, the world as it is now, without Gogo.

And this makes me very, very sad.

I realize now that all those things I tried to prove to Gogo before, all those things that I thought made him who he is, or was—it doesn't matter.

Because Gogo, in any form, is the man I'm supposed to be with.

And I have no idea what I'm going to do about it or how I'm going to go about getting him back.

The only thing I know for sure right now is that I miss Gogo.

I have to get him back.

10.

As soon as I get home from meeting Gogo, all I want to do is get into bed and stay there. It's four in the afternoon, but I just want to go to sleep for the rest of the night. I peel off my tight jeans and throw them into the pile I left this morning.

I want Gogo back. I want him back with me now. I miss him so much. Just looking at him across from me today, no matter what he said, made me want him more. What will I do? How will I get over this? As I put my head on the pillow and throw the covers over me, my mind is going back and forth: leave him alone or fight for him? There's no right answer because either way, nothing will be the same.

I try to think about it this way: What will make me happy? Will it be convincing Gogo to leave Rhonda and be with me, even though he's not the same person, or leaving him alone and just knowing he's okay. He's alive.

The next thing I know, I open my eyes when I hear the phone ringing. When did it get dark out? When did I fall asleep? It must be Gogo calling. I guess he's working late. What time is it? The phone rings again, and suddenly I'm back to reality. I'm in my own home, the one with the freezer that's a block of ice. The one with all the clothes thrown everywhere. The house I don't share with Gogo. Everything that's happened is real.

"Hello?" I ask, groggily picking up the phone on the third ring.

"Lily?" the voice answers, "It's Rose. I called to see how you were doing. What happened?"

"Hi," I say, pulling the covers over me. "I'm, uh, I'm okay."

"You sound like crap, so that can't be good. Tell me what's going on."

So I tell her all about my meeting with Gogo, all about going to Continental Mid-town and eating the sundaes, and how my mind keeps going back and forth.

"I just don't know what to do. He's not mine anymore. He doesn't like brussels sprouts and he doesn't sleep on his back. He doesn't even play video games," I say, and I pause. "He's not the man I knew."

"And he pinched you and nothing happened?"

"Nothing."

"There's got to be something, though. You're telling me that you couldn't find any resemblance to the guy you used to know?"

"Nothing. The most that I can say is that he still eats hot fudge sundaes when he's upset and he still doesn't crumple up his napkin, but you know, that could be a coincidence."

"That's great!" she shouts.

"No, it's not great. I'm hanging on the fact that he eats hot fudge sundaes?"

"Well," she says, "it's a start, isn't it?"

"I don't know anymore." I sigh. "I think I'm just going to give up. I just don't see what I can do."

"Look," she tells me, "I think you're forgetting something here. *He* called *you*. You didn't call him. *He* wanted to know how you knew his real name. He didn't have to call you. He could have just chalked it up to some crazy lady, but he didn't. Not only did he call you, but he met you for *coffee*! Not only did he meet you for coffee, *he* was the one who wanted to get the ice cream! And then you asked him to *pinch you*, and he *pinched you*! You wanted to walk away. Right now, you have to look at the facts. If he didn't want anything from you, he wouldn't have bothered you. Do you see what I'm getting at here?"

"Yes, but there was no spark to him when he saw me. He was just a nice guy who felt bad seeing a woman cry."

"You cried?"

"I did. I couldn't help myself. What would you do if you were in this situation?"

"Oh God, I'd be on the ground crying in the fetal position for days. I really admire the stability you have, by the way."

"Thank you."

"The thing I'm getting at here, though, is," she continues, "some part of him has to know that you're not making all of this up. Some part of him, a place that he doesn't even recognize, realizes that you are his soul mate. Jeez, anyone could see that and I've never even met the guy."

"You think?"

"I don't think. I know. There's a part of him that wants to see what his life could have been, or is, or was. This is not over, Lily. This is just the beginning. Look, let me ask you something. Let's just say if—God forbid, God forbid, of course—none of this curse ever happened and, God forbid, he got into some accident, wouldn't you be there for him? Wouldn't you be there helping him to get better?"

"Of course I would, but this is a little different, don't you think?"

"No. A curse was put on the guy, just like if something, God forbid, happened to him, you'd be there helping him to rehabilitate. You wouldn't leave his side if something like that happened, would you? Why is this any different?"

Her words are really making sense to me.

"You can't give up now. You just can't."

"So what should I do?"

"You need to get your man back to the way he was. Make him remember who he was and all that he had."

"And take him from his wife?"

"No, forget the wife."

"How can I forget the wife?"

"Because she doesn't exist. He's not in the right dimension or whatever. This isn't his life. You have to get him back to the life he knows with you."

Her words stop me cold.

"So I get him back. I rehab him. I teach him who he used to be. He'll like himself so much better that he'll want to be with me."

"Yes, it's like that movie *Regarding Henry*, except he got boring instead of nice."

I sit up in bed and think about my cousin's words. Is she right?

Yes, she's right. I shouldn't feel bad for the wife or the life he's lived up until now. The whole thing isn't real anyway; even though it is, it's really not.

"This curse is so confusing," she says.

"I was just thinking the same thing," I answer. "So what do you think I should do?"

There's silence on the other end of the phone.

"Rose?" I call out. "Rose?"

"I'm thinking," she tells me.

We sit there on the phone in silence for a few moments.

"Well?" I ask her.

"Here's what you do," she says as if she's come to a conclusion. "First of all, you rehab him. It's like, think of his life as a book. When the curse happened, at a certain point, the book went in a different direction. What you have to do is find that part in the book where he was still on his way to becoming Gogo, your Gogo, and then tear out the rest of the book. Start from that part of his story. Do you get what I'm saying? Start at the last page where he was still your Gogo."

I have no idea what she's saying. "What am I supposed to do, build a time machine and go back in time?"

"No, not physically go back in time. I mean quiz him, let him tell you his life story. You know the story of his life when you were with him, right?"

"Of course."

"Well, that's how he came to be the man he is. There was some point in the life he's living now that's caused him to be the way he's become. Get me?"

"Yeah, and then I find that place where his life changed course."

"Exactly."

"But that won't work at all."

"Why?" she asks.

"Because if I get him back to remembering who he was and he falls back in love with me, the curse is going to hit him again! It could be worse the second time!"

"So we'll make sure that we lift the curse by then. If he starts to fall in love with you, so you'll start being mean to him. Start acting crazy so he doesn't like you anymore."

"But in the meantime, I'm going to remind him of the way he used to look. Teach him the ways the old Gogo lived his life."

"Yes! You said he's thin and tired? Send him to a gym. His clothes are out of style and look like they came from a surplus store? Get the guy some new clothes."

"You are absolutely right." I smile, getting excited, and then I suddenly realize . . . "Only . . ."

"What?" she asks.

"How the heck am I going to spend the time with him? He's not going to suddenly allow me to pop into his life."

"Oh yeah," she says, deflated. "So we'll think of a way. You keep your thinking cap on and I'll keep mine on and I'll call you if I think of something."

"Me too."

I hang up with Rose and grab a piece of paper and a pen.

WAYS TO TURN GOGO BACK INTO GOGO

1. Get him to a gym.
2. Get him some new clothes.
3. Buy him some video games.
4. Make him eat brussels sprouts.

My list is not turning out the way it should. So I cross everything out and start all over again.

1. Build up his confidence.

Just then, my doorbell rings.

"Jonah," I say, exasperated, expecting to see him standing there, only he's not standing. He's kneeling. "Jonah, what the hell are you doing?"

"Lily, I know you said you were married, but I'm pretty sure that's just a ruse. I've been staking out your house for the last two days and I haven't seen any guy come around here, so I'm pretty sure that's something you've made up. Look, I know you're scared. I'm scared too, but we have something here. I think we're meant to be with each other." He digs into his jacket side pocket and pulls out a small black velvet box. He starts to open it. "Lily, will you—"

"No!" I shout out, grabbing the box with the ring from him and throwing it on the ground. "Don't say it!" I yell, warning him. "Take it back! Take back what you were going say, quickly!"

Jonah sits there, still on his knee, looking like he's in shock.

"I'm sorry, Jonah, I really am, but trust me, it's for your own good."

"Wow, you really know how to hurt a guy," he says, bending down and grabbing the velvet box, which landed on the steps.

"I'm sorry, I really am, but please, don't ever ask me to marry you. I beg of you, please."

"You're even more screwed up than I thought you were," he says.

"Yes, I'm totally screwed up. They should take me away in a straitjacket. Jonah, you've got to stop this already."

"Okay, just tell me this. Are you really married? Is there really another guy in your life?"

"Yes!" I shout out. "There really is someone else that I'm with."

"So where is he?"

"He's, he's gunning for head of Northeast downspout operations."

"Of what?"

"Oh, it doesn't matter. Unless you're interested in buying some downspouts?"

"To help my competition?"

"Yes?" I ask hopefully.

"What kind of a moron do you take me for?"

"Just thought I'd ask."

"Okay, I'm going to go," he says, starting to walk away, "but this isn't the end of things. I'm still going to fight for you," he says, walking over to his bright yellow Hummer.

I shut the door. I'm thinking of the words that both Jonah and Rose have said to me tonight: *Fight for you. Win back your man. Don't give up. Find the place in Gogo's book where he went off course.*

I pick up my phone and dial Rose.

"Hey," she answers.

"I've got it!"

"What is it?" she asks excitedly.

"Do Golden Bakeries need new downspouts?"

"They do now." She smiles through the phone.

"You are awesome!" I say. "Okay, we'll discuss more later. I just wanted to see if that was a possibility. If I can just spend time with him, you know, oversee the operation, then I can build up his confidence and, at the same time, find that place he went off track. I can get him back!"

"Excellent idea," she says. "And to tell you the truth, I think we really do need our downspouts replaced."

"You know what downspouts are?"

"Of course. They're the pipes that are attached to the gutters on the sides of buildings and houses."

"Rose?"

"Yeah?"

"You're the best thing that's come out of this crazy situation. You really are."

"I hate to admit it with all you're going through, but I thought the same thing."

"I'll talk to you later."

"Will do."

I hang up and push the speed dial.

"Hello?" I hear my mother's voice.

"Mom?" I tell her. "Are you home?"

"You called me."

"Is Dolly there too?"

"She's on the front lawn planting some begonias. Bert Poolson is across the street washing his car. So sad."

"At night? Why is she planting flowers and why is he washing his car?"

"You have to ask?"

"Tell her I'm coming over. I need a favor from you both."

"Is this about the curse?" she asks.

"Of course it's about the curse."

"You've got a plan?" she asks, sounding downtrodden.

"I've got a plan," I say proudly.

"Oh, Lily, how many times do I have to tell you? It's useless."

"It's not useless, Mom. Look, can you just hear me out? Can you just listen to what I have to say?"

I arrive at my childhood home a half hour later to find Dolly and Selma sitting on the front porch staring across the street. Bert Poolson is buffing up his Oldsmobile Cutlass Supreme.

"Hi, Mr. Poolson," I call over to him as I get out of my car.

"I'll ask you to ask your grandmother not to put on her sprinklers. I've just finished washing my car while she was doing some gardening. Your grandmother always seems to be gardening when I wash my car, and your grandmother always puts the sprinklers on afterward, which sprinkle all over my car and I have to wash it all over again."

"Did you hear that, Gram? Mr. Poolson doesn't want you to put on your sprinklers tonight."

"Will do, Poolson." She smiles.

"Don't get the man exasperated, please, Gram?"

"That poor man is so brokenhearted," Selma tells us.

"So am I." Dolly sighs. "So am I."

"Well, this is exactly why I've come here tonight, Mom, Gram. Come on inside," I tell them as I usher them through the door. "Let's go into the living room."

Dolly and Selma take a seat on the couch as I pace back and forth in front of them.

"Okay," I start. "Here's the thing. We can sit here and accept this curse and resolve to be miserable all our lives and die alone, or we can change it."

"So what's the plan?" Selma asks.

"Yeah, what's the plan? I've got to go turn on the sprinklers as soon as Poolson walks in his house," Dolly adds.

"Why would you do that to him?" I plead.

"He loves it. Trust me." She nods.

"Ma, Gram, I want you both to buy some downspouts."

"What's wrong with the ones we have?"

"Nothing, but I need to get Gogo some business so he'll spend some more time with me, so he'll fall in love with me again, and maybe in that time I'll think of some way to break the curse."

"This is your big idea?" Selma asks. "Buy some downspouts?"

"Wait a minute, wait a minute." Dolly puts her hand on Selma's arm. "I think Lily has something here. I think we should buy some downspouts for the whole neighborhood."

"Copper ones," I add.

"Copper ones?" Selma says, taken aback. "And who's going to pay for them?"

"You," Dolly and I say at the same time.

"Oh no, I won't use that money. I just can't, I won't!" Selma folds her arms.

"Five husbands come and go and along the way they leave you with over ten million dollars. You haven't spent a single cent of it; God knows how much the interest is on all that money."

"I can't use that money for anything. I'd feel awful doing it. I'd feel dirty."

"So what's the point in having it?" I ask her.

"I just thought that maybe one day the spell would be broken and all the husbands would come back to me. They'll need something to live on, won't they?"

"And how do you expect the curse to be broken if you don't even try to break it?" I ask her.

"Oh God, vicious circle. What do I do? What do I do? Okay." She slaps her hand down. "I'll do it."

"Good, so you're in?" I ask her.

"But how is buying the entire neighborhood some downspouts going to help break the curse?" Selma asks me.

"I'm going to figure out the point in his life where the curse veered him off track and figure out a way to break the curse. In the meantime, I'm going to show Gogo what his life used to be like, before the curse started. I won't let him fall in love with me, of course, but I do want him to be happy again, strong. The only way to do that is to rehab him."

"This is wonderful!" Dolly smiles. "You're a genius, though I already knew that. I'm going to go and tell Bert Poolson right now!" she says, jumping up and heading toward the door.

"I'm still confused," Selma says, looking bewildered.

"Just trust me on this, okay?" I ask her.

"Okay," she says. "We'll get the money in the morning."

Suddenly we hear water hitting the living room window. Dolly has turned on the sprinklers.

"Dolly!" We hear Bert Poolson shout from outside.

"Hey, Poolson," Dolly shouts to him. "I'm buying you some new downspouts for your house."

"I don't need any new downspouts, I just had some new ones installed last year, and I especially don't want them from you!"

"Yeah, well, you're going to get your downspouts done and that's that."

"Are they copper?" he asks.

"I'm not some cheapo like you; of course they're going to be copper."

"Fine!" Poolson calls out. "And thank your granddaughter for reminding you not to get my car wet. I'm going to have to wash this thing all over again. I could be here all night."

"You better not bother me. I'm still doing my gardening out here."

She walks back into the living room, where Selma and I are sitting.

"Lily," she says, grinning excitedly as she gives me a big kiss on the cheek. "This is the best idea you've had yet! Now, I just hope those same plants I keep planting will stay up. Oy. The things we do for the men we love—planting, installing downspouts. What romance we have in our lives."

"So true." Selma sighs, patting my leg.

"So true." I nod back.

11.

"You did what?" Gogo asks for the fourth time since I entered his office and walked over to his cubicle. When Gogo saw me walk in, he looked like he thought I was going to start screaming that I was really his wife and had damaging evidence that could destroy his life.

"I got you some great jobs. An entire block of homes in Bala Cynwyd *and* the entire Golden Bakery chain!"

"But how? Why? Why would you do this for me?"

"Take it as a thank-you for the sundae."

"I appreciate it, Lily, but that's just too nice. I can't accept this."

"Why not?" I shrug. "What's the big deal? You sell and install downspouts, and I have a bunch of people who need them. It's as simple as that."

"Golden Bakeries has twenty-five stores all along the tristate area. Morning Hill Lane has what, ten houses?"

"Fifteen." I smile.

Gogo smiles in that way where I know I've got him. It's the same smile he had the night in Paris at the George V when I told him I wanted to marry him.

"I don't— This is— I don't know how to—"

"Just do a good job," I tell him. "That's all the thanks I need."

"Well"—he pauses—"thank you. I appreciate this. I really do."

"Oh, and they want all copper drains," I add.

If he wasn't sitting, I think he'd collapse.

"Hey, buddy, what'cha got here?"

"Hey, Brad," Gogo says, "this is Lily . . ."

"Burns," I say, introducing myself.

"This is Brad Sandringham," Gogo announces. "Brad and I share the Northeast sales. Lily has some work for us," he says proudly.

"Nice to meet you." Brad flirts as he sticks his hand out for me to shake it. I immediately see Brad as the kind of guy who has made Gogo's life at work a living nightmare. The way his pecs are bulging through his black Carverman Downspouts polo shirt, you'd think he spends more time in the gym than anywhere else, that or he carries the downspouts around with him all day. I look back at Gogo in his black Carverman Downspouts polo shirt. His polo shirt is so big on him, he could fit another person and a small child in it if he wanted to.

"What is it?" Brad asks cunningly. "Your house needs a new downspout?"

"Golden Bakeries." Gogo smiles.

"One Golden Bakery?" Brad asks hopefully.

"The entire chain." Gogo nods.

"Not bad," Brad answers as if he's happy for Gogo, but the look on his face tells me otherwise.

"That, and fifteen homes on Morning Hill Lane," Gogo brags on.

"What are you, the downspout fairy?" Brad laughs.

"I guess she is." Gogo smiles, looking at me as I smile back.

"Hi, Brad." An older guy walks in with the same muscle-bound body busting out of his black Carverman Downspouts polo shirt. I know this is Rhonda's father. "We still on for the gym this afternoon?"

"You know it," Brad answers. "I'm benching two twenty-five now."

"Two twenty-five? You could carry two of my son-in-law here." He laughs and Brad laughs, but Gogo doesn't.

"Goldblatt"—the guy turns to Gogo, changing his tune—"I'm

going to need you to go out and look in on that development in Cherry Hill. They say they've had some leaks, and with the rain coming, I don't want any more problems."

"Will do," Gogo answers. "By the way, Tank, this is Lily Burns. Lily, this is my father-in-law, Tank Carverman."

"Nice to meet you." I smile.

"Lily has some business for us this morning," Gogo says, looking like he won't be able to contain himself much longer.

"Good for you," Tank responds, assuming Gogo couldn't possibly have brought in anything more than a tiny job.

"Morning Hill Lane," Gogo says.

"Nice street," Tank says, turning to me. "Nice houses. Which one is yours?"

"Twenty-nine fifty-six," I tell him, "but we're going to need the whole street done. Morning Hill Lane decided they wanted the houses to look more unified."

"What's that, five houses?" he asks.

"Fifteen," Brad, Gogo, and I say at the same time.

"Gogo came to us and, I've got to say, his sales pitch was so convincing, he had the whole neighborhood on board. We were eating out of his hand." I give a discreet nod to Gogo, who nods back appreciatively.

"Really? Gogo?" Tank asks, trying to process this startling bit of news.

"Oh yes, he's an amazing salesman. That's probably what won over the Golden Bakeries too."

"Golden Bakeries? Not the whole chain?" Tank's face is a mix of delight and shock.

Gogo calmly says, "Copper."

"Copper!" Tank looks like he's about to blow a gasket.

"Copper." I nod assuringly. "We were going to go with aluminum, but Gogo explained the advantages of copper to us and it was a no-brainer in the end."

"Now, hold on, we're talking about this guy right here?" he asks, pointing at Gogo.

"If they made platinum, he probably could have convinced us to buy those," I tell Tank.

Tank puts his beefy hand on Gogo's shoulder. "Good work, son," Tank congratulates Gogo, obviously impressed. I have the feeling this is the first time this man has ever called Gogo "son."

Tank lingers there for a moment, a huge smile on his face. Brad puts his head down. Gogo's smile could light up a small town.

Tank finally says, "I guess we'll need to get on this immediately."

"Sure, right after I come back from Cherry Hill," Gogo says, getting up.

"You know what," he says, turning to Brad, "Brad, why don't you take Cherry Hill. Let's get Gogo on these projects ASAP."

"But I've got the Broomall site to go out to," Brad whines. "I won't get back until late. We were going to work out tonight."

"Brad," Tank says sternly, "I think it would be best if you went."

"Fine." Brad pouts as he walks away.

"Good to meet you, Lily," Tank tells me. "Now, let's get on this, shall we? Are you the contact person for all of this?"

"I am," I tell him. "Rose Golden of Golden Bakeries and Selma Burns from Morning Hill Lane will be taking care of payments, but I'll be overseeing the whole thing."

"Maybe I'll take over on this. I don't know if Gogo here is up to all of it," Tank says.

"Actually," I interrupt, "I've heard a lot of good things about Gogo, uh, Mr. Goldblatt. The stuff he was doing downtown—a lot of people are talking. That's how I got here. I think I'd like Gogo to head up the project."

"Don't screw this up," Tank quietly warns Gogo.

"I won't," Gogo answers.

Tank heads off.

"He's never called me 'son' before," Gogo says, surprised. "I've got to call Rhonda and tell her the news. Thanks, thanks a lot, Lily."

"My pleasure." I swallow, trying to keep a smile.

For the first time since I've entered it, I notice invoices are tacked all along the wall of Gogo's cubicle. He's got only one picture. It's a framed photo of Rhonda and it's placed right by his phone. It looks like one of those glamour shots you get at the mall. She's sprawled out on a bench with a pink background behind her. She isn't smiling in the picture. I think she must have been going for something sexy, only it doesn't look sexy. Her face looks more like someone caught her off guard and made her angry. She looks like an angry, surprised woman in a sexy pose. Not that I'm putting down my husband's wife or anything. I'm just describing what I see.

I watch Gogo pick up the phone and dial excitedly.

"You know what?" I say, getting up. "I'm going to get out of here. Why don't you give me a call later and we'll go over the plans."

"This will only take a minute."

"No, you celebrate with your wife. Give me a call later."

"Hi, hon," Gogo says into the phone. "Hold on one sec." Then he looks up at me as I start to walk out of his cubicle.

"I'll give you a call this afternoon," he says.

"Great, I'll be expecting it."

"And Lily," he whispers, putting his hand over the phone's mouthpiece, "thanks again."

"No problem," I mouth.

"Hey," I hear him say into the phone as I walk away, just like all the times he called me from work.

"It's not his wife, it's not his wife. This is an alternate reality.

There is no reason to get upset," I whisper softly to myself as I walk through the office toward the door.

"Thanks for giving Gogo some business," I hear Brad's voice behind me. "You saved him from losing his job."

"Excuse me?"

"The only reason the guy stays on is because he's the boss's son-in-law. He's not the best salesman."

"He won me over," I tell him. "A lot of people are talking about him."

"Yeah?" He looks surprised.

"If I were you, I'd be worrying about my job a little more."

"Yeah, right." He laughs.

Brad's cubicle looks a lot like Gogo's, with invoices tacked on the walls, only his desk is covered with muscle magazines and a big jug of protein powder. Beyond the jug is a picture of an attractive blond woman and two blond-haired children.

"Is this your family?" I ask, pointing to the picture.

"This?" he says, taking the picture in his hand. "No, this is the picture that came with the frame. I'm not married. Clients like it, though, if they see you've got a family."

"Nice." I feign interest.

"Are you single?" he asks.

"No," I tell him. "I'm married. Very married."

"Good for him." He smiles as if he's got an ulterior motive.

"Well, I guess I'll see you around," I tell him.

"Guess I will," he says, flirting.

"Ugh," I mutter as I walk away.

12.

Dear Homeowners of Morning Hill Lane,

Let's cut to the chase here, folks:

Our street looks like crap.

When I first moved into our house twenty-five years ago, what a gorgeous street this was. It looked like a paradise of stone colonials, each uniform in look and yet with its own personal charm to it. Remember how Mrs. Fabrezi would put the American flag out each Fourth of July? We all still love Mr. Saulbrook's perennials. Many of you through the years have complimented my mother's gardening expertise. This was what set our homes apart while keeping that tranquil uniformity our street was known for.

When the Fishbounds put in their circular driveway, no one raised a big fuss, and why should we? This isn't a development where no one is free to express their own individual tastes. Everyone is free to do what they want. Some may have whispered when Agnes Southy put pink flamingos on her lawn to go with the hot pink trim on her house, but no one really gave it a second thought. We're all too caught up in our own lives to worry about such things, aren't we? Then, in early 2000, the Rindchecks moved in and tore down Mrs. Kornhart's home and built that McMansion, and Old Man Poolson took them to court. Who could have blamed him? His house never sees the sun anymore. That house shadows his entire home. Have any of you been in Old Man Poolson's house? It looks like the dead of night at noon!

Let's be frank: Our block used to look like a Shangri-la. Now? It looks like a hodgepodge of shacks.

This is why I am writing you today.

I have been in touch with a lovely gentleman named Gogo Goldblatt over at Carverman Downspouts.* AT NO COST TO YOU, I have decided to install identical copper downspouts* on each of your homes. Let me repeat: THIS IS AT NO COST TO YOU. This is my gift to you, the fine neighbors of Morning Hill Lane. Did I mention the downspouts will be made of copper? They'll last forever!

All you have to do is add your name to the list of neighbors who want to help turn our block back into the elegant street it once was.

And if you're still not sure about taking me up on my gift to you, chew on this: Housing prices are falling fast. Has anyone seen the comps on this block? Adding copper downspouts will only raise the resale value on our homes.

Now, will you sign your name to this list?

I thought you would.

Many thanks and my pleasure,

Selma Ruben Garf Sloan Bucazzi Lonagin Burns

*P.S. Downspouts are those drainpipes on the side of everyone's house that catch the water when it rains.

"Can you believe I got every neighbor to agree?" Selma exclaims as I walk through the door. "The Rindchecks had a little problem with it, but when I swore up and down that I was paying for everything, they finally came through. I'm a hero to the block! Can you believe it?"

"Now, shouldn't Gogo be here by now?" Dolly asks me, holding a tray of crudités and dip. "I was going to make my famous empanadas, but I didn't know if Gogo liked empanadas. Does Gogo like empanadas? I'm just so nervous."

"Crudités is fine, Gram," I tell her.

The two of them are in such a frenzied state, they don't seem to notice that Rose is standing behind me holding a big Golden Bakery box in her hand. Finally Selma looks beyond me.

"Hello," Selma happily exclaims. "Are you from the downspout place?"

"Actually, no. Ma, Gram, come into the living room," I say as Dolly heads in with the tray of crudités in her hands. I motion Rose to follow.

"Ma? Gram? This is Rose Golden."

"A pleasure." Selma holds out her hand.

"So nice to meet you too," Rose tells her genuinely. "Here, I bought you a gift."

"How sweet," Selma says, taking the box from Rose and setting it on the coffee table.

"Can I offer you something to drink?" Selma asks, holding her own glass in her hand. I pour myself some mineral water.

"Are you a friend of Lily's from work?" Dolly asks.

"Well . . ." Rose looks at me as I look back.

"Ma, Gram . . ." I dramatically pause as Selma takes a sip of her mineral water. "Rose is our cousin. She's Emmalina's great-great-granddaughter."

"*Ahhhhhh!*" Selma shouts, doing a spit take with the mineral water as Dolly drops the entire tray of crudités on the floor and throws her hands on her face in horror.

"I come in peace! I come in peace!" Rose shouts as I grab Selma, who looks like she's going to faint.

"Ma, Gram, she's on our side! She knows all about the curse and she feels terrible about it. She's trying to help us!"

"I am," Rose says, as she bends down to help pick up the carrots and celery scattered all over the floor. "Look," she says, picking up the bakery box, "I brought you a gift!" She opens the lid and hands the box to Selma.

"*Chocolate chip cookies!*" Selma shrieks as if they are tainted. Like Dracula being presented with a box of garlic, she throws the box on the couch. Cookies fly everywhere.

"Don't touch them!" Dolly shouts. "Chocolate chip cookies are what got us into this mess in the first place!"

"*Would you two calm down for a second?*" I shout at them.

"Get them away!" Selma says, shielding her eyes from the couch. "Take the cookies away!"

"I'm sorry!" Rose apologetically exclaims, grabbing the box. "I'm so sorry." She turns to me and mutters under her breath, "I think this was a mistake."

"It's no mistake. Mom, Gram, please, get it together and control yourselves for a moment. Would you just sit down and let us explain. Gogo is going to be here with the plans any minute, and can you imagine what he'll think if he walks into this mass of hysteria?"

"The peppermint schnapps," Dolly utters, taking a seat on the couch, fanning herself. "Get the peppermint schnapps."

I run over to the liquor cabinet and pull out the schnapps and two glasses. When I return, Selma has taken a seat next to Dolly. The two look like they're both about to suffer coronaries.

I hand Dolly a glass.

"Not needed," Dolly says, shooting away the glass and grabbing the bottle of schnapps from my hand. She takes a big swig and then hands it to Selma, who gulps down a quarter of the bottle.

"We're going to need to get some more liquor in this house." Dolly sounds resigned.

"Are you calm now?" I ask them.

"Is there anything that I can do?" Rose asks.

"How did you find us?" Selma asks.

"You know, now that I look at the two of them together, they could really be sisters," Dolly says, looking up at Rose and me.

"They really do." Selma sighs. "The four of them."

Rose looks at me, confused. I take the bottle of schnapps out of Selma's hand just as she's about to take another swig.

"No more for you," I tell her.

"So you're Emmalina's great-great-granddaughter." Dolly looks deep into Rose's eyes.

"I found her," I explain. "I thought that maybe she could reverse the curse."

"I knew about the curse. My grandfather used to tell me all about it as a bedtime story when I was little."

"More like a horror story," Dolly interjects.

"I never knew if it was true. I always wondered. Then when Lily showed up at my door, I just couldn't believe it. I just can't believe what all of you have gone through. How could I not try and help you?" Rose sighs. "After all, Emmalina was just as bad as Astrid for what she did to you. Maybe even worse."

"See, Mom? Gram? Rose is here to help us. She knows all about Gogo."

"I'm having him install new downspouts in all our bakeries in the tristate area," Rose announces proudly.

"Wait a minute!" Selma looks at the box. "You're *Golden Bakeries*? They're known for their chocolate chip cookies!"

"They're not . . ." Dolly gasps.

"Yes, Emmalina's recipe," Rose says proudly and then quickly regrets it. "I mean, well, not exactly Emmalina's recipe, kind of Emmalina's recipe—sugar, eggs, chocolate bits, no big deal."

"They're only the reason our family is cursed, but yeah, no big deal." Selma cringes. "Oh, sorry, I know it's not your fault, Emmalina's great-great-granddaughter, it's just—what did you say your name was?"

"It's Rose, and I know." Rose sighs, going over to Selma and putting her arm around her.

"What we've been through," Dolly whimpers as she takes Rose's hand. "But we don't blame you, really we don't."

"Of course not," Selma tells her. "It was just such a shock when Lily introduced you. We just weren't ready." Selma burps.

"And that's why I'm here to help Lily," Rose says. "I'll do anything to help Lily get Gogo back."

Silence fills the room as Selma, Dolly, and Rose smile at each other in a truce.

And as if on cue, the doorbell rings.

"It's him!" Dolly whispers with anticipation.

"Oh, one more thing," I whisper. "Please don't mention that Gogo and I are actually married."

"I thought you told him," Selma whispers.

"I did, but he seems to be letting that part slide. He's so excited about all the work he's getting, he doesn't care how I got to him. So let's not remind him, okay? I don't want to spook him."

"But what if he brings it up?" Selma asks. "Should I act like I don't know what he's talking about?"

"He's not going to bring it up," I tell her. "Why would he bring it up?"

"But what if he brings it up?" Dolly asks nervously.

"He won't," I insist. "Now, promise me you won't act like you're meeting your son-in-law for the first time. Just act natural. Do you promise?"

"I'm so nervous." Dolly shakes. "Who's going to get the door?"

"I can't even feel my feet," Selma answers. A quarter of a bottle of schnapps and she's smashed.

"Do you promise?" I ask them again.

"I promise," Dolly says. "I'll be so cool, you won't believe it."

The doorbell rings again as I look at Selma.

"I'll be so casual, you'll think I don't know anything." Selma crosses her heart.

The doorbell rings one more time.

"Should I get it?" Rose asks me.

"I'll get it," I say, heading toward the door as I smooth my hair.

The front door of my childhood home has a window on the top part of it. The window is so high that you can never see who it is. If the person is over six feet tall, you can just see the top of their head, and that's what I see as I walk over to the door. Gogo's once-luxurious hair, now a bit flattened, is peeking through the bottom of the window. When I open the door, he's standing there in the Carverman Downspout polo shirt and khaki pants I've become oddly accustomed to.

"Hey." He smiles as I open the door. His smile is so warm and genuine, for a split second I feel the urge to jump into his arms.

I don't do this, of course, and I chalk up the smile to his delight in having so much work.

"Hey." I smile back, hiding my excitement at seeing him in my childhood home.

This is not the way it should be when he first meets Dolly and Selma. I should be taking his hand and leading him into the living room where Dolly and Selma are sitting, but I have to get that out of my mind.

"Ma, Gram, this is your son-in-law," I wish I could announce. But I'm not holding his hand. He's not holding some flowers or a bottle of wine for Dolly and Selma. Instead, he's got two big file folders under his arm labeled Morning Hill Lane and Golden Bakeries, and without touching him, I motion him into the living room, where Selma, Dolly, and Rose are standing, anticipating his arrival. The three of them have these plastic smiles on their faces. In the time it took me to answer the door, the cookies and crudités have been cleaned up and put back in their proper containers.

"This is Gogo Goldblatt," I announce.

The three continue to stand there with those nervous smiles.

"Hello," Gogo casually announces.

But they still stand there. I don't know what's going on in their heads, so I give Rose a quick nod with my head so she'll snap out of it and give me a little help. Knowing Selma and Dolly as well as I do, I know they're hopeless right now.

"Nice to meet you," Rose approaches him, breaking the stagnancy of the room.

"And this is my mother, Selma, and my grandmother, Dolly Burns."

They continue to stand there.

"Ma!" I call out.

"Gogo," Selma states in an affected voice, sounding like a movie from the 1940s, "it is so lovely to have you in our home."

"Thank you," he says as she comes a little too close to him, invading his personal space, looking up at him, and staring deep into his eyes.

"Gogo," Dolly says in amazement, walking toward him and standing next to Selma.

"What a handsome face he has," Selma states.

"He looks tired, though. Poor thing."

Gogo looks at me for any kind of help.

"We had a little cocktail just before you got here," I tell him, pulling the women to the side. "Can I offer you anything to drink?" I ask. "Maybe you'd like a cookie?" I say, lifting the box.

"No, no cookies!" Dolly states firmly, stealing the box from me, as if the curse might get even worse from looking at the box. "Crudités. Gogo, I spent all morning chopping the carrots and celery for you and I make my own ranch dressing. Here." She takes a carrot, dips it in the ranch dressing, and offers it to him.

"No, thank you, I'm fine," Gogo says, taking the files from under his arm and placing them on the coffee table.

"Not even a little taste?" Dolly begs.

"Um, okay," he agrees, and Dolly stuffs the carrot in his mouth.

"It's good." He nods as Dolly takes a napkin and wipes the excess dressing off his face.

I put my head in my hands.

"So should we get down to business?" I ask. "Ma, Gram, take a seat."

Dolly and Selma sit down on either side of Gogo, unable to take their eyes off him.

"Now." Gogo pulls a sheet of paper from the Morning Hill Lane folder and shows it to Selma who doesn't even move her eyes to look at it. "I've added up the estimated cost for copper piping for all fifteen homes. I've given you a ten percent break, since this is such a big job."

"Is he sweet or what?" Dolly asks me. "I mean, he doesn't know us from Adam—it's not like you two were married and a curse was put on him—and he's giving us a break for no good reason."

I look at Rose for help.

"Gogo," Selma says, pulling the sheet from him and placing it on the table. "Tell me something, I'm curious. You don't remember our gorgeous girl here? You don't remember anything that's ever happened between you?"

"*Ma!*" I shout.

"To tell you the truth, Ms. Burns," Gogo answers, "I'd rather just get to the work at hand."

"Yeah, Ma," I say, picking up the sheet. "Let's take a look at the cost estimates."

"I'm just wondering about the curse." She doesn't give up. "I mean, I don't mean to pry, but I'm so curious as to what it feels like from the male perspective. I never asked my husbands because I didn't believe in the curse until they were all gone."

I give her a look like I'd just want to put a curse on her if there wasn't one already.

"What?" Selma shrugs. "You can't fault me for asking."

"She's got a point." Dolly nods.

Gogo looks up at me. "This isn't a joke, right?" he asks, not angry, but as if he's panicked that he might have been tricked into something. "You're really putting in downspouts, right? I mean, I'm not wasting my time here, right?"

"She swears," Rose answers. "I promise you, we're only here for the new downspouts."

"We are," I state firmly. "Aren't we, Ma? Gram?"

Selma and Dolly grimace at each other like children not getting their way.

"Fine." Dolly pouts.

"Fine." Selma crosses her arms. "Let's get back to the downspouts."

"Yes, tell me about these downspouts." Dolly rolls her eyes as I give her a harsh look.

"Well," he says, taking the folder in his hand and pulling out some more sheets, "I figure the Morning Hill Lane job, Ms. Burns, will take about a month, and then Rose—I can call you Rose, right?"

"Of course." Rose smiles.

"And then I'll move on to the bakeries. That's a bigger job with transporting everything. I'd say both jobs will take me about three months in total."

"Will it just be you installing the pipes?" Selma asks.

"No." He laughs. "I'll have a crew here."

"But you'll be overseeing the job?" I ask.

"Oh sure," he says, and I breathe a sigh of relief.

"And when do you think you'll start?" Rose asks.

"We can start as early as Monday, if that's okay with everyone?"

"Monday is good for me." Dolly smiles.

All of us nod in unison.

"Excellent. Now, we've got a couple of different copper pipes I want to show you," he says, taking a catalog from the folder.

I cannot get the huge smile off my face that formed when he said the words "three months." I'll have three months to win Gogo back. I'll get to spend all of that time by his side. I can't begin to contain my happiness. Out of the corner of my eye, I catch Selma looking at me.

"That won't be necessary," Selma says, taking the catalog from his hand. "We want the best. Whatever you think are the best copper downspouts, then that's what we want."

"Well, it might be a little more than the estimated cost," he says, picking up the first sheet.

"I don't care how much it costs." Selma takes the sheet and rips it in two. "Whatever the cost, however long it takes."

Gogo smiles with delight.

"Okay then." Gogo closes the folder and stands. "I guess I'll see you here on Monday."

"We'll be here." Dolly smiles, excited.

"We'll be starting at about seven."

"We'll be here." Selma gets up and puts her arm around him.

"Great," he says hesitantly. "And just so we're clear here, you mentioned this stuff about Lily and me being married, and I just want to say, you know, I'm flattered, but I'm married. I'd appreciate it if we didn't bring that up again, especially once the crew arrives."

"Oh that." Selma throws up her hand. "Let's forget about that. We're just some crazy ladies here, don't mind us. We promise we won't bring that up again."

"We won't?" Dolly asks.

"No, Ma, we won't," Selma tells her.

"It was lovely to meet you," Selma says, walking Gogo to the door.

"Nice to meet you too, all of you," he says as Rose opens the door and we crowd around it.

"Good to see you again, Lily," he tells me, though there's no hint of romance in it, strictly formal.

"Good to see you too, Gogo," I answer.

Gogo walks through the door, folders in hand, and heads down the walkway as Selma closes the door.

I look at Selma, kind of amazed. "You had a quick turnaround," I say to her.

"Sweetheart, when I saw that smile on your face, just at the thought that you could spend some time with him, I said to myself, 'This is Lily's true love.' And I have to help you any way I can. I want you to be happy, darling, to make up for all that's happened to you. If I can make you happy, then all of this is worth it."

I put my arms around my mother.

"She speaks the truth." Dolly nods. "At the very least, if I could just say a kind word to Poolson, let him know that my feelings for him are the same as he feels for me—just that little thing, that would make me so happy. Instead, the poor man has to put up with all of my hammering and hawing."

"Are you married?" Selma asks Rose.

"I'm engaged."

"What's he like?"

Rose sighs. "He's the best thing that's ever happened to me."

The four of us take a collective sigh.

"Ma, Gram, Rose?"

They turn to me.

"Thank you," I tell them. "Thank you so much."

"It's our pleasure." Dolly puts her arm around me.

"I wish I could do more," Selma says, putting her arm around me. "Who knows, maybe you can break the spell without hurting Gogo any more than the curse already has. If anyone can get this spell broken, you can. It's worth the try."

"We're going to break this spell," Rose says, putting her arm around Selma.

And as the four of us hug, I can't help but think, *This could work. This could actually work.*

13.

I feel like such an idiot right now. When I devised this plan, I had a timeline for how it would work:

Week 1:   Sharing laughs, etc.
Week 2:   Increasing Gogo's comfort level, casual touching, brushing up against each other.
Week 3:   Working late one night, a couple of beers . . .

That's not how it's going.

You know that feeling when someone comes to fix something in your house? You wait all day for the person to come and fix the cable or the washing machine, and when the guy finally arrives, you show him to the area, you explain the problem . . . and then you stand there like you don't know what to do with yourself as the guy fixes whatever needs to be fixed? Like he rules the roost now and you're invading his space?

That's pretty much how I'm feeling right now.

Usually, when I'm home and someone comes to fix something in the house, I go over to my computer and play a video game (Gold Conqueror: the one where you try and get all the gold you can in a pile, but if the pile tumbles you lose? Gogo makes fun of me whenever he catches me playing this game, but I find it very relaxing), or check out People.com (what's Lindsay gotten herself into this week?), until I'll hear a "Ma'am, can you show me where your fuse box is?" That's when I jump up and take him over to the fuse box, but then I go back to my Gold Conqueror game and act like I'm busy working.

How I wish I could play some Gold Conqueror now.

Instead, I'm standing out here in front of the Fishbounds' house on Morning Hill Lane on a chilly fall morning watching some sweaty guys (and not even the hot Chippendale kind, but the kind that show the cracks of their fat asses when they bend down; I've seen more men's ass cracks today than over years when I was single) install copper downspouts. Gogo is really into overseeing the operation. The most he's said to me all day has been "You really don't have to stick around," but then I put on my smile and lie, "It's just so interesting! I'm having so much fun watching the whole process. Now tell me what they're doing now. Are those brackets that they're installing? Is that to keep the pipes in their place?"

Gogo, however, has no time to explain to me the obvious reason for the brackets. He's been looking over blueprints (the sexiest thing I've seen him do all day) and measuring pipes. The biggest drama all morning was when one pipe was three-quarters of an inch off.

Still, this is the best way I could find to spend time with Gogo, and I've certainly done nothing but watch him.

Maybe I'm asking too much. I mean, it's only the first day. Baby steps.

God, my feet hurt standing in heels on this grass, and damn they're cold. I really wanted to look sexy, though, and Gogo always liked the black heels I'm wearing. He always said they made my legs look longer, as in "Why don't you wear the black heels that make your legs look longer?"

The bright spot, though, was that he did make a comment about my black heels. "You might want to put on something a little more comfortable if you're going to stay out here all day," he said, pointing to my shoes.

"What? These?" I said, turning my leg to the side, hoping he'll get some kind of thrill seeing how long my legs look.

Nothing. Crickets.

"They feel like sneakers!" I exclaimed as I hid the excruciating pain I was feeling from the no doubt bloody blister forming just under my big toe.

Tomorrow I'm wearing the ballet flats.

It's not like I'm trying to seduce him, because I'm not. It's just, can you imagine standing around the husband who always loved your legs and now he doesn't remember he liked them at all?

Then, around eleven, Selma came jogging by with some granola bars for the crew that Dolly whipped up. She put them on the table Dolly set up with the big coffee urn. It's now noon and none of the bars have been touched.

So that's the extent of all the excitement that's happened since I got here at 7 a.m. For five hours, I've been walking back and forth with my arms folded as if I'm concerned about the whole construction. Except for Gogo's few comments, none of the crew has spoken to me, unless you count the four workers who passed me and nodded as they headed toward the Porta-Potty located in front of Old Man Poolson's house (Dolly insisted it be placed there).

Hence, I feel like such an idiot right now.

I hear a horn playing "La Cucaracha," and I turn my head to see a roach coach coming down our street.

"Lunch!" Gogo calls out, and the men drop whatever they're doing right on cue. I figure I'll head over to the roach coach myself as I am a bit hungry. I've never eaten from one of these things before, but it's as good a chance as any to grab some time with Gogo or make friends with the other workers. There's about ten of us standing around the cart right now. These guys are grabbing at sandwiches like they haven't eaten in days. I grab a cellophane-wrapped chicken salad sandwich and a bottle of water from the cart and pay for it, but as I turn around, I notice that no one is asking me to sit with them. Three of the guys have taken a seat on the curb, opening their sandwiches and speaking to each other in such hushed tones, I can't begin to make out what they're saying. Another few guys have walked back up to the job site and they're leaning against the ladders. I start to turn in the other direction—maybe I'll just head back to Selma and Dolly's house, throw this sandwich in the trash, and grab something out of the refrigerator—when I hear the music to my ears.

"Hey," I hear Gogo's voice. "We've got some room here by the coffee if you want to come eat with us."

"Thanks!" I say happily. "Day one is turning out really well."

"It's looking pretty good," Gogo says, surveying the pipes. "I think everyone should be really happy with what we've done here."

"I guess this is something you see every day," I say, unwrapping my sandwich and taking the top bread off so I can peel the tomatoes off the chicken salad and place them to the side. "I'm finding it all so interesting."

"You said that before." Gogo laughs. "I guess if you've never seen anyone install downspouts, it could be considered interesting. I don't know. Maybe I've been doing this for so long, the thrill has gone out of it for me."

"That's how I feel about advertising," I tell him. "But then, I'll be watching television, and one of my ads will come on, and," I say, taking a bite of my sandwich, "it's the same thrill I have when I saw my first ad on television."

"How many ads have you worked on?" he asks.

"Oh God, I've never counted, but over the years, I guess I'd have to say close to a thousand, maybe more if you consider print, internet, and additional television spots."

I take another bite of my sandwich, and as luck would have it, I bite right into a piece of fat. I suddenly remember I don't have a napkin.

"Come to think of it, I guess it's true for me too. I get a nice feeling when I drive by a building with downspouts I installed. It's like I've left a piece of myself there."

I'm trying desperately to swallow the piece of fat, but it's making me want to gag. I'm so grossed out with this bite of chicken lingering in my mouth that I could vomit all over the table. I take a sip of my water, but it's only making the situation worse. Now I've got a watered-down piece of chicken fat in my mouth. I feel myself starting to gag. I've just got to get this out of my mouth. The situation has become unmanageable.

"*Oh no, I missed lunch!*" we hear in a high-pitched squeal. Thank God for Dolly, who is running with a tray of sandwiches in her hand. As Gogo turns his head, I bend down under the table and spit out the aforementioned.

"I slow-cooked some brisket for eight hours and got the bread from the bakery on Montgomery Ave. just as the Amoroso truck delivered it this morning!" Dolly screeches sadly as she approaches the table. "What are you doing down there, hon?" she asks just as I finish burying the contents of my mouth.

"Nothing," I say, shooting back up and grabbing my water bottle. "That's so sweet, Gram. And these look great!" I say, pushing my chicken sandwich to the side.

"That's very kind of you, Ms. Burns, but you didn't have to go to all this trouble."

"Trouble?" Dolly exclaims. "What trouble? It was my pleasure! And here's some plates for all of you and forks and spoons and knives . . . ," she says, setting them down on the table. "Wait, I made potato salad and cole slaw too, all homemade! Let me just run back and get it." She hurries away.

Gogo and I chuckle to each other as we look down at the beautiful presentation in front of us.

"She would be really upset if no one ate it," I tell him. "She lives for this kind of thing."

"Hey, guys?" Gogo calls out. "We've got some brisket sandwiches over here."

"*And Amoroso bread!*" we heard Dolly call from three houses over.

"And Amoroso bread," Gogo corrects himself with a chuckle.

"I'm sorry, you were interrupted. You were telling me the feeling of passing a building with downspouts you put up."

"Oh yeah," he says, making an embarrassed face. "It's not important."

"No, it is," I tell him, taking a plate and grabbing a sandwich. "Please, go on."

"Well . . . it's just a nice feeling to know that if there's been a really bad rain—"

"Hey, Gogo, can I get in here?" a worker asks as Gogo moves from the side. Six other workers follow him as Gogo moves out of the way and allows them to huddle around the table, grabbing plates and sandwiches.

"You were talking about when the rain comes and you drive by one of your downspouts," I shout over the commotion in front of me.

"It's . . . it's not important . . . Another time," he tells me as he walks away, leaving me standing around the table with the other workers grabbing at sandwiches and plates.

"This is one great sandwich," the guy next to me says as he bumps me in the arm with his elbow. We're bunched so close around this table now that we can't lift our sandwiches without hitting someone.

"It is," I say, swallowing a bite, elbowing him back.

I guess it's good. I can't taste it. All I see is Gogo with his plate heading toward the job site and taking a look at the pipes. He looks down at the pipes on the ground and then takes a bite of his sandwich.

"Cole slaw and potato salad!" Dolly calls out as the men cheer. Two of the guys run over to her and take them out of her hands and head back to the table.

I turn around again and see Gogo, still standing by the pipes, all alone with his sandwich.

I put down my sandwich and head over to him. My heels are sinking into the ground, so I'm kind of wobbly when Gogo notices me heading his way.

"You were telling me about driving by places where you've installed downspouts."

"You know, it's really not a big deal," he says, a bit embarrassed. "Just drop it."

"No," I answer, "I really want to know."

Gogo takes a seat on the ground and continues to eat his sandwich. I know that if I sit on the ground next to him, I'll have a huge dirt stain on the seat of my pants. I bend down and sit next to him. This will be the second pair of pants that I'll throw out in a month.

"I'm always interested in what drives people. I'd like to hear what you were going to say," I tell him.

"It's just that it's nice to know I've helped people, even if it's in the smallest way. Even if it was just a downspout," he says.

And right there, that's Gogo. That's the old Gogo. And I can't help but smile. Even in a job where he hangs drainpipes, he has the soul of a kindhearted pediatrician.

"Well, I think that's cool," I tell him.

"Cool?" he says, a bit surprised.

"Neat, cool, whatever. I like that you feel like you help people."

I walk back to the table and return to my original spot with the guys.

"That's my sandwich, lady," the guy next to me tells me.

"What happened to mine?" I ask.

He looks over at the guy standing to the other side of me.

"I thought it was mine," the guy says sheepishly.

I grab another sandwich off the platter and start eating.

Suddenly, though, I'm full.

It's been a couple of hours now since lunch and I'm ready to tear my eyes out, I'm so bored. Tearing my eyes out would at least give me something to do.

The Fishbounds' house, however, is pretty much done and tomorrow it's on to the Saulbrooks'.

At least it's a different house to look at.

Dolly has come by two different times since lunch, first with lemonade (yes, she squeezed the lemons herself), and then with blondies and brownies about an hour ago. "Normally I don't bake, but I know you boys and Lily might need a sugar rush at three o'clock." Selma ran by on her way to the gym. The bright spot of my day was anticipating seeing her run back from the gym.

Gogo could not be bothered with me. He's taking this operation so seriously, you'd think he really was a doctor. The thing is, though, he was never as tense as he is now. Sure, he'd be worried if some kid came in with something really bad, but there was a difference. As a doctor, he experienced pure worry. This is a worry mixed with a lot of stress. When I asked him if he was sure the paint on the downspout really matched the Fishbounds' house, I thought he was going to kick me off the property for good.

"Look, we checked and rechecked the paint three times," he told me angrily.

To tell you the truth, I was only asking him so that I could get him to talk to me. He used the same paint color as the one that was on the house. I thought it was an easy question to ask.

"Four o'clock!" Gogo suddenly shouted. "That's it for today, fellas."

Suddenly, the men around me drop whatever is in their hands and start walking toward their trucks.

"Great day!" I say cheerfully, as Gogo heads my way.

"Yeah, I think it looks pretty good," he says, turning around and looking at the house.

"You know, I keep thinking about what you were telling me. You know, about how good you feel when you drive past some of the places you put up your pipes."

"Uh-huh." He nods, looking down.

"I feel that way too a lot, you know, when I see one of my ads on television. I think to myself, 'Someone is laughing about this,' or 'Maybe someone has a headache right now and my Excedrin commercial is reminding them that they could take a pill for that.'"

Gogo looks at me like I'm crazy, but I keep blabbing.

"Sure, a lot of people might call my ads 'those things I fast-forward through on my DVR,' but there's always that chance that someone has seen my ad and I've helped them in some way. I don't know. Maybe I'm grabbing at straws with this . . ."

"I guess." He shrugs. "I mean, not to diminish what you do, but I just don't see ads as being all that important."

"Not important?" I say, reacting in a more dramatic way than I normally would. "Hey, have you ever heard of consumerism, that thing that helps keep our nation running?"

"So that's how you help people?" He balks. "By trying to get them to spend their money?"

Now I'm pissed. What is wrong with this guy?

"Hey, I'm sorry if my line of work doesn't meet your approval. I don't think downspouts are exactly saving lives."

"Really?" he asks. "A rainstorm comes to a house without downspouts, and do you know what kind of damage it could do?"

"And how do you expect people to pay for these downspouts if there's no money to buy them?"

"How's that?" he asks, as I give him the stink eye.

"If people don't spend money, then places close, people lose their jobs, no one gets downspouts."

"If they don't get downspouts, then their house gets ruined."

"If they don't contribute to the economy, they don't have the money to get the downspouts. Or the house, for that matter."

We're nose to nose with this ridiculous argument. Literally. I'm right in his face now, voicing a passion for advertising that, frankly, I know I'm kind of putting on.

"Look, what's your problem anyway?" I ask him angrily. "Are you always this rude to your clients?"

Gogo takes a deep breath. I take a step back and look into his eyes. I want to say to him, "Why are we getting into this stupid argument?" But I don't. We just stand there and look at each other.

"I guess I'm a little nervous about getting this job done right," I tell him. "I'm sorry if I've made you anxious too."

"You know what?" he says, looking contrite. "It's my fault. I am sorry. I'm really sorry. You're right. I'm nervous about this whole thing too. I had no right to react the way I just did."

"Oh, it's okay." I smile as I hold out my hand. "Truce?"

"Huh?" he asks, puzzled.

"Truce," I offer again.

And just as I'm saying this, I can see in his eyes that this statement strikes him as familiar. I continue to hold out my hand.

"Truce," he says tentatively, as he takes my hand and shakes it.

"Something wrong?" I ask him.

"No." He smiles. "That's cute. It's a good way to end an argument."

"That's cute. It's a good way to end an argument."

It was about six months ago. Gogo and I were at the market debating what we were going to have for dinner. I was in the mood for pasta. They were having a sale on San Marzano tomatoes—the really good ones from Italy. Gogo wanted to make roast chicken. We'd had Mexican the night before, his choice.

"Because last night we had what you wanted to have and it's only fair now that I get what I want to have," I told him.

Somehow this escalated into a whole thing. Gogo walked away and I put the San Marzano tomatoes in the cart.

Walking through the market, I started to feel like a fool. It had been a bad week at work. We were going to debut some new Holiday Inn Family Vacation ads featuring a big basketball star and his family. The day before the ads started airing, the guy was caught being less than a family man. Then there was a stomach virus going around the sixth-grade class at Welsh Valley Middle School and it was spreading to the seventh graders. Gogo said his office was starting to feel like a bad afterschool special. It wasn't often that Gogo and I got into a fight, but whenever we did, it was always something stupid like this. I wheeled the cart to the front of the store and started to look for him. When I finally found him, he was in the frozen foods section.

He looked so lonely standing there staring at the frozen pizzas. Like pepperoni and sausage were the last thing on his mind. When he saw me, I knew he wasn't mad at me anymore. He was looking at me with these fake-sad eyes, enough to make me smile. I put on a similar fake grimace and walked the cart over to him.

"Truce?" I apologized, putting out my hand.

"Huh?"

"Truce." I repeated.

"Truce." He smiled as he shook my hand.

We kissed and hugged each other for a moment. Over the loud-speaker, we heard Hall and Oates begin to sing:

Because your kiss . . .

"Can I have this dance?" Gogo asked, holding out his hand to me.

"Where, here?" I pursed my lips.

"It's a nice big dance floor, big enough to try my moves out on you." He shimmied back and forth.

"No, Gogo," I resisted, as a woman with two kids walked by giving us suspicious stares.

"You're afraid of what *that* woman is going to think?" he asked me.

"No," I said, "I mean yes, oh." I shoved him a little as he put one arm around me while taking my other hand in his and rocking me back and forth.

Because your kiss . . .

And then we just started dancing, right there in the frozen food section. And I started to enjoy it, Gogo dipping me, me picking up our arms for Gogo to go under. People were walking by looking at us like we were crazy, but you know what? Who really cared?

And then we just let loose, singing at the top of our lungs:

Because your kiss . . .

"That's cute," he said as the song and our dance ended. "It's a good way to end an argument."

"What?"

"The truce thing. Where did you come up with that?"

"I don't know." I shrugged my shoulders. "It just came to me."

And every time after that if there was ever a disagreement, no matter what it was, one of us would always hold our hand out before it got ugly.

"Truce?"

"Truce."

And that was that.

Back on the lawn, Gogo smiles as if he's got a million thoughts going through his head, a million memories that have just come to him. This is great! He remembers something. It's all starting to come back to him. This is going to be easier than I thought!

"I'll have to try that truce thing with Rhonda," he remarks. "Seems like an easy way to get out of an argument."

I'm suddenly deflated.

"So I guess I'll see you tomorrow," I say, trying to act as if the damp grass hasn't just swallowed me up.

"Tomorrow, seven a.m." He opens the door to his Carverman Downspouts truck. "Oh, and tomorrow, you might want to think about wearing some sneakers and some jeans you don't care about. It can get really dirty out here."

"I'll make a note of it," I say, as he starts his car.

And when I see Gogo drive away and turn the corner, I kick off my heels and wobble back to Selma and Dolly's house.

14.

Day four.

Old Man Poolson's house.

I might just leave. In the four days I've been standing out here, I've tried to ask Gogo questions, naïve questions about the work, but the answers are always minimal: "*Yes,*" "*No,*" "*Downspouts don't require electricity.*"

I'm starting to doubt this whole idea, but Rose keeps reminding me that this is the only way I would get to see him and find that place in his life where he veered off course and thereby get him to fall in love with me again.

Phase two of getting Gogo back to the old Gogo isn't working out well either. Yesterday, I had Dolly roast Gogo's favorite brussels sprouts in olive oil and balsamic vinegar. When she brought the tray out, I immediately took a sprout and shoved it into my mouth making yummy sounds, sounds usually reserved for things like french fries and fried chicken and milkshakes.

"You've got to try these, Gogo," I tell him as Raul, one of the carpenters, also remarks how great they are. Frankly, Raul the carpenter is showing more signs of the old Gogo than Gogo!

"They're so crunchy and flavorful," Raul says in broken English. "Did she use kosher salt or regular salt?"

"Kosher salt," I say, nodding in delight as I take another sprout. "Gogo, you don't know what you're missing here."

"Thanks, but no thanks. I've always hated brussels sprouts."

Frankly, I'm less depressed than fed up. Maybe it's just not worth it. I mean, what's the point anyway? When I dream about actually getting Gogo back, really having him back in my arms and going on with our life again, the sinking feeling comes when I remember that something else might happen to him. So what's the point of all of it?

The point is that I still love him.

Each morning when I see him drive up in his cute little Ford truck with the Carverman Downspouts logo on it, and then he gets out of the car in his cute little Carverman Downspouts black polo shirt with his cute little khaki pants, I melt. He still looks sad and tired and everything, but I don't see that anymore. I seriously melt looking at those gorgeous blue eyes (even though they've got bags under them) and seeing him take his hand and comb it through his hair (even though the shape isn't the same as it was, it's much shorter than it was, and I think he's going to a cheap hairdresser or using cheap shampoo or something because his hair just doesn't look as good). That's when I remember that if this is the closest I'll be able to get to him, then this is what it's got to be.

Mostly, though, I just sit and daydream about my past with Gogo and wish it could be what it was. I wonder sometimes what we would be doing now. I wonder if it will ever be that way again, and that makes me sad, so that's when I go to Gogo for comfort. That's when I ask him stupid questions just to hear his voice talking to me:

"Now, that hose Maurilio is using—is that just a regular hose or is that made specifically for the downspout industry?"

"It's just a regular hose." He laughs.

I've decided to stop asking such moronic questions. After four days, standing here all day long has started to feel ridiculous, so I've decided to go into Dolly and Selma's house across the street and rest for a while.

"What's with you?" Dolly asks as she walks in the house and sees me lying on the couch. She's trailing two grocery carts with her, the kind with two wheels on one side that elderly women like Dolly drag to and from supermarkets.

"I just came in for a while to lie down. What's that you've got there?"

"This?" she says, pointing down at the carts. "I just came back from Costco. I got ten chickens to make for the workers' lunch tomorrow. How's it going? You know, with Gogal?" She sits down beside me.

"Gogo. It's awful."

"You're not making any headway?" she asks.

"I've tried everything but stripping down to my underwear and I can't seem to break through to him. I've tried to engage him in conversation so I could find out more about his life, but I just can't get him to speak. I thought this was going to be great: you know, we have some small chitchat and then that leads into a bigger conversation and gradually he falls back in love with me and we live happily ever after."

"Even the brussels sprouts didn't work?" she asks.

"He looked at them like they were laced with arsenic. I mean, I'm at a loss now. I really thought I could break through to him. That was the whole reason for this."

"In a perfect world he'd fall right back in love with you." Dolly sighs. "But you knew what you were getting into here."

"Yeah, I did. So I just needed a break for a while."

"Rest up, sweetheart," she says, patting me on the leg as she gets up and heads toward the front door again. "You want something to eat? You want to stay for dinner? I'm making meatloaf."

"Thanks, but I'm going to go home and go to sleep early. Standing outside doing nothing can make a person incredibly tired."

"Suit yourself," she says. A moment later she returns carrying a handful of long metal rods with her.

"What the heck are those for?" I ask.

"I'm going to rotisserie the chicken. I'm going to build a bonfire in the front yard and I'll put the chickens on the rotisserie. That's the best way to cook them, you know. I think rotisserie is better than roasting in the oven."

"You're going to build a bonfire in the front yard?"

"Do you think anyone will complain?"

"Do I think anyone will complain about you standing in a beautiful suburban neighborhood cooking ten chickens over a bonfire? I think it's possible."

"It's only for a few hours," she says sheepishly.

"Whatever," I say, giving up.

A little time later, I've fallen asleep. I'm having a great dream too. Gogo and I are on a desert island. It's just Gogo and me and we're sharing a coconut. I can taste the coconut juice.

"I love you so much," Gogo tells me as he feeds me chunks of coconut.

"I love you too." I smile lovingly.

Suddenly, though, the sun starts shining right in our faces. It's so bright that we have to shield our eyes from it. It's like someone took a huge piece of aluminum and pointed it at the sun so it would reflect back at us.

Suddenly Old Man Poolson is standing over us. "Jesus Christ, you're going to burn the whole neighborhood down!" he is shouting. How did he get on our desert island?

I try to ignore him and open my mouth for another chunk of coconut. But for some reason, Gogo begins yelling, "Get some water!"

"It's just a little fire!" Dolly shouts. The island is getting extremely crowded now.

That's when I open my eyes. Through the big bay window in the living room, I see Dolly standing outside. She's got a fire going in front of her that's about seven feet high.

"Oh, crap," I say to myself as I jump off the couch and head outside.

"Do you know that you're purposely causing a fire hazard?" Poolson yells at Dolly.

"So who's going to call the police?" she yells back.

"Ms. Burns," Gogo tries to reason, "we have a lot of flammable items we're using here. Maybe it's not the best time to be roasting chickens outside your house."

"You mean there's a right time to roast chickens outside someone's house?" Poolson asks.

"Can it!" Dolly shouts at him as she continues to turn the rotisserie wheel.

"Gram, I knew this would be a bad idea," I say as a breeze swells the fire and smoke in our direction. "Why don't you just roast the chickens in the oven? Like a normal person?"

The four of us cough from the billowing smoke.

"Ms. Burns, let me give you a hand here. Let's dismantle this whole thing. The guys will appreciate anything you make for them. We've all gained five pounds from your wonderful food."

"Oh, Gogo." Dolly giggles. "Five pounds? Really?"

"I can hardly fit into my pants here." Gogo smiles. "Come on, let me help you bring this in the house."

"I should call the police on you for this!" Poolson tells her.

"You know, old man, if you took a little less time to be angry and a little more time to be a gentleman, you'd have a lot more fun in life." Dolly wags her finger in his face.

"Do you know how many years I've had to put up with this woman?" he complains to us.

"Do you know how many years I've had to put up with all of his haranguing?" Dolly asks Gogo.

"She's been nothing but an old crow from the first day I met her," Poolson complains to Gogo.

"And you've been nothing but an angry old man. How old were you when we first moved in? Eighty?"

"Old crow!" Poolson shouts in her face.

"Angry old man!" Dolly returns right back in his face.

They are a half an inch apart from each other. One step and their noses will be doing an Alaskan kiss. Both of them keep lifting their hands up and down, like they're going to either come to blows or grab each other in a fit of passion. Dolly puts her arms up in the air as if Poolson should fall right into them. Then she shakes her hands like she knows she just has to relent for fear of what could happen next. Poolson's face goes from angry to suddenly sweet and vulnerable.

"All right!" Dolly relents. "Let's put out the fire and bring the chickens inside. Lily, you and Gogo do it. I'm too old and tired for this."

Dolly looks like she suddenly wants to cry, and I just want to cry along with her. She turns and walks into the house. Poolson looks surprised, as if here was his chance finally to get Dolly in his arms. Gogo and I look at him. He looks so alone even though he's standing next to us.

"And see that you don't do anything like this again!" he exclaims heatedly as he backs away and crosses the street to his house.

"What was that all about?" Gogo asks me.

"It's a long story," I say as I take a look at the work in front of me. "You want to give me some help here?"

"Yeah, let me get the hose, you know, the 'special' one you asked me about earlier, so I can put the fire out."

"You're so funny," I deadpan. "I'm going to run in and get some roasting pans for the chickens. Then you can help me get them off the spit."

"Okay," he says, heading off to get the hose.

Suddenly I'm in no mood to deal with Gogo. This is truly the first time I've seen Dolly upset about the way her life has gone, what the curse has done to her, what it's done to the man she loves. All I want to do is run in the house and tell Dolly it's okay, that she's not alone here. She's got me and she's got Selma and we're a team. I know that kind of talk is not going to help her, though. She's lived her whole life under the burden of that stupid curse. How many times has she had to run away from love? How many other suitors have come into her life, and even though she's wanted love so badly, how many times has she just had to turn away?

I know she must have tried to get it out of her head. I know she and Selma have accepted the fact that romance is not an option. This has probably broken them in ways I don't even know. They've kept so much pain from me. I've only known about it for a couple of weeks and it's nearly killed me. What must it have been like to deal with this for a lifetime?

And now there are two people in their homes, Dolly and Poolson, alone in grief and sadness. How many times has Dolly lain on her bed and cried about love she can never show? How many barbells has Selma lifted, how many miles has she run in hopes of getting that pain (not to mention sexual frustration) to go away? How many meals has Dolly cooked just to get the mere thought of male affection out of her system?

I'll tell you something. Thinking about it is making me angry right now. I'm angry and sad. I'm so brokenhearted for Dolly and for Selma that I can't think of anything else.

I head into the house and toward the kitchen thinking this whole thing might be hurting more than it's helping anything. What is the point of it all? Am I wasting my time? My mind is racing back and forth with all these thoughts in my head as I turn the oven on and grab two large roasting pans and some oven gloves and bring them outside. Gogo has dragged the hose from across the street and fastened it to our spigot outside my childhood home.

"Those two should just get a room already," Gogo jokes.

"Can you just help me get these chickens off of here so I can put them in these pans?" I tell him irritably.

"Your grandmother is a kook," he tells me. "Between your grandmother and your mother, I can't imagine what it could have been like growing up in this loony bin."

"Excuse me?" I say, taking a step back.

"Sorry, that was rude," he says.

"Yes, that was rude."

"You're right. I'm sorry. It's just that, well, who sets up a bonfire in their front yard? Why does she think she needs to feed all of us anyway?"

Gogo turns on the hose and begins to bring the hose toward the fire, but I run over to the spigot and turn it off just as he's about to spray the flames.

"Gogo, let's get something straight. Those two women I grew up with in this house you've just referred to as the 'loony bin'? I'll have you know that those women are the bravest, most amazing two women that you'll ever meet in your life. Do you have any idea how much they've had to endure in their lives? Do you have any idea how much these women have sacrificed, not just for me, but for themselves and plenty of other people?"

I can see that Gogo is a little taken aback by this sudden eruption, but I really don't care. "You're right, I don't know anything about you or your family," he tells me.

"You're damn well right you don't!" I shoot back at him. "So don't go pointing fingers when you don't know the half of what's going on."

I'm standing there looking into Gogo's eyes, furious as he stands there not knowing what to do next. He doesn't look like he's particularly sorry. He looks more like he's dealing with a client who's overreacting to a situation. This is just getting me angrier.

There's silence between us. It's silent in the rest of the neighborhood too, as all of the workers have left for the day. It's getting dark as Gogo goes back to the spigot, turns on the hose, and begins to spray the fire. When he finally puts out the blaze, the only light we have, other than the streetlamps, is the glow coming from the living room window.

"Just help me get these chickens off the spits and you can go home for the night." I hand him the oven gloves I brought from inside.

"Sure," he says as I pick up one of the roasting pans I've placed on the front path.

As Gogo takes each chicken off the spit and places it on the roasting pan I'm holding, all I can think about is my wonderful grandmother sitting upstairs. All I want to do is go and be with her.

When Gogo finishes putting the last chicken on the last slot in the roasting pan I'm holding, he takes the other pan, now full of chickens, and we head into the house.

"I'll clean up the bonfire tomorrow, when it's light out," I tell him.

"No need," he says. "I'll get my guys on it when they get here in the morning. Those logs she set up are pretty heavy. I don't know how she got it all out here."

"Thank you. I guess the logs can wait until tomorrow."

We walk into the house and through the living room.

"Well, thanks for helping me," I say as we enter the kitchen.

But as we enter the kitchen, I start to smile. That crazy lady. That crazy kook of a grandmother I have has set up the kitchen table with a home-cooked meal fit for a family of five. There's a note on one of the plates.

I'm tired so I went to bed. Selma is taking three spinning classes back to back tonight, so she won't be home for dinner. Maybe Mr. Gogol would like to join you for some meatloaf and brussels sprouts?

    With love,
    Gram

"You want to stay for dinner?" I ask Gogo, handing him the note.

"Do you think she'll ever get my name right?" He laughs.

"Not likely." I smile.

"That's really sweet of her, but I should be heading home," he tells me. "Rhonda is expecting me."

"I'd hate for all her food to go to waste here," I say.

"Is that homemade corn soufflé?" he asks.

"What do you think?" I crack. "Do you think Dolly would serve anything store-bought?"

"Well, I guess it couldn't hurt," he says hesitantly. "Uh, let me give a call to my wife and let her know I won't be home for dinner." He takes out his cell phone from the holster on his belt.

"Sure," I tell him.

"I'm just going to walk outside to get a little privacy for a moment."

"Sure," I say. "I'm going to go and check in on my grandmother."

"Good," he says.

Gogo walks outside as I head up to Dolly's room.

"Gram?" I say softly as I open the door. She's lying in bed reading a book.

"Thanks for dinner downstairs."

"Is Gogol staying?" she asks.

"Gogo."

"That's what I said, right?"

"Yes, he's staying," I say, sitting next to her on her bed.

Dolly smiles brightly.

"So my plan worked." She beams.

"It did." I laugh.

"And do you see I made the brussels sprouts again? Maybe he'll take some this time."

"I saw them." I take her hand.

"And what did you think of Poolson out there?" She leans in, confiding in me. "Didn't you think he was going to grab me and smother me with kisses?"

"He looked like he wanted to violate you in ways I don't want to think about."

"That's what I'm going to dream about tonight," she whispers as she smiles faintly.

"Gram," I whisper, "I just want to thank you for all of this. For all the meals you've made for the crew and how much money Mom is putting up. I just want you to know how much I truly appreciate everything."

She shoos me with her hands.

"Oh sweetheart, please, all we want to do is see you happy. If this is what's going to make you happy, then that's all I want."

"But I know now how much you and Mom have suffered with this curse. Now I know why you tried to steer me away from men, and I understand all of it. I know you were looking out for me. I just want to thank you for this one last chance. I love you so much, Gram." I lean and give her a kiss.

"I love you too, darling," she tells me. "I'm glad Gogo is staying for dinner. Maybe he'll snap out of the curse and realize what he's missing with you."

"We'll see," I tell her as I get up to leave.

"You'll give me all the juicy details in the morning," she says with a giggle.

"I don't think there's going to be many details, but okay." I laugh.

"'Night, sweetheart."

"'Night, Gram, sweet dreams," I tell her.

"I plan on it." She smiles.

As I come downstairs, I hear Gogo still talking on his phone outside. I stop in midstep to listen a little.

"No, for the last time, can't you trust me? I'm not going to have an affair with her. Her grandmother invited me for dinner. It's her grandmother and her mother and Lily. What do you think? I'm going to throw her over the table on top of the meatloaf and make mad passionate love to her? . . . Look, this is a part of the business, ask your father. You have to wine and dine your clients and this is the biggest client I've had yet . . . I know your father would be okay with it too . . . What do you want? Do you want me to come home? Do you want me to tell them forget it? . . . I won't be late . . . I love you too."

Wait a minute. Is this what's going on here? The wife doesn't want Gogo to be around me, so he's ignoring me? Could that be what's going on here? Is that why he's been so standoffish toward me? Of course that's the reason! Of course the wife doesn't want her husband to be around a woman who came to her house claiming he was my husband. God, what an idiot I am!

But wait. Should I feel bad about this? Am I doing something wrong? No. Think back to what Rose said: Rhonda doesn't exist. This world doesn't exist, where Gogo is this person and we're in this situation. I'm not having an affair with Rhonda Goldblatt's husband. I repeat: *I am not having an affair with Rhonda Gold-blatt's husband!* He's my husband, right? *Right?* This is what's going through my head as I stand on the stairs listening to him. Oh God, I'm trying to have an affair with my husband! I'm trying to seduce my husband with meatloaf and corn soufflé and brussels sprouts!

He enters the house as I continue down the stairs. Should I tell him I suddenly feel sick? Should I tell him I'm suddenly not hungry anymore? Think. *Think!*

"Oh hey," he says, startled by my standing at the bottom of the stairs. Not knowing what else to do, I smile at him. *Think!*

"I don't know what to eat first." He smiles, looking at the kitchen table full of food as he puts the phone back in its holster.

"Dig in," I say, sitting down and helping myself. Screw it.

We're silent for the moment as Gogo takes some meatloaf and puts it on his plate.

"How about some corn soufflé?" I ask, spooning some on his plate.

"Roll?" he offers, holding up the bread basket.

"Thank you." I take one and put it on my plate.

"So, tell me about your life. Where did you grow up again?" I ask as I begin my search to find out where Gogo's life went off course.

"You know I have a scar on my stomach, but you don't know where I grew up?" He smirks. "I thought we're married in some other dimension. Shouldn't you know that too?"

This is so Gogo to figure me out and it makes me smile.

"So now we're laughing about it?" I flirt.

"I'm starting to think it's all kind of funny."

"Well, in my world you're married to me, not someone else, so maybe you grew up somewhere else." I shrug.

"Where do you think I grew up?" he asks quizzically.

"You were born here in Philly," I say confidently, "but your parents moved to Beachwood, Ohio, when you were twelve. You went to University of Pennsylvania undergrad and, in my world, Harvard Medical School, but that's not right now, right?"

"No, it's not right," he answers, grumpy. "I never went to medical school, much less Harvard."

"I'm sorry," I utter, knowing I just hit a dark spot.

"It's okay. You got the first part right about Philly and Ohio."

"But you still think I'm crazy, right?"

"Sure, I think you're crazy, but to be honest, I'll take even the craziest person if it means getting some business right now. We're really tight for cash in my house and if I can just get that promotion, maybe things will be okay."

"Well"—I shrug—"I'm glad I could help in some way."

Gogo takes a bite of his corn soufflé.

"So after all the time we've spent together lately, you still don't remember me?" I ask him straight out. "You really don't believe anything I've told you about yourself, about us."

"To be honest, sometimes I don't know whether to feel sorry for you for this stuff you've thought up in your head, or to call a mental health facility and get you into a straitjacket."

"And the only reason you're here is to put in those downspouts? Really, Gogo? You're not here because you're curious?"

"Of course I'm curious. You know so much about me, how could anyone not be curious? It's just that it's all so crazy, all you're saying to me, all the money you're spending to have me around."

"Are you happy in your life?"

"You've asked me that before," he says, putting down his fork. "And I've told you, how many people in the world are always happy?"

"You used to be," I say. "When you were with me, we were very happy." The words just shoot out of my mouth before I can stop them.

Gogo shakes his head. There's silence between us.

"How about some brussels sprouts," I say, stabbing my fork into one.

"No, really, it's enough with the brussels sprouts already. I don't like them."

"Just try one for me, for Dolly," I say, forcing it over to his mouth.

"No, really, I don't like . . ." He tries to fend it off until I've got it right to his mouth and he's got no other choice than to take a bite. "I'm telling you—" He takes a bite. His face immediately looks like he's eaten sour candy, but it calms down as he continues to chew. "You know what? It's not that bad."

"I knew it!" I smile.

"Yes, it's all coming back to me now thanks to this magic brussels sprout," he mocks. "We were married and now I live a different life."

"But you like them." I nod. "That's the important part."

"They're not bad," he says, taking another one and putting it on his plate. "But it doesn't mean I believe you." He laughs.

"I know." I smile back.

All of a sudden we hear a scream outside. It's a bloodcurdling scream that jolts both of us out of our seats. Gogo and I look at each other in panic and then we hurry toward the door.

Once out there, we find Selma sprawled on the lawn, grabbing her leg. Beside her is one of the logs from Dolly's bonfire.

My leg! she shouts as we find her. "Who put this goddamned log out here? The pain! My leg!"

Dolly comes outside behind us as we both reach down to try to soothe Selma.

"What happened?" Dolly asks her.

"I tripped over this godforsaken log. *Where the hell did it come from?*" she screams as tears start forming in her eyes.

"Ms. Burns," Gogo says, hunching down beside the leg she's holding. "Can you bend your leg for me?"

"No, I can't bend my goddamned leg. *Mother!*" she shouts at

Dolly. "Did you put up that bonfire again to make chickens? Did I tell you not to build a spit? Don't you remember what happened last time? The whole house almost caught on fire! You promised you'd never build a rotisserie on the lawn again!"

"Mom, just calm down," I say.

"I'm sorry, chicken is always better on a rotisserie and there are so many men working out here!" Dolly shrugs.

"Ms. Burns," Gogo says, observing the leg, "I'm not going to hurt you, I just want to see how bad it is. Can you move your ankle for me?" Then he puts his hands on her leg. "Why don't you just take a deep breath for me so I can see how bad it is. Dolly, Lily, why don't you hold her hands and just remind her to breathe right now?"

"Mom, listen to me, breathe, just breathe in and out right now so Gogo can check your leg to see if it's broken."

"Yes, Selma, breathe in and out."

"Mother, I could shoot you," she seethes.

"Ms. Burns." Gogo sighs. "Can you move your ankle?"

"The pain! The pain!"

"It could be your tibia, but I'm also concerned about your ankle." He takes her ankle in his hand. "Can you move this for me, Ms. Burns?"

"No!" she shouts in pain.

"Can you point to where the pain might be situated?" he asks her calmly.

"The whole damn thing!"

"And you don't think you can walk?"

"Honey, Gogo, I can barely breathe." She rocks back and forth.

"Okay," he says, patting her leg. He turns to me and whispers. "I'm afraid it might be a bad fracture. I think we should get her to the emergency room and have some X-rays done. That's the only way we'll really know."

"Okay, I'll get my car keys," I say, jumping up. "Ma, we're going to take you over to the hospital."

"And grab my jacket," Gogo calls out. "It's on the chair where I was sitting in the kitchen."

"Okay," I call back.

"Oh Jesus, how am I going to work out now?" I hear Selma gripe from outside.

"Selma—it's okay if I call you Selma, right?" Gogo asks.

"Yes?" She whimpers like a child.

"That's a very pretty name, Selma," he tells her.

"Thank you," she answers as he pats her arm.

"Now if it's okay, Selma, I'm just going to pick you up and carry you over to Lily's car. I'm going to do it nice and easy, so it shouldn't hurt you."

"Are you sure you can lift me?"

Gogo laughs. "You're so fit and trim, I could lift you with one arm."

I come back outside and see that for the first time since we found her, Selma is smiling.

"Oh, Gogo," she says demurely.

"Let's put her in the back seat," he instructs me.

I run over to the car and open the back door. Gogo carefully places her in.

"Jesus, watch the leg!" she shouts.

"I know," Gogo soothes her. "I know you're in a lot of pain right now, but we're going to make it better, and soon enough you'll be right back at the gym."

I run around to the other side of the car and open it so I can drag her in by her arms.

"You know something?" Selma whispers to me. "He really is a doctor."

"Lily, do you have that jacket?" he asks. I remember it's in my hand. I run around to the other side of the car and hand it to him.

"I'm so sorry if I hurt you, but I'm trying to ease you in here the best that I can." He folds the jacket into a ball and places it under Selma's bad leg. "I'm just putting my jacket under your ankle so we can elevate it, Selma. That way, the swelling won't be as bad. I hope this isn't hurting you."

"It's okay. It hurts like hell, but you're doing a good job there, Gogo," she tells him.

I can't stop staring at Gogo. For the last several moments, he has transformed into the doctor he always was: kind, gentle, with a wonderful bedside manner.

"Gogo," I say to him.

"Yeah?" he asks.

"Where did you learn how to do this? How did you know how to check her leg? How do you know that it's a fracture?"

He stops for a second and looks up at me.

"I don't know," he answers, a bit shocked.

15.

"Look, I've been working in construction for twelve years," Gogo tells me, exasperated. "There are a lot of injuries that can happen. Anyone can check a leg or an ankle to see if it's broken."

"Yes, but the way you handled her. Only a doctor would know how to do that."

"You said I was a pediatrician."

"A doctor is a doctor. You can diagnose a leg injury on a five-year-old the same way you can on a fifty-five-year-old."

"Can we just drop it, please?" he pleads.

"All I'm saying is that if you could think about what you did for my mother, how you handled that whole situation, maybe you'd start to think I wasn't crazy."

We've been sitting in the hospital waiting room for over an hour now, waiting for Selma to come out. Since there was no more room in the car, Dolly has been waiting back at the house, calling every twenty minutes for updates.

"I'm not asking you to believe me. I'm just asking you to think about it."

"You think I haven't thought about it?" he asks. "You think I haven't wondered why someone like you would go to such lengths to make me believe I'm your husband in some past life?"

"Alternate dimension," I correct him.

"Life, dimension, whatever," he says, "I'm still trying to get past the idea that this is the most elaborate practical joke that's ever been pulled." He moves closer to me. "Look, I can't deny that I'm flattered by all of your attention. But the truth is, and please understand this: I'm married. I've lived an entire life that I can remember, with memories and pictures to document those memories. If we were married, how come there are no pictures? Are you telling me that they've disappeared too?"

"It's the curse," I try to explain. "There are no pictures, no documents, no memories, no nothing. It's like it never happened. I'm the only one who can remember."

"A curse." He laughs.

"A curse," I insist.

"And why me? I'm no one. I'm a guy who sells drainpipes. I'm a boring, nothing person."

"Because you're not that to me."

"To you I'm a doctor."

"Well that, but it's much more than that."

"And who am I?"

"You're . . . you're . . ."

I want to tell him he's the love of my life. I want to tell him how he's changed my world and made me the happiest woman on the face of the earth. I want to tell him that before I met him, my life was lonely and full of heartbreak. He changed all of that for me.

"Like I said, because in some other dimension, we're married."

Gogo looks at me with those baby-blue eyes. He doesn't say anything, as if he's really trying to remember anything. In my mind I'm begging him to remember anything. *Remember how you send me little notes, all the flowers you've given me over the past year, the beautiful things you've said to me. Please remember; please let it all come back to you.*

"Fractured. In three places," I hear Selma's voice call out before I see her. She's sitting in a wheelchair being wheeled out. The bottom half of her leg is covered in a cast. The doctor says eight weeks in this godforsaken thing. I don't know how I'm going to live through it," she tells us.

"We've just given her some pain medication," the nurse wheeling her out informs us. "She might start to act a little loopy in about ten minutes."

"Well, that will be nothing new." Gogo smiles. "How are you feeling, Selma?"

"Like a moron in this thing," she answers. "Let's get out of here, Lily."

"Thank you," I tell the nurse as she continues to wheel Selma out of the hospital.

Gogo and I haven't spoken since we got Selma in the car and I drove out of the hospital. I can't help but sneak peeks at Gogo, looking at the expression on his face. Gogo is sitting in the passenger seat full of thoughts in his head. He looks pained. A part of me wants to tell him to forget it all. The other part wants to convince him even more.

"I've got to call my wife and tell her I'm on my way. Would you mind not saying anything for a moment?"

"Sure," I tell him.

He takes out his phone and dials. I can hear the ringing coming from the earpiece, followed by Rhonda's voice.

"Hi. One of the clients had a little accident and I had to take her over to the hospital."

"A little accident?" Selma announces from the back seat.

"What was that?" Rhonda asks.

"That's the client. She's sitting in the back seat—"

"Of whose car?"

"The other client."

"That woman?"

"Yes."

"Lily, you're driving so beautifully. Are we airborne?" Selma mutters from the back seat.

"No, Ma," I whisper as I hit a pothole.

"Turbulence." Selma laughs. "I love turbulence."

"No," Gogo says into the phone, "I'm not on an airplane. The client is hopped up on drugs right now."

"Paris," Selma utters. "That's where you got engaged. Such a romantic story, right at the Eiffel Tower. Gogo, what made you think of proposing to Lily at the Eiffel Tower? It's so romantic. Are we on our way to Paris?" she asks.

"I'm on my way home, right after I get the client home . . . Yes, I'm on the way home."

"Ma," I whisper, "can you please keep it down?"

"Gogo, you're a wonderful son-in-law," she mutters. "Even if you don't know it."

"She's on drugs!" he says again into the phone. "I'll be home in twenty minutes. The woman is strange even when she's not on painkillers. Twenty minutes and I'm home, I promise." He hangs up the phone.

"Sorry about that," I tell him.

"It was my fault, I shouldn't have called her in the car like this. I just didn't want her to worry."

"Right when we get to Paris, I want to go to the Eiffel Tower," Selma mutters.

"*Ma!*" I shout. "Would you just shut up and go to sleep already?"

"Okay, Lily." She sighs.

Gogo looks in the back seat. "She's out."

"Finally." I exhale.

"What was she talking about?"

"We got engaged at the Eiffel Tower."

"Who did?"

"*Who?*" I shout. "You and me!"

"Enough," Gogo says. "It's enough for the night. I can't take any more of this tonight."

"I'm sorry."

"No, I'm sorry that I took this job. This was crazy for me to think that I could do this. I don't even know what's going to happen to me when I get home."

"I'm sorry, Gogo, I really am."

"Just . . . just forget it," he says.

Gogo and I are silent all the way back to Selma and Dolly's house. When we pull up, Dolly opens the door and comes out.

"How is she?" Dolly asks Gogo.

"It's fractured in three places," he says, opening the back door of the car.

"Selma?" Gogo says to her. "I'm just going to put your arm around my shoulder so I can get you out of the car and into your house. Is that okay?"

"He's a wonderful son-in-law," Selma says, waking up and smiling to me.

"That's right," he says, pulling her out of the car. "Let's get you into the house for a good night's sleep."

"And in the morning we're off to Paris." She smiles.

"That's right, Ma," I tell her.

"Paris?" Dolly asks.

"Drugs," I tell her.

"Ah." Dolly nods.

Gogo carries Selma up to her bedroom as I go into the kitchen to clean up, only to find that Dolly has taken care of that.

It's quiet at last, and all I can wonder is what's going to happen when Gogo comes back downstairs.

I take a seat at the kitchen table and wait. And wonder. Is this really helping to break the curse? Should I just let Gogo live this life? Would I be able to go on without seeing him, even if it's not on a romantic level?

I've been sitting down here for about five minutes wrestling with these thoughts in my head. *What is best for Gogo?*

"She's in bed and she's fast asleep," Gogo tells me as he comes into the kitchen. "Your grandmother has gone to sleep too. She says to tell you good night."

"Thanks."

"Look." He sighs. "This has been a really strange night."

"Gogo, I—"

"I'm not going to deny that I had a hand in staying here," he interrupts me, "but I don't know, all of this might be a little too much for me."

"I'm sorry, I really am," I tell him.

"Look, I'm going to just get out of here. I've got to get home."

"Of course," I say, getting up.

"Well, thanks for the dinner," he tells me.

"Of course."

"So I'll see you tomorrow then," he says, grabbing his folders and putting them under his arm.

"Yep," I say as casually as I can, trying to hide my surprise and suppress a smile, "I'll see you tomorrow."

16.

Remember how when you were younger and you made out with someone or if you found out that a boy liked you, you'd spend the next day unable to look him in the eye? You'd be sitting in math class watching the boy working on a problem, or measuring liquids in test tubes in chemistry class, and as quickly as you could, you'd steal a glance at him here and there? And then at some point in the day, most likely in the cafeteria, you'd try to steal another glance and he would be stealing a glance at the exact same time?

That's kind of the way today feels.

And it feels like heaven.

One of the workers didn't show up today, so Gogo is pitching in, taking old pipes off the side of the house and installing new ones. I'm oddly keeping myself busy today. We're working on the Saulbrook property, and Mr. Saulbrook begged me to please make sure that workers stomping in his garden don't damage his prized perennials. You'd be surprised how hard this task is. I've had to reprimand them all morning.

But of course, every so often, I get a break from perennial security, and that's when I get to steal my glance. Like right now.

There's Gogo, holding up a gutter with another worker, Maurilio, centering it so it fits perfectly over the drainpipe. Maurillo just said something funny and Gogo chuckled. Gogo is too busy to catch me looking at him, so I continue to watch as Gogo jimmies the gutter into place, then presses on it to make sure it's stable, which it is. He's really observing the gutter, making sure it's snug against the house . . . oh jeez, God. He just turned around and caught me staring at him. I immediately look down at the perennials, and although nothing is wrong, I bend down and spread the soil around. When I look up again, he's back looking at his gutter. Whew.

"*Rotisserie chicken, Spanish rice, roasted potatoes, and sautéed mushrooms!*" I hear Dolly shout as I turn around.

"*Lunch!*" Gogo shouts.

The workers start coming my way, so I hold my hands out over the perennials to shield them from danger as the men walk by.

"You're really taking this seriously," Gogo says, smiling as he walks over to me.

"Yeah, well, Mr. Saulbrook really takes pride in these flowers and I gave him my word that nothing would happen to them. Mr. Saulbrook has always been a really nice guy."

"You've known him all your life?" Gogo asks.

"Oh yeah," I go on. "I used to sell Girl Scout cookies all along this block. I sold more Thin Mints than any other scout in the entire Philadelphia tristate area," I say proudly.

"I personally liked the chocolate chip cookies," he casually mentions.

Ugh. Chocolate chip cookies. I decide to change the subject.

"You looked like you knew your stuff back there," I gesture to the gutter Gogo just fitted as we walk to the card tables Dolly has set up on the lawn.

"Yeah, it's funny. I rarely need to pitch in and help. Usually I'm overseeing things, but we need to get moving here if we're going to make it to the Golden Bakeries project on time. I'll tell you," he says as he plops down in a seat at a card table and picks up a napkin to wipe his brow, "doing this kind of work makes me realize how out of shape I am. I've got to get to a gym."

"You don't work out?" I ask him and then look him up and down, realizing the obvious, not that Gogo is fat of course, the opposite in fact. He's so unmuscular that I wonder for a second how he was even able to lift those gutters at all. I want to tell him how he always worked out in his other life, but after last night's drama, bringing it up today doesn't seem prudent.

"I haven't worked out since college. God, I used to go to the college pool every day and swim laps in my junior year. I was pretty fit back then."

"So what happened?" I ask, preparing to jot his answer down in my mental log of where Gogo's life went off course.

"Uh . . ."—he starts to think—"I guess I started dating Rhonda."

"And now?"

"Now there's no time. I know I should make time, but I wouldn't even know where to start. I don't even know of a good gym."

Lightbulb!

"Would you excuse me for a second?" I ask him.

"Where do you think you're going, *missy?*" Dolly asks as she prepares a plate for Raul, who's standing next to her.

"I just want to go in and see how Mom is doing today," I tell her.

"Send her a hello from me," Gogo tells me. "Maybe I'll come by later to see how the patient is doing."

"Will do," I tell him.

I run the five house-lengths to Selma and Dolly's and swing open the front screen door like I did when I was a kid and one of them would shout out, "You're going to ruin the house!"

"Ma?" I shout.

"Yeah?" I hear her answer from the family room downstairs.

I go down the steps to find Selma lying on the couch. Her leg is propped up with a bunch of pillows. She looks catatonic sitting there staring at the television.

"Ma," I say, "I just came in to see how you were feeling."

"I feel my muscles shrinking by the second," she says listlessly, still staring at the television.

"Gogo asked how you were feeling," I say, sitting down by her side. "Why don't you go outside and thank him for last night?"

"That's nice," she tells me. "What a sweet boy he is."

"Yeah." I smile.

"Hey," she says, picking up her head, "I was wondering. I hope I didn't say anything out of line last night. Those drugs were pretty powerful. I woke up in the middle of the night and I could have sworn I was in Paris. I even saw the Eiffel Tower out my window."

"You were fine," I lie, figuring why upset her even more since it doesn't seem to have done any damage.

"You know what?" I say, getting up and grabbing her crutches. "Why don't you take a walk with me outside? Go thank Gogo. Everyone is eating lunch. Dolly made rotisserie chicken."

"Please don't mention *Dolly* or *rotisserie chicken*." She grimaces.

"Oh, it's not like she did it on purpose."

"I have to stay off of this leg for six weeks. Next week they're going to put a pin in my ankle, *a pin*! For the rest of my life I'm going to be that annoying person in the security line at the airport who has to explain why the bells and whistles keep going off. Most people my age who work out as much as I do have had to have hips and joints and cartilage removed, but not me. Now it's all going to go to pot from here on out."

"Oh, it is not and you know it," I tell her. "You'll be up and back exercising in no time. It's good to take a break."

"Break? I don't care about a break. How am I going to see my little Carter, the Adonis? He's going to be so worried about me. I don't know how to tell him. Who is going to believe that I tripped over a log in my front yard because my mother built a bonfire to make chicken? What are we, the Beverly Hillbillies? I've had it with that woman."

"So what are you going to do?"

"I'll tell you what I'm going to do," she says, grabbing the remote and putting the television on mute. "I'm going to move out. It's about time I moved out of my mother's house and got a place on my own."

"This is *your* house," I remind her. "Your mother lives with *you*."

"Oh yeah." She nods wearily, looking back at the television and then looking at me again. "Then I'm sending her off to a retirement home. When I tell them what she did, anyone would believe she's gone to Dementia City."

I wince. "Oh come on, would you kill the drama already? Now get your butt up and come outside with me and have lunch with the workers. It's a beautiful day today."

"I have nothing to live for!" she cries out dramatically. "No men, no exercising—what have I got left for God to take? Huh, God?" she exclaims, looking up at the ceiling as if God is hanging out up there. "You want my soul? How about taking my soul too?" She squints her eyes to get a better look at the ceiling. "Oh goodness," she says in her normal tone, "the paint up there looks like it's had its last day." She looks around the room. "Come to think of it, this whole room could use some redecorating."

"And there's your next project," I tell her as I shove the crutches toward her. "But for now, let's get you up and get you some lunch outside."

"Great, fatten me up," she says, sitting up and grabbing a crutch. "That's just what I need right now."

"The crutches should be great on your biceps," I remind her. "You could really build up some strength in your upper arms."

"That's true," she tells me as she stands with the crutches firmly underneath her arms. "Maybe I could fasten some weights to these things," she says, studying them.

"See, there's a silver lining to everything."

Just then, the phone rings. I walk over to get it.

"Don't bother," she says, hobbling toward the stairs, "it's Carter. He's called four times wondering where I am today."

"Why don't you take his call?" I ask as I help her.

"Oh, he'll come over here and want to take care of me, and I don't want that kind of relationship with him. I like having the upper hand with him. I can't let him see me in such a vulnerable state."

"You're going to have to speak to him sooner or later."

"So I'll speak to him later than sooner," she tells me. "Now, which house are they at today?"

"Mr. Saulbrook's."

"Has he got you watching those perennials?"

"I'm guarding them like they're the royal jewels."

"You're such a sweet girl," she tells me as she hops up the stairs. "And so committed to getting your Gogo back. I just don't understand it. He should be salivating for you by now."

"Slowly but surely," I tell her. "Now come on, let's go outside."

"Fine," she pouts, heading out.

As we make our way down the street toward Mr. Saulbrook's, we see the group sitting at the tables. Dolly is standing over everyone, spooning more food onto their plates. Juan is the first one to see Selma and me walking down the street. He stands up and starts clapping like they do in sports when a team member is hurt and then able to get up again. Then the other workers, including Gogo, turn around and stand and start clapping. Selma looks at me and smiles.

"Oh come on, fellas, it's just a little fractured ankle," she flirts.

"Here, Selma," Gogo calls out, getting out of his seat and

pushing his food to the side as the clapping dies down. "Have a seat."

"Yes, Sel," Dolly says, hurrying over to her. "It's good to see you up. I'll make up a nice plate for you."

"I'm still not speaking to you, Ma." She winces.

"Oh come on, you can't stay mad at me," she says like the mother she is, talking to her young child. "I'm planning a big bridge tournament for us tonight. Maurilio and Raul are going to join us. Did you know they're brothers?"

"No, I didn't," Selma answers.

"Yes, Ms. Burns, brothers," Maurilio explains to her in broken English. "But I'm playing with Ms. Burns . . . *this* one." He points up to Dolly. "My brother, Raul over here, gets sloppy."

"I said *two* no trump that time," Raul says. "You didn't hear me correctly. You always blame me for that every time."

"You play bridge?" Selma asks, digging into the plate Dolly has just put in front of her.

"Yes, ma'am," he exclaims. "It's what saved us from boredom over on the raft from Cuba."

"That's why he didn't hear me correctly. The waves were big that day." Raul nods as Maurilio crosses his arms.

"I've been hearing this argument for ten years now," Gogo throws in as an aside.

"You've all been working together for ten years?" I ask.

"Ten years," Maurilio tells us. "Gogo is the best guy to work with at Carverman's. Gogo is a third brother to us."

"That's right," Raul interjects.

"You want to watch yourself when you work with that Brad," Maurilio continues. "He treats you like dirt."

"Dirt," Raul repeats.

"Not like Gogo. Gogo is one of us."

"Thanks, guys." Gogo timidly nods.

This makes me smile. That's Gogo for you. At least that hasn't changed in him.

"But what got you into playing bridge?" Dolly asks.

"Our mother was a big Omar Sharif fan," Raul explains. "His bridge books were prized possessions in our house. My mother had his syndicated bridge column smuggled in from the States. We've seen *Funny Lady* and *Doctor Zhivago* more times than any straight boys growing up in Havana ever should." Raul turns to Maurilio, who shakes his head, cringing at the memory.

"That's sweet of all of you, but I'm a little sad today. I don't think I'll be much of a bridge player tonight."

"What is it, Selma?" Gogo asks in a soothing tone. "Are you still in pain?"

"No, the pain has lessened a lot. I'm strong, I can take this kind of thing. Thank you for asking. And by the way, Gogo, thank you so much for taking care of me last night. I don't know what we would have done if you hadn't been here."

"Oh, it was nothing, Selma, don't worry about it."

"Well, I owe you one. If there's anything I can do to make this up to you, the way you took charge of the situation—if there's anything I can do to thank you, please let me know."

"Selma, you've done enough. I was happy to be there for you. It was the least I could do. I should be thanking you."

"What have I done to make you so appreciative?" she asks.

"What have you done?" he exclaims. "Take a look around."

Selma looks around at the houses and the table.

"With the economy the way it is, you've provided Carverman Downspouts with a huge job. You've given jobs to all these men. We don't even know how to begin to thank you enough for your business."

Selma is obviously touched. She looks over at Juan and Maurilio.

"Yes." Raul nods. "We were off from work for over a month."

"*Sí.*" Maurilio smiles.

"And Dolly," Gogo continues, "the way you've fed us all and kept our energy up. I think this is the best job we've done so far. And may I go further to say that your hospitality has touched us far more than we could ever let on."

"Oh Gogo." Dolly sighs. "That's all you have to say." She caresses his cheek. "That's the best thing I could ever hear."

Selma takes her napkin and dabs her eyes.

"You've really done a wonderful thing here," Dolly says to Selma. Selma pauses and looks at her plate. Then she looks up at her mother.

"And you've done a good thing here too, Ma."

"Thank you, sweetheart." Dolly smiles.

"No problem, Ma." Selma smiles back.

The fight is over. Dolly will not be going to a retirement home any time soon. Not that I ever thought she would be.

Selma turns to Gogo. "You know, I was asking Lily, but I don't know if she was being truthful. I didn't do or say anything embarrassing under the influence of the drugs last night, did I?" she asks him. "Did I do something I can't remember last night? I didn't say anything irrational, did I? Those drugs were so powerful."

I look over at Gogo, who looks at me and smiles as if he knows exactly what I'm worried about.

"You were fine, Selma. The perfect patient."

My smile is huge now. I look at Gogo to thank him, but when he looks at me, I suddenly become a little embarrassed with my enthusiasm, so I take my fork and dig into my plate again.

"Well, besides all of that"—Selma turns to Gogo again—"Gogo, there must be some way I can thank you for last night. Isn't there anything I can do?"

"I know what you could do," I announce.

"What?" Selma asks.

"Gogo, didn't you just say that you wanted to get into better shape?"

"Well . . . yes, but . . ." Gogo looks like he wants to take it back.

"Selma is the queen of the gym. She can work you out better than any trainer can. She'd love to take you over to her gym."

Selma gasps in excitement. "Oh yes! Gogo, let me do this for you, please. You won't regret it!"

Gogo waves his hands to say no way. "That's not necessary," he tells her. "It was just something I mentioned to Lily off the cuff. Really, you don't need to bother with me. I'm in pretty good shape as it is."

"Gogo," Selma confides, "if you don't mind me saying, you are a very good-looking man."

"Thank you," he says, looking shy.

"But you could be better. Sometimes I worry about how tired you look when I see you in the morning as I'm running by."

"Well, the job really takes a lot out of me."

"So let this be my gift to you. Every day after work I'll take you over to the gym and we'll do a little circuit training. In fact, I have a great trainer there, Carter, who could really help us out."

"I think that's a great idea!" Dolly says. "Gogo, you won't believe how great Selma is with the weights. She's kept Lily and me in such good shape all these years. Why do you think we can afford to eat so much?"

"You should do it," Juan tells him.

"I'd do it. Ms. Burns looks like she's in great shape," Maurilio puts in his two cents.

"Oh Maurilio," Selma says bashfully.

"What have you got to lose?" I ask Gogo.

"Only a little pudginess replaced with some hard muscle," he jokes.

"So it's settled!" Selma claps her hands. "Ma, hand me my crutches." She gestures as Dolly hands them to her and she places them under her arms.

"I'm going to go and call Carter and tell him that we'll be over tonight!" she says as she skips briskly on one leg back to the house.

Gogo sighs.

"What have you gotten me into?" he asks me.

"Trust me, you'll have a good time," I tell him.

"And if I don't?" he asks.

"Then I'll owe you," I tell him in a flirtatious way, and Gogo flashes a flirtatious smile right back.

I look around the table and suddenly notice that Dolly, Juan, Raul, and Maurilio have all witnessed this little interlude.

I put my head down, bashfully, and start eating again.

Hee hee hee.

17.

You would have thought that we were in an episode of *Extreme Home Makeover* and Ty Pennington was going to come out any minute and scream, *"Move that bus!"* Only there was no bus, even though every single resident of Morning Hill Lane was out in the street acting like their homes had just been turned into newly remodeled, ultra-state-of-the-art dwellings of the future. Dolly grilled up hot dogs and hamburgers and corn and barbecued ribs (on her barbecue in her backyard, not another bonfire), and everyone had a feast. Mrs. Fabrezi took out some fireworks left over from the Fourth of July. The Fishbounds rented a cotton candy machine, and Mr. Saulbrook made balloon animals for all the kids. The Rindchecks' teenage son, an aspiring DJ, brought out his turntables, and Mrs. Southy and Old Man Poolson have been dancing the night away (much to the chagrin of Dolly who made it her business to dance with Mr. Feldman, Mr. Marra, and Mr. Rozsa, which made Poolson look noticeably disturbed). Even Rose and Leo came down from New York to celebrate the completion of phase one of the Morning Hill Lane/Golden Bakeries job. Rose has been dancing with Maurilio, and Raul has been teaching Leo, Juan, and Alejandro the finer points of contract bridge. Even Mr. Carverman, Gogo's boss and father-in-law, is having a great time. He came by to look over Gogo's work, and Dolly invited him to join the party. Brad is with him too, but he doesn't look like he's having much fun. He's been following Mr. Carverman around like a puppy dog, a jealous puppy dog at that.

"This job has done wonders for my son-in-law," Mr. Carverman told me. "He's not the chump anymore that my daughter brought home all those years ago, right, Brad?"

"He's certainly a changed man." Brad sighs with a tinge of sarcasm in his voice.

"Did you hear how much he's been working out? I hear he's already benching one eighty," Tank brags. "Pretty soon he'll be benching more than you." Tank laughs, but Brad doesn't.

And everyone has been fawning all over Selma, thanking her for such an incredible gift. You'd think that she paid all their mortgages. Instead, this entire celebration, the whole reason everyone is outside their homes and dancing in the street—a block of people whose socializing never went further than a hello on their way into their own homes or, at the most, a call to pick up their mail while on vacation—the whole reason for this revelry is that everyone got a new set of drainpipes along the sides of their homes.

Gogo isn't even here yet to join in the celebration. He's still at the gym working out with Carter. Selma, who arrived late because she was spotting Gogo on the weights (the only person in the world with a fractured ankle who could safely spot someone), said he'd be coming along with Carter in a little bit.

It's unbelievable what three weeks of weight training, followed by daily doses of Dolly's massive protein-heavy meals can do to a person. In such a short time, he's not only starting to look like the man I once knew, but he's starting to act like it too.

"So when's he getting here?" Rose asks as a song ends and she comes back to her seat next to me.

"I think he should be here any minute."

"I have to say, even his voice on the phone sounds different than it did when I met him the first time. He just seems more upbeat, more sure of himself every time I talk to him about the plans for our new downspouts."

"You know," I confide, "it's funny. He's gotten into the habit of walking me back to Selma and Dolly's each night so he can pick up Selma and take her to the gym with him to work out. It's a short walk each time—you know, a couple of houses—but in that walk, I swear, sometimes I forget that all this happened. Something about the way he looks at me and the comfortable way we talk to each other now. Sometimes I have to stop myself from instinctively taking his hand or putting my arm around him. I forget for a second that there's actually a curse and he's married to someone else."

"So have you?" Rose prods.

"Have I what?"

"Have you kissed him yet?"

"What are you, crazy? He's married."

"You're still allowing him to be faithful to his wife? I mean . . . his other wife?"

"What do you take me for, some hussy? And what will kissing him do? The most important thing I've figured out is to not let my emotions take over. This is just like you said, it's rehab, and you don't want to shock the patient."

"I didn't exactly say that. What if he made a move on you? What if on one of your evening walks he leans over and casually slips you some tongue?"

"Then I would stop him!" I exclaim. "I'm trying to reverse that curse!"

Rose looks at me in awe. "You know, you're like the strongest woman I've ever met in my life."

"Nah, actually, I'm one of the lucky ones. Most women who have bad luck with men only think that they're under some curse. I actually *know* I've been cursed."

"Well, I guess if there is a bright side in all this, it's that."

"Yeah," I grunt, "real bright."

"Look at these two young ladies sitting here, Selma," Dolly calls over to Selma as she cha-chas. "Two girls with all the energy their twenty-something bodies have, and they're sitting here like bumps on a log . . ."

We look over at Selma, who gives her mother the stink eye.

"I mean, two bumps on a stump. Sorry, Sel, my bad."

"That's okay, Ma," Selma says as she hobbles over to us and takes a seat. "So what were you two talking about?"

"Oh, I was telling her about Gogo and how much he's changed in the past couple of weeks."

"That boy." Selma sighs. "He's the apple of my eye."

"Gogo is the greatest," Dolly coos. "He's so helpful and kind."

"Speak of the Gogo, here he comes now!" Rose announces as Gogo's car drives up.

Now, if this were a movie, you'd see Gogo getting out of his truck. The only thing you'd see is the top of Gogo's body as he sees us and smiles as he waves. We all wave back, no big deal, it's just Gogo.

Then as he walks around the truck, this part of the movie starts to go in slow motion. The camera pans up his body. The Carverman Downspout polo shirt has been replaced by a black T-shirt, not form-fitting or anything, but tight enough so you can see his obvious pecs. His shoulders are now sculpted, his arms are now cut, not obnoxiously like Mr. Carverman's or Brad's, but chiseled just enough to look healthy, perfect. Cut to Tank, who is beaming. Then the camera pans to Brad, who could not be more disgusted. Cut to Rose as her jaw drops. I mean, a swarm of birds could fly in there and build a nest. I'm just smiling, proud. Look at what I've created.

"Holy sh . . ." Rose gasps. "He's like a model in a Calvin Klein ad!"

Oh, and by the way, Carter, the hot young trainer, has ridden over with Gogo and is walking with him on the lawn. If this were the movie, I'm thinking in my head though, Gogo would have walked up by himself.

"Hi!" Gogo announces. Selma holds her cheek out as Gogo kisses it. Carter follows his lead, but Selma brushes him away (poor Selma, she's become good at averting the curse).

"Look at all this," Gogo says, taking in the big celebration going on.

"There are so many people here, I think some of them don't even live on this block," I crack.

"Gogo." Rose closes her mouth. "If you don't mind my saying so, you look amazing!"

"Thanks." He smiles and sits down as Dolly sets a hamburger in front of him and hands him a napkin.

"Gogo!" Mr. Carverman walks over.

"Hi, Tank," Gogo says, shaking his hand. "Hey, Brad."

"Goldblatt." Brad nods.

"I gotta hand it to you." Tank smiles, shaking Gogo's hand. "You've done a great job here, son."

"Thanks." Gogo nods. "The neighborhood really seems to like it."

"You should call my daughter to come over and see this," Tank tells him. "This should put a smile on that sour face of hers."

"Yeah," Gogo answers, "this kind of thing just isn't her scene. Rhonda would never want to come to something like this."

"Did you ask her?" Tank asks.

"Sure, I asked her to come over, but she has her knitting club tonight, so she couldn't come anyway, even if I begged her. The knitting club is always the highlight of her week," Gogo explains.

"Knitting club?" Selma asks. "Who are you married to, Old Mother Hubbard?"

Tank, Gogo, and Brad glance at her, looking slightly offended at this statement.

"Ma!" I mouth.

"Oh, I guess I said the wrong thing." She puts her hand over her mouth.

"No, that's okay," Tank tells her. "It would be good for my daughter to let loose once in a while like her husband is." He pats Gogo on the back again.

"Hey Dolly," Raul shouts, "you're getting a little low here on the hot dogs."

"Oh goodness." She slaps her forehead. "I've got a whole tray of them keeping warm in the oven. I'll go get them."

"No, Gram, you stay here. I'll go and get it for you," I tell her.

"I'll help you." Gogo jumps up.

"Excellent," I tell him as we walk off together.

"So you'll be coming with us on the Golden project, right?" Gogo asks me.

"Of course." I smile.

"Good." He smiles back. "I mean, you're really good at overseeing everything, you know, for the client."

"Thanks." In the kitchen we look in the oven. Dolly must have about ten dozen hot dogs in a aluminum pan.

"I've never seen anyone cook as much as your grandmother," he tells me incredulously. "Why didn't she become a caterer?"

"She'd been asked to a million times," I tell him as I turn off the oven and grab two pot holders. "She would have, but Selma had to work a lot when I was growing up, so Dolly really took care of me."

"Ah," he says, and sighs. "It must have been nice growing up in this house with Dolly and Selma. Those two really have a lot of life in them."

"Yeah," I tell him as I grab the pan of hot dogs.

"Here, let me get that." He tries to take hold of it.

"You know what, I'm afraid this aluminum pan is going to buckle under the weight of the hot dogs. I'll be able to carry it," I tell him, as Gogo slides the grill shelf back in and shuts the oven door.

"I'll get the door for you," he says, rushing in front of me.

I walk out with the tray in my hands as Gogo walks next to me.

"What was your house like growing up?" I ask him as if I don't know.

"It was normal—two parents, a sister, growing up in the suburbs, your basic upbringing."

Suddenly the roasting pan starts to buckle. I'm trying to keep it steady in my hands, but the pot holders don't give me a strong grip.

"Oh no," I shout to him as I stop and bend my knees to save the pan from falling. The two sides of the pan are now buckled together like a large metal hot dog taco. Gogo runs in front of me and bends down as he puts a hand underneath the pan to keep it steady, but it's too hot and he quickly flinches from the burn.

"Ouch!" he shouts out. The pan buckles even more, and now I'm bending over Gogo, causing him to fall to the ground as I trip over his legs. The hot dogs fall all over him and I fall right on top of Gogo with only the dogs to cushion my fall.

"*Noooo!*" I shout as I fall right on top of Gogo's body. Our lips even skim each other, so I roll over quickly onto the ground.

Both of us are laughing hysterically at each other as Gogo leans over and takes some flattened hot dogs off my stomach as I brush the mess off him. We can't stop laughing at the sight of ourselves. I roll toward Gogo and he rolls toward me. We stare at each other, laughing uncontrollably, inches away from each other's faces. I want to kiss him so badly. I know that he feels the same way. It's an urge that I just can't seem to fight, and before I know it, I'm bending in a little closer to him as Gogo begins to meet me halfway.

Suddenly I come to my senses when I realize that the street has gotten quiet. I look up and everyone is staring at us, Tank

Carverman especially. Gogo notices as well and immediately stops laughing. We sit up and I grab the roasting pan and bend it back into shape. I get up and start throwing the hot dogs into it. Gogo gets up and begins throwing hot dogs into the pan, too.

"It's okay," I tell him. "I've got this."

He nods and walks over to Tank, who is giving him a hard stare. Brad is behind Tank, beaming.

"That's okay," Dolly announces, walking over to me, "I've got more hot dogs in the fridge. It will only take me a little while to grill a new batch." She bends down and grabs the hot dogs. "Lily, why don't you come help me?" She motions.

"Sure," I say, feeling very uncomfortable as I see Tank crossing his arms and Brad pointing at Gogo behind Tank's back, like an annoying little brother shouting, "*Ooh*, you're in trouble now."

We walk toward the house. Dolly looks a little perturbed.

"What's the matter?" I ask her.

"Wait until we get inside," she murmurs.

Once we get through the front door, Dolly takes the hot dogs and puts them on the kitchen table.

"Love," she begins. "I just need to tell you this. I understand what you're doing here, trying to reverse the curse, and you've really turned Gogo's life around, but I'm asking you, please, don't go any further with him romantically until you break the curse."

"What are you talking about?" I feign ignorance.

"I saw you on the street, rolling around with him. We all saw it."

"Gram, I'm not getting him to fall in love with me, you don't have to worry about that."

"All I'm saying is, we don't want anything else to happen to Gogo. We don't want to make the situation worse than it already is."

"You're acting crazy," I tell her. "Gogo is not falling in love with me. I know Gogo. I know *this* Gogo too, and *this* Gogo is in love with his wife. If I thought for one second that he was falling in love with me, I'd leave him alone."

"Just . . . please watch yourself," she warns me. "Don't get so close to him anymore. It's all fun and games until the word *love* comes out, and then you're scraping his flattened body off the highway."

"Did that happen to someone?"

"What?"

"To one of the husbands? I don't remember any of them ever being roadkill."

"I'm serious here, *missy*," she tells me, slightly angry.

"You're crazy," I tell her like a teenager. "I'm going back outside."

"Promise me you won't let things go any further with Gogo."

"Fine," I whine as I head outside.

I make a beeline over to sit with Rose, who is giggling at me.

"Great, your first almost-kiss and you do it in front of the father-in-law. Really smart there, Lil."

"Oh shut up." I smirk and then giggle along with her.

"So, I think I'm gonna get out of here," Gogo announces as he walks up to us.

"But we haven't even had cake yet," I tell him. "Rose brought a huge cake."

"A Golden Bakery specialty," she brags, "strawberry and blueberry cake with custard and our famous angel food cake."

"Oh, I love that!" I tell her. "I could eat a whole thing myself. You have to stay, Gogo, you just have to!" I beg.

"I'm sure you'll keep us in sweets as much as Dolly has kept us in proteins when we start the project next week," he tells Rose.

"Gogo," Brad taunts, "Tank is waiting."

"Yeah, I gotta get out of here. This was really fun, though."

"What's going on?" Dolly asks, appearing from the house.

"Gogo is leaving," I tell her, as if to say, *See, he's leaving, he's not in love with me.*

"Rhonda should be home soon," he explains.

"He's leaving?" Selma comes hobbling up. "Before cake?"

"Aw man, you can't leave before cake," Carter says, walking behind Selma. "You deserve a piece of cake with all the training you've done."

"That's what I said," I tell them.

Tank approaches. "Thanks, ladies, but Gogo here has a wife at home that he needs to get back to."

"That's right," Dolly announces. "Why don't I cut you all a piece to take with you?" she asks. "How about a piece to bring home for the wife?"

"Rhonda isn't much for sweets," Gogo tells us.

"How did I guess that?" Rose leans into me.

"Well"—Dolly opens her arms to hug Gogo—"Gogo, spending this time with you was wonderful."

"Yes, Gogo, but I'll still see you at the gym tomorrow, right?" Carter asks.

"Yes," Selma adds, "tomorrow, same time, right?"

"Sure," Gogo answers, but I'm not so sure it's true. "You have a way to get home tonight, right, Carter?" he asks.

"Well . . ." He looks at Selma, flirting.

"Lily will take him," she says. Carter pouts.

Gogo looks down at me as I start to get up.

"See you later, Lily," he tells me, seeming somewhat sad.

"See you, Gogo," I tell him.

"Thanks for having us," Tank tells Dolly.

"Yeah, this was great!" Brad tells her enthusiastically.

"Glad to have you," she tells them.

The party is still in full swing as I watch the three men head to their cars. I'm watching Gogo's back as he walks to the driver's side of his car. This time, it's not in slow motion and it's definitely not a scene from a movie. It's just normal. My normal. I'm watching my husband go home to his other wife. I've got Dolly's warning in my head and I know that I can't go any further. And this makes me sad.

Gogo turns the corner of his truck to the driver's side. He opens the car door and gets in. Everyone else has gone on with the party, Tank and Brad are already in their cars, and since they're parked in back of him, there is no one left to see this.

Gogo looks over at me. His stare says everything. We can never be together.

I look back at him. We stare at each other for a moment.

Then Gogo starts his car and I watch as he drives off.

18.

I got up early this morning and now I'm out on the street taking a long run. It's been two days since the infamous almost-kiss, and my head is swimming. Of course I want to listen to Dolly. Of course I want to obey everything that she's warned me about. I've seen firsthand what this curse can do to a person.

Still, the wanting, the need to be near Gogo is an itch that can't be relieved, no matter how many coats of calamine lotion I put on it.

"You're acting crazy!" Rose told me this morning when I told her I won't be able to come up to New York. "What could happen to him? How much worse can it get? He's already cursed! Curses don't work like that. It's like double jeopardy!"

"How do you know?" I asked her.

"Well, I don't know, but how do you know that something else will happen to him if he remembers he's married to you?"

The truth is, I don't. I can only go by what's happened to Selma and Dolly and all of their husbands, my father, Dolly's father, Selma's father.

"This is a really powerful curse, might I remind you?"

"I just don't see how you can stop right now. You've come so far!"

"I know, I know, and maybe I've made a mistake. Maybe I did too much."

"I think you're just scared," she tells me. "I think you're paranoid that if you make one wrong move, you'll ruin everything. You haven't even found out where his life went off the track. How are you going to do that if you don't hang around him?"

She has a point there, but still, I just don't know what's right.

That's why I went for the run, thinking it would clear my head.

And then, wouldn't luck have it . . .

"Lily!" I hear my name being called so loud that even with my iPod turned all the way up, I can't mistake the call.

I stop in midrun and turn around.

There's Selma hobbling alongside me.

"What the hell are you doing?" I ask her as I turn my volume down. "You just got out of surgery yesterday and you're jogging on crutches?"

"I've got my leg elevated," She tells me. I notice her leg is extended a foot off the ground. The muscle ability this woman has. "Now slow down. I want to have a word with you."

I know what she's going to say and I don't want to hear more input.

"I'm in a groove," I tell her. "My adrenaline is really rolling right now. I don't want to stop."

"Lily!" she insists. "Slow down!"

So I obey my mother and slow to an easy jog.

"Listen, I spoke to Dolly," she says, keeping up with me. "I think she's right. I think this has gone too far."

"I know!" I tell her. "I know it might have gone too far, but I don't think I should stop now. How am I going to break the curse if I don't spend time with him?"

"Because if you spend more time with him, God knows what could happen to him. Look at you. You're a gorgeous, smart, sexy woman. Did I tell you to gain some weight? Did your grandmother tell you to wear your clothes two sizes too big so no man could become enamored with those voluptuous breasts of yours? It's time to stop. It's time to let things be and go on with your life."

"So why did you let me do all of this if you knew it would lead to him falling in love with me again?"

"When you're a mother, you'll understand," she tells me.

"And how do you expect me to become a mother if I can't spend time with my husband?"

"You'll adopt!" she tells me. "You'll get donor sperm, some anonymous sperm donor you'll never meet who's a rocket scientist and a part-time model. Life doesn't end just because you can't be married to the man you love. There are ways around it."

"But that's not what I want!" I cry out as I stop jogging. "I want my husband back! I want my life back!" Tears form in my eyes.

"And you don't think I want my life back?" she asks angrily, as if all the years of frustration are packed into that one sentence. "You just have to give up now for Gogo's sake before it gets any worse. I've gotten to know that man and I've gotten to love him. Dolly loves him. We know why you were with him. We understand why you kept him from us when you were dating him. But let me ask you something, think about it, what's better? Having him in this world, even though you can't be with him, or not having him in this world at all?"

Her words stun me into silence.

"Think about it, Lily. Think about Gogo. Think about the consequences. Make the right goddamned choice," she orders as she turns around and begins to jog on her crutches in the other direction. I stand there watching her, the muscles bulging out of her arms; she looks like Madonna on steroids.

I turn around and walk the other way back to my house.

I'm so confused.

So now I'm sitting in my house going over this whole thing, once again, deciding which way to turn. Which way is right? My clothes are strewn all over the floor. The only time I've spent here during the Morning Hill Lane construction was to sleep, shower, and change clothes. Not knowing how else to get rid of this energy, I start picking up my clothes, taking the clean clothes and folding them up and putting them back in their drawers and taking the dirty ones and throwing them into the washing machine.

While I'm waiting for the wash to get done, I take a broom (which incidentally I didn't know I had) and begin to sweep the hardwood floors. I pick up the dust bunnies in my hand, one by one, all over the house. Where does all this dust come from?

I'm working up a sweat as I go at that freezer with a hair dryer and an ice pick, stabbing that block of ice that's formed over the years. If my life is going to stay this way, and I'm going to stay in this house, I might as well have a freezer that I can put stuff in.

I'm halfway through the ice in the freezer. As I continue to blast the hair dryer on it, there's a puddle forming on the floor of my kitchen in front of me, but I don't really care. I continue to stab with the ice pick, and I have to say, it feels really good. I'm getting rid of so much tension, so much that has built up inside me over this time. My anger is at an all-time high, and when I stab the ice, all I can think of is Emmalina and how much I wish that I could take it out on her, a woman who has been dead for over sixty years. I want to show her what she's done to our lives, Dolly's and Selma's and mine. I want to ask her, Why? Why would she curse us? What did we do to deserve this? We weren't even born when she lost her man. We are good people. Why do we have to suffer because of Astrid's spoiled ways? Emmalina could have found her backbone in some other way. She could have gone on with her life and found someone else without cursing our bloodline. Maybe Astrid and Hermann's marriage wouldn't have worked out, being that Astrid was such a despicable human being, who could live with her? Maybe that would have been her punishment. Why couldn't Emmalina just have thought rationally?

"Damn her!" I shout at the ice as if it can hear me.

I want to curse her now, wherever she is. I wish I could make sure that if there is a heaven, she's not on the highest plane, like seventh heaven or something. Maybe she's on the third or fourth plane of heaven, where everything that heaven is supposed to be has a catch. Maybe on the fourth plane in heaven, she gets to eat all the most incredibly delectable chocolate chip cookies she wants, but she's got bad teeth and has to spend her afternoons at the dentist.

I know I'm talking crazy, and the last thing I'd want to do is put a curse on Emmalina and her descendants. I mean, oh God, obviously I would never want anything to happen to Rose. She's the best thing that's happened to me in this whole ordeal.

There just has to be some way to resolve it. There just has to be some way to end this curse. I don't see any other way. This is not the way that life is supposed to be.

And as all these thoughts keep going through my head, and all these emotions from anger to depression to sadness have put me in a tailspin, I just break down. I start to cry, more than I ever have in my life. The bottom line is this: I miss my husband. I miss Gogo so much. I miss everything about him. I miss his hugs, his kisses, his smile when he looks at me. I miss the scent of him when I put my arms around him and breathe in that mix of sandalwood aftershave and Pantene conditioner. I miss the feeling of seeing him when we get home from work at night and that feeling in the dark of night when I brush my leg against his. I miss eating brussels sprouts and watching him play video games and sleeping next to him and talking and laughing and being loved by him. I want my husband back. I want him with me now!

I throw the ice pick on the floor as I start crying even louder now.

I just want my best friend back.

I want the love of my life to be here with me.

"Screw it all!" I shout to myself as I run around the house, searching furiously for my keys. I've cleaned this house so well that I can't find anything now.

Finally I find them in a bowl next to the door and I charge out of the house toward my car.

I drive like a maniac over to Gogo's house. I know I could kill someone with the way I'm going through stop signs and flooring the gas after a stoplight turns green. It's not like there's so much traffic here in the suburbs of Philadelphia. They don't do traffic reports for Fairview Road in Narberth, Pennsylvania. Still, I'm reminding myself to at least keep my eyes on the road, watch for children playing in the street like the yellow sign with the silhouette of young children playing tells me to.

I pull up to Gogo's house, my house, and jump out of the door before I've even got my car keys out of the ignition.

I run up to the door and start pressing the doorbell. I'm not thinking of anything except for Gogo. I want to tell him that I want him to be with me. We'll watch for falling rocks and we'll wrap him in bubble wrap like we once joked.

I can hardly contain myself as I hear footsteps coming to the door.

"Who is it?" I hear the female voice call out.

"It's Lily Burns," I try to say as normally as I can, though even I can hear the exasperation as my voice cracks a little.

The door opens and there's Rhonda. This time she's in a pink sweatsuit to match her pink house with her pink walls and her pink roses, but I don't have time to mock.

"Hi," I tell her. "Is Gogo here?" I ask her as normally as I can. I know I've got sweat beading at my brow and my T-shirt still is wet in places from the freezer ice. "I wanted to come by and talk about the plans for the New York job," I lie.

"Lily." She inhales. "I guess you haven't heard. Gogo won't be working on the Golden Bakery project."

"What do you mean?" I ask her.

She exhales. "Brad is going to take over."

I wince. "But I'm the one who hired Carverman Downspouts on this project. I hired Carverman because of Gogo. If we don't have Gogo on this project, then there is no project."

"I don't think you mean that," she tells me. "You want to put all those people out of work because my husband isn't working on it?"

"Yes," I tell her, thinking of Raul and Maurilio and all the guys. They'll just have to understand.

"Well, then I guess you'll have to go with another company."

"Why isn't Gogo working on it?" I ask, even though I know the answer.

"Lily," she says, "why don't you come in for a moment."

This sets me back. I don't want to walk into that house. I don't want to see my home that's now shared with another woman with her decorations and her memories.

"Thanks, but I don't need to come in," I tell her emphatically. "Can you just tell me where Gogo is so we can take care of this?"

"Gogo is taking a break from work," she tells me.

"He is?"

"Yes, he is. Come on, Lily, stop lying to me. I know what you're up to. I know that you're trying to steal my husband."

"Because he's my husband!" I shout.

Rhonda looks outside to see if any neighbors have heard me. I turn around to see a neighbor, Janice Lopsky—the only reason I even know her name is that we always got her mail by accident—staring at us as she takes groceries from her car.

"Come inside." Rhonda grabs me and pulls me in the house.

I walk inside my home. It looks so familiar to me, and yet this isn't my home at all. I immediately spot Rhonda and Gogo's wedding picture in a silver frame on the mantle above the fireplace. Neither is smiling in the picture. If it wasn't in color, and Rhonda wasn't wearing that frilly off-the-shoulder dress with a skirt blooming so wide it looks like ten children could be hiding under it, I swear it could be a wedding photo from the 1920s when people didn't smile in pictures.

"Look," she seethes as she shuts the front door, "I've had just about enough of this."

"Well I'm sick of this too," I tell her, equally angry.

"Just who the hell do you think you are coming into my life and trying to steal my husband away from me? What is it about Gogo that's got you so enraptured with him anyway? I mean, who do you think you are, trying to turn Gogo into some handsome, happy guy anyway?"

This stops me before I can even get a sentence out.

"What?" I ask her.

"You're a very attractive woman. Why are you wasting your time on a married man who isn't even worth stealing?" she asks me. "What is it about Gogo that's got you so crazy?"

I'm seriously stunned into silence. I cannot believe that a person would say these things about her own husband. She's waiting for an answer from me, and I swear, I almost feel sorry for this woman.

"Are you out of your mind?" I ask her.

"Am I out of my mind?" she counters. "You're the one who's gone to all this trouble to get Gogo work, give him confidence, get him to work out, eat right. I just don't understand why."

"Because Gogo deserves much better than this!" I shout.

"Well"—she smiles snidely—"you're too late."

"And why is that?" I ask firmly.

"Because I'm six weeks pregnant," she says, rubbing her belly.

"You may be a crazy lady, but are you crazy enough to take a father away from his child?" she asks me. "You know Gogo so well, do you really think he'd leave his wife and unborn child?"

And the truth is, I don't think he would. I know he wouldn't be able to do that.

"Does Gogo know?"

"I'm telling him tonight." She smiles.

"Well, congratulations," I manage to mumble.

"Thank you very much," she responds, as I stand there looking sullen.

She motions me to sit down on the couch, so I do. She takes a seat next to me.

"Don't get me wrong. Gogo is a good person. He's too good. When I think back to when we first met, you know, I was dating his roommate at the time. Every time I'd walk into their dorm room, there was Gogo sitting at his desk studying his premed books, and when he wasn't there, he was swimming at the college pool or shopping for vegetables at that horrible co-op supermarket. He was really handsome back then; all the girls wanted him. My sorority sister at Kappa Kappa Lambda, Debby Larkin, she wanted him bad. She kept asking me to fix her up. She was so scared to approach him, she didn't have the nerve. I was going to be the matchmaker. One morning, as Gogo was leaving for his class, I told him that I was going to tell Debby to meet him in the quad that afternoon. They didn't have cell phones or email back then, so I was the messenger. I had a class with Debby that morning, so I had planned to tell her then. When Gogo left the dorm room, though, his roommate—Zach was his name—Zach told me that he needed to talk to me." Suddenly she looks depressed.

"What did he say?" I ask.

"He told me that he wanted to break up with me. He told me

that he thought I was spoiled. Spoiled? Can you imagine? I was fixing his roommate up with a nice, pretty girl and he was calling me spoiled."

"Wait, why did he say you were spoiled?" I ask, trying to make sense of the whole thing.

"Oh," she tries to brush it off, "you have to understand, I'm an only child. My mother had trouble getting pregnant. There were complications with her pregnancy. So when I was finally born healthy, my parents made sure I had the best of everything."

This conversation is starting to freak me out as I begin to realize what's going on here.

"So you went from the top bunk to the bottom bunk," I say, repeating the same line Gogo had told me when we first met.

And then I think about the story that Gogo told me. Gogo had been dating Rhonda first; it wasn't the other way around. In this life, this dimension, it was the roommate who dumped Rhonda, and not Rhonda who dumped Gogo.

I've found the page in Gogo's book! The page where everything changed!

"I was so upset that day. I had forgotten all about telling Debby about Gogo. I just happened to be sitting in the quad when Gogo came out of class and was coming to the quad for his date with Debby.

"What did he do when he saw you?" I ask.

"He asked why I was crying. And I told him. He was so sweet. He took a handkerchief out of his pocket. What man carries a handkerchief?"

"Gogo," we both say at the same time.

"And as I told Gogo what had happened with Zach, it occurred to me: I never want to have this feeling again. I'm not the sort of person who should be dumped. I should be with someone I know for sure is going to stay with me forever. Gogo was so kind, such a pushover. I knew that he would never leave me. I was sure of it."

"So you made your move on Gogo?"

"I seduced that boy like he'd never seen before."

"And what happened to Debby?"

"Oh, she hated me. She still hates me, I guess. I'm banned from the Kappa Kappa Lambda reunions. They exiled me from the sisterhood. Everyone took Debby's side. So what? I got the guy, didn't I?"

"So you used Gogo's good heart to entice him into marrying you right out of college? You wouldn't let him have his dream of becoming a doctor?"

"Well, I wouldn't put it that harshly," she interrupts.

"I would," I tell her.

"It doesn't matter now anyway." She folds her arms.

"You did all this because you didn't want another man to ever leave you again? That's how weak you are? You made him dislike brussels spouts and other vegetables because you wanted to turn him into some pasty guy who wouldn't attract other women?"

"He's still good-looking," she reminds me.

I shake my head. "So you did exactly what Astrid did. You stole someone's man for your own benefit. Is that true?"

"Who's Astrid?" she asks me.

"It doesn't matter," I tell her. "Okay, you've got me." I throw my arms in the air in defeat. "You're right."

"And so all this nonsense about your being in love with Gogo and thinking he should be your husband: you understand that with a child on the way, he'll never leave me no matter how much you entice him, build him up, and lift his spirits? He's with me for life and that's that."

"You're right." I nod. "And I'm sorry. I've tried to steal him away from you for the same reasons you want to keep him. He's too good a person to walk away from you. He would never do that. I'm sorry I told you I thought he was supposed to be my husband. I'm sorry that I ever met Gogo."

"I thought you'd see it my way." She smiles in victory.

"Well," I tell her as I stand up to leave, "I'm going to go now, out of your life, and I promise I won't bother Gogo anymore."

"I appreciate that, Lily. And believe me, there are other fish in the sea. You've got a nice figure. You'll be able to snare a good guy for yourself one of these days."

"Thank you," I tell her, walking out the door.

"Truce?" She puts her hand out to me.

"Huh?" I ask.

"Oh"—she laughs—"it's just a funny thing that Gogo says to end an argument. "I guess it's caught on with me."

"Truce," I say, shaking her hand.

19.

I'm so excited that I'm shaking. I can hardly get the key in the ignition because I'm shaking so much. When I finally do, I rev the gas and hightail it out of there. Because I know the next time I go back to that house, it will be mine again.

I grab my phone and dial Rose.

"Hey," I say before she can finish saying hello, "is Gogo up there?"

"No," she says, "I've been trying to call you. I've left like ten messages! Gogo called and said he wouldn't be able to make it on the job. He said he's taking some personal time off. What the hell, Lily? This guy Brad is here overseeing the construction. He's such an asshole."

"I know, I'm going to go find Gogo. Lily, you were right. You were right about everything. This life, his wife—she doesn't exist. You were right all along!"

"What happened?" she asks me.

"I'll explain it later, I need to keep my eyes on the road. I need to find Gogo! I can't imagine where he might be right now. Rhonda is pregnant."

"She's what?"

"It's bullshit, I know it's bullshit. She's telling him tonight and I know it's a lie. I know she's just telling him that. I know it. But I also know that he would never leave her if she told him she was pregnant. I have to find him and tell him what I know."

"Oh my God, Lily, think, think! Where could he be?"

"I don't know!" I tell her. "I'm driving by all the places he's put in downspouts—he was so proud of all that—but I don't see him anywhere. Look, I'm going to hang up so I can keep an eye out for him. See if you can get anything out of Brad, maybe he knows."

"Will do," she tells me.

I head toward Morning Hill Lane and search up and down the street. I see no sign of him.

I drive around to some of the other buildings he's told me about, but there's no sign of him.

After two hours of driving, I finally pull over as I try to think of other places. I turn onto Montgomery Avenue, heading toward Hymie's Deli. Gogo put some lovely downspouts on there. My stomach is starting to gurgle, reminding me that I haven't had anything to eat all day. Maybe I'll get a sandwich while I'm there.

And then suddenly it hits me, right in the middle of busy downtown suburban traffic.

I know exactly where he is.

I hold my hand out of the car and beep my horn, halting other motorists as I make the most illegal U-turn imaginable.

"What the hell?" a woman in a white Jaguar screams out as I shout to her, "I'm sorry! I'm sorry!"

I head down to the City Line Avenue entrance to get on the expressway, and wouldn't you know that there's goddamned traffic everywhere.

After twenty minutes on the expressway, I'm not getting anywhere. I'm weaving in and out of cars, but I'm not making any headway.

"Oh screw it!" I shout to myself. I veer my car over to the shoulder and begin driving. It feels so liberating passing all these cars. I must be doing seventy miles an hour. My eyes are staring intently at the road for fear that some other car will swerve into the shoulder, but I'm still gunning the gas pedal, seventy-five miles an hour, eighty. And no sooner do I reach eighty-five, then I hear the sound of a police siren in back of me.

"This isn't real!" I say to myself out loud as I keep going. "It doesn't matter if you get a ticket or get killed, because this life isn't real!"

I floor the gas as I drive like a madwoman down the shoulder of the expressway. The cop is right on my tail and I'm scared out of my mind, but I keep reminding myself, "THIS ISN'T REAL!" I shout inside the car at the top of my lungs. "THIS ISN'T REALITY!"

I swing a sharp right and head off the Twenty-third Street exit, zigzagging in and out of cars with the cops still trailing me. I nearly hit an elderly couple as the guy pushes her out of the way.

"*You're a good man!*" I shout out my window to him.

I go right through a red light on Market Street as I head up toward Chestnut Street and take a sharp left. The fact that I haven't gotten into an accident is completely amazing. It's becoming increasingly clear that none of this is real. This is not reality, just as I keep telling myself. How can it be? Only the greatest race car drivers could go through a red light on Market Street without getting killed or killing someone.

I finally make it to the restaurant and pull up onto the curb as I throw the car into park and jump out, looking into the restaurant.

Sure enough, there's Gogo, sitting at our table, eating a hot fudge sundae.

"Gogo!" I shout. "IT'S NOT REAL! ALL OF THIS ISN'T REAL!"

"What are you talking about?" he asks as he looks behind me.

Suddenly I'm thrown to the ground. I feel someone grab my hands and pull them behind me.

"You have the right to remain silent. Anything you do or say—"

"What the hell is going on here?" Gogo shouts as he walks over to my body, now lying sprawled on the floor.

"Gogo"—I smile as the cops pull me up—"none of this is reality. It's all a part of the curse. This life you're living now is a part of the curse. It's been made to resemble Astrid and Emmalina's story!" I tell him.

"Who are Astrid and Emmalina?" he asks as the cops pull me toward the door.

"I'll explain later." The cops take me through the door of the restaurant and onto the street. "Gogo!" I shout to him as he stands at the door watching me.

"Yeah?" he asks.

"Do you think you could come bail me out? I'll explain everything then. I'll be at . . ." I turn to one of the cops. "Do you know where you're taking me?"

"Ninth district station," he tells me.

"I'll be at the Ninth district station. And maybe, if there's a lawyer that you know . . ." The cops put me in the patrol car and shut the door.

"Do you know how many laws you just broke?" one of the cops says to me as he gets into the front seat and turns around to me.

"Yep," I tell him smiling, "but I don't care. I just don't care," I say matter-of-factly as I take a deep breath and rest my head on the back of the seat.

"You know, you've flipped," he tells me.

"Yeah," I tell him. "And it feels great." I smile.

20

Damn, I must be cursed too," Charity, a prostitute in a short sequined miniskirt I actually have, tells me as she straightens her bra and readjusts her cleavage. "With the way some of these men have treated me over the years. You don't walk the streets to be nice."

"You've got that right." Trinket, another pro with way too much makeup, nods. "How do you find out if you've got a curse?" she asks.

"Ask your mother."

"I don't have to," Charity adds. "She married my father. If she went with him, there's got to be a curse."

"Burns, your bail has been paid," a female guard announces as she comes to our cell.

"He came to bail you out. He's a good one," Charity tells me. "He's worth fighting for."

"I know," I tell her. "It's been nice meeting you." I shake her hand.

"You too," she tells me.

"Does Gogo have a brother?" Trinket laughs. "Even with the curse, he's better than the guys I've been with."

I give the ladies a hug as the guard opens the door for me.

"See you around," I tell them.

"Break that curse, Lily!" Charity shouts.

"Go, Lily!" Trinket follows.

"I will!" I smile to them as I go through the doors to the front of the station.

There's Gogo standing there waiting for me.

"Thanks for getting me, Gogo," I tell him. "I'll pay you back."

"No need," he tells me as we leave the police station. "What the hell got into you? I was going to call Selma and Dolly, but I didn't want them to worry about you."

"Oh, thank you for not calling them. That was a good move," I say, thinking about what they might do if they knew I was still going on with this.

"What the hell has gotten into you?"

"Oh, Gogo," I say as we head down the steps of the police station. I stop on the last step and walk to the side.

"Come sit for a second," I tell him.

Gogo sits by my side.

"Gogo," I start, "I went to your house. I saw Rhonda."

"Oh," he breathes.

"And she told me everything."

"What did she tell you?" he asks.

"She told me about how you met. She told me about how she got you to marry her. She told me about how she discouraged you from going to medical school. She told me everything."

"I wouldn't say that she discouraged me from going to medical school," he says, a bit offended.

"I would!" I counter. "Gogo," I continue, "this is the thing. You have to believe me, for real this time. All of this, your being married to Rhonda, working in her father's downspout company—none of it is real. I'm telling you. You have to believe me. You just have to know that none of this is real. In another life, in another dimension of your life, it wasn't Rhonda who was dumped by your roommate; it was Rhonda who dumped you! That's where the curse first put you on a different course. It took over your life from there and all of your dreams for your future, becoming a doctor, meeting me, all of it went out the window. You just have to believe me, Gogo. You just have to."

"Lily." He stops me. "Rhonda is pregnant. She just called with the news."

"She might say she is, but are you positive that she is?" I ask him.

"What's that supposed to mean?" he asks me.

"I mean, did you see the positive result? Are you one hundred percent sure that she's pregnant? Tell her to send a copy of the pregnancy test."

"Why would she lie?"

"Because she knows the truth!" I tell him. "She knows that you've fallen in love with me."

"Who says I've fallen in love with you?" he asks.

"I do," I tell him.

"And how do you know that?"

"Because I've seen you fall in love with me before. I know the feeling of being loved by you. I know it by the way that you look at me and the way that you talk to me. I know it by the way you hold your head up. Gogo, when I see you smile at me, it's a smile I know better than I know myself. It's this warm, inviting smile that tells me I am loved. It tells me that everything is okay in this world because a wonderful person like you loves me."

"Look." He stands. "I'm not going to deny that I have feelings for you. I'm not going to deny that I've thought about you every moment that I'm not with you."

"I knew you loved me!" I smile. "I just knew it."

"But that doesn't mean that I can just go off and be with you. That doesn't mean that I can just leave my wife and unborn child and go off and live another life. I made a promise to Rhonda a long time ago and I've sacrificed a lot because of it. I won't give up on that."

"Even if you don't love her?" I ask.

"I do love Rhonda," he tells me. "Rhonda and I have a life together."

"But are you in love with her?"

"We've been married for a long time," he tells me. "It's . . . I don't want to get into my relationship with my wife. It's just . . . when you've been married for as long as we have and have gone through as much as we have, being *in* love is just not something that stays with you."

"But it does!" I tell him. "Of course it does. When you're with the right woman."

"So what do you want me to do?" he asks, sitting down again. "Do you want me to tell you that I'm in love with you? Do you want me to tell you that all I want to do is leave my wife and the life I have now? Do you want me to tell you how much it kills me that we can't be together? How much I ache knowing that there's a person in this world who makes me feel like the man I really want to be? This curse you keep talking about? The curse that got me this way? If it's true, then it's a curse that can't be broken. If you think you've been cursed, I'm the one who is taking the brunt of it. And the best thing that could come out of it is that I've got a child coming into this world, a child that cost many painful years of fertility shots and pregnancies that only came to nothing in the end. To have this child come into my life, a life that isn't great by any standards, but now at least there's something amazing to look forward to—I don't want to ruin that hope."

His words sting. And now I know that no matter what I do, I can never get Gogo back. Just like Rhonda, if Gogo left with me now, who knows what would happen. Even though this is a different dimension, this is still real enough. Stealing Gogo from Rhonda would be doing exactly what Astrid did to Emmalina. And I know I can't do it. I know now that I can't be with him no matter what I do.

"Lily," he says softly, "I . . . lo—"

"Don't say it." I stop him. "Don't tell me what you were going to say."

"But I want to," he says.

"Please don't." I stand up, starting to cry. "You're right. This is all my fault. I've tried to change it. I've tried to stop it, but I can see there's nothing I can do anymore. I don't want anything else to happen to you," I tell him. "I've been selfish. I did all this because I thought I could get you back, but in the end, I just can't . . . I can't break this curse."

"I believe you," he tells me. "As strange as it sounds, I believe you when you say that there's been a curse."

"You do?" I ask him.

"I've tried to think of any other explanation for what's happened to me in these last few months with you. I've tried to think about why a beautiful woman like you, someone who seems to have a smart sense of reality, would go to all these lengths to make me believe that I am a stronger person. I have to make a confession to you."

I sit down again and look at him.

"That first night you called me on the phone? When you asked if I was okay? Your voice that night? I don't know what it was, but I just knew that voice from somewhere. I knew it so well and I couldn't put my finger on it. Your voice? It sounded like home to me. It sounded so familiar and so comforting that it just scared me. Who was it? Why was she claiming that we were married? I couldn't sleep after that. I just kept tossing and turning, trying to remember that voice. And then when I saw you, I'm not going to deny it, the first time I saw you at my office, you were someone that I knew, very well, but I still couldn't pinpoint it. It felt like we'd gone through school together or maybe we'd worked side by side together, someplace where I saw you every day. I looked through my yearbooks." He starts to laugh. "I tried to figure out where I knew you from, how did I know your face, your voice so well? The reason I took the job from you? All that you said about the curse? I couldn't deny you might be telling the truth. I had to take the job, not just because I needed the business. Who cares about the business? I took that job because being with you made me more myself than I had been in any time I could remember in a very long time. So what choice do I have now? If I leave my wife and go with you, I'll still be cursed, because knowing Rhonda, I'll never get to see my child. I'll never be able to see it grow up. I just don't know what the right answer is."

He looks at me with such sadness in his eyes. I know what the right choice is. I know that I can't keep hurting Gogo anymore.

"I am so sorry about all of this. I am so sorry that all of this happened to you. This is all my fault, a curse on my family that has affected you, and this is something that I have to live with. This whole thing started because my great-great-grandmother stole my great-great-grandaunt's fiancé. I love you so much, Gogo, but someone in my family has to put a stop to this cycle of misery. I would rather spend the rest of my life alone than cause another woman to feel a pain that deep. If there's anything that I've learned from all this, from my own heart, from Emmalina's heart, it's that losing someone you love is the worst pain imaginable. In Emmalina's case, it was so painful that it gave her the ability to curse Astrid's entire bloodline. I couldn't do that to another person. Rhonda is your wife, and no matter how I feel about her, whether she's real or not, I can't do this to another person. At this point, the only option I have is to let you alone. I am a strong person. I will go on with my life without you. It won't be easy, but at least I'll have the knowledge that somewhere in this world, someone loves me."

Gogo takes my hand in his. We look at each other, knowing that this is the last time we'll see each other.

"So what will you do?" he asks me.

"I'll go on," I tell him, not knowing what else to say. "I'll go on with my life and try to make the best of it, just like Selma and Dolly have."

"Selma and Dolly." He sighs. "I'm really going to miss them."

"They're going to miss you too," I tell him, stroking his hand. "They understand why I did this. If there's anything good that came out of this, it's knowing that they got to meet you and spend time with you and love you as much as I do."

We look into each other's eyes one more time. I look at Gogo's lips, wishing I could kiss them one last time, but I know that I can't. There's no sense in letting this go on any further.

"So this is it," I tell him.

"I don't want you to go," he tells me.

"I don't want to go either," I say.

But I look down at our hands as I take my hand off his.

"I wish you all the happiness with your life," he tells me.

"And I wish the same for you," I tell him. "That's all I really want. Just tell me one thing before I go."

"Sure."

"Tell me that you're going to be okay. Tell me that you'll go on with your life and that you'll be happy. Tell me that I'll never have to worry about you."

"I promise you," he tells me. "I promise you I'm going to be okay. You've changed me for the better. You think that you've cursed me, but meeting you has been a blessing. I'm going to be okay. You never have to worry."

He smiles at me.

I smile back at him.

I touch his hand one more time.

And then I get up.

I will be okay. I know I will. I know I'll be okay, because Gogo is going to be okay. After all, that's all I ever really wanted out of this, right? Though I know that I'll never again be able to wake up next to Gogo or talk to him or even share a meal with him, somehow, that's okay. I feel an incredible comfort in knowing that he is all right. He'll be fine. He won't be cursed anymore because he'll take what he's learned from all this and he'll live his life better. I know he won't allow people, especially Rhonda, to walk all over him. He won't allow that.

It's not perfect. My life will never be perfect again. But I can still be happy. I can still live the rest of my life knowing that Gogo will be okay.

If anything, the comfort in knowing that is worth everything in the world to me.

And as I look out onto the street, the world goes on. Life goes on. On the front steps of this police station, cops are coming in and out of the doors. The sun is shining bright. People are passing by on their way to wherever they're going.

I join them on the street. Just another person on her way to someplace else.

I turn around one more time to find Gogo watching me as I head down the street.

I hold my hand up and give him a little wave.

Gogo stands up and we smile at each other one last time.

And then Gogo turns and walks away in the other direction.

Life, this dimension of life, goes on.

21.

It's 6:00 when I arrive home. There's a bunch of mail in the box, electric bills for energy I don't remember using, a bill from Bloomingdale's for a very expensive blouse I don't remember buying. My new *Vanity Fair* is there and I wonder who was on the cover last month or the month before that. Did the covers change in this dimension of life? I go inside and throw the mail on the console next to the door.

This house is quiet as I stop and take a look at the foyer and living room in front of me. A decorative pillow from the couch is lying on the seat of the chair, and it occurs to me that no one moved that pillow but me. There's no one else who moved that pillow and no one else is going to move it back to its place until I do. I throw myself on the couch as I take the pillow and put it behind my head, curling myself in the fetal position. Staring at the back of the couch, I begin to pick tiny pieces of lint and flick them behind me.

I turn onto my back and look up at the ceiling. What will I do now?

I have no job, no man. I have a criminal record. I have to start my life over.

Maybe tomorrow.

I lean over, grab the remote on the coffee table in front of me, and turn on the television.

It's some soap opera. I recognize the couple on the screen from when, as a teenager, I used to watch this show with Dolly. They've gotten a bit older. Who did this poor woman's face-lift? HD television has not been good to her. Or him. He couldn't wait until the hair plugs healed?

"But if I can't have you, what will I do?" The fifty-something woman asks the same guy she asked when I watched this same show fifteen years ago.

"Jesus, get a life," I tell her as I switch the channel.

It's some talk show.

"In this envelope," the host says, "I've got the results from the paternity test. We're all about to find out if Timothy really is the father of Leanne's baby."

"He better be!" Timothy shouts out.

"He is! I swear it!" Leanne pleads. "I never slept with Leon!"

The host opens the envelope and reads to himself what's on the paper. We all wait with bated breath.

"The report is ninety-nine-point-nine percent positive—the baby is not Timothy's!"

"Ha ha!" I laugh as Timothy jumps out of his chair and throws it at the audience. I switch the channel.

"It's a royal wedding unlike anything we've seen since Diana and Charles."

"And look at where it got them," I say out loud.

Switch. An ad for engagement rings.

"Three months' salary can last a lifetime of happiness . . ."

"Up yours."

Switch. The news.

"Coming up after the break, how to watch out for traps in your marriage."

"Now they tell me."

Switch.

The Way We Were.

"What kind of pie?" Hubble asks.

This line gets my eyes watery. I sit up and begin to cry.

I'm alone. I'm all alone in the world and I always will be. There will never be romance or love or walks on the beach or romantic vacations or Valentine's Day chocolates or anything else that might put a little softness in my heart. I'm an old maid at twenty-nine. I might as well get some cats.

I grab the remote and shut off the television. I've got to do something, anything to keep my mind off my misery.

I contemplate dinner. I can't remember the last time I've eaten anything, but I don't seem to be hungry. I go over to the refrigerator anyway and open the door, only to find one lone box of baking soda in the back. I think about going to the supermarket, but for what? Before I met Gogo, going to the supermarket was a quick in and out for laundry detergent, some juice, and whatever I was going to have for dinner that night. Life wasn't about picking vegetables and making sure there were enough eggs or bread. It was all about going to the hot section or the deli section or the salad bar and getting a small container of whatever caught my eye on my way to the checkout. Hey, there's a new career for me, opening a supermarket geared for single people. Eggs are individual; one stick of butter is available. I see the ad now: *Got a sudden need to bake a pie, but don't want the frustration of having to buy flour and sugar by the pound? Look no further and head on down to your local Single Shop, where sugar is available by the cup. Say good-bye to three-year-old bags of flour infested with bugs. Yuck! And at the Single Shop, you'll never have to worry about long lines. Every line is an express line!*

People will wonder, though, why you can't get a cup of chocolate chips or even buy a single chocolate chip cookie. I'll just tell them it's a religious thing.

"*F* this," I say as I shut the refrigerator door.

So what? So what if I can't find love. I can still live, can't I? There's nothing preventing me from having a good time, is there?

Jonah.

I start to weigh the pros and cons. Okay, so he's not perfect, he's nowhere near perfect, but he's kind of perfect because I know I'll never fall in love with him or want to have his babies or worry if he's happy with me. I'll never get jealous if any other women are interested and God knows I'll never feel upset if I catch him with someone else. We'll live by my rules and my rules alone. If I don't want to see him, I don't have to. If I don't want to talk, I don't have to. I don't have to care if he's had a bad day or if he's in a bad mood. I will not buy a new dress or get a facial or get my hair done if it's to look good for him. I don't care who's trying to take business from him or ruin his career. Sucks for you! We'll only see chick flicks and go to restaurants I want to go to. There will be no meeting of the parents or holidays spent together unless I feel like it. If relatives or friends come in from out of town, you won't see me at the Liberty Bell or Independence Hall, and forget any explanation on how to order a cheesesteak from Pat's or Gino's. There will never be a gift bought for a niece's bat mitzvah or a nephew's graduation from high school. There will be no gifts for him either, or little notes sent to brighten up his day. And above all, sex (as extremely infrequent as it will be) will always be with the lights off and for my pleasure and he is to leave the second I say he's not needed anymore.

The fact is, if I'm going to be cursed, I'm not going to let it ruin me. I'm not going to be like Selma and Dolly, pining over men they'll never be able to have. I'm going to do what they brought me up to do: find some jerk I'll never love and make sure he'll always feel as bad as I do.

I go over to the phone and dial Jonah.

"Hey," I say in a brash tone the second he picks up the phone.

"Hi!" he breathes warmly, totally surprised.

"Eight o'clock, Le Bec-Fin, and don't forget to bring your credit card this time because I won't be footing the bill."

"But it's impossible to get a table," he cries.

"Find a way," I say wickedly.

"What time should I pick you up?" he asks.

"One hour. And if you're a minute past seven, the door stays locked."

I hang up without waiting for an answer and walk over to my closet. I realize that I haven't even showered since spending time in jail, but I don't really care. The first thing I pull out is some sweatpants. That will show him.

I start to put them on, but then I see a form-fitting black shift, one that's always been a favorite of mine; it's one of those rare magical dresses we all have that seem to always fit perfectly without the need of a body shaper or push-up bra.

I throw the sweats on the floor and pull out the dress and get myself into it. I take a look in the mirror.

I look too good.

So I take it off and throw it on the ground.

Pretty soon I've got half my closet on the floor of my bedroom. There's one pair of jeans in my closet. I stare at the jeans like I'm staring at Gogo, feeling the fabric folded on the hanger. I haven't worn these jeans since the night I got married in Vegas. The night I promised to stay with Gogo in sickness and in health, for richer or for poorer, for better or for worse.

I take the jeans off the hanger and hold them in front of me, begging them to remind me of that night, the happiest night of my life. I wish they could talk. I wish that they could tell me how all this happened, how I was so thrilled and delighted one second and the next second I was in utter misery.

I put the jeans on leg by leg, fasten the button, and pull up the zipper. I've lost weight since I wore these last. I take a look in the mirror at my butt and smooth the fabric.

And then I feel something in my back pocket. It's a card, like a credit card. I take it out of my pocket and look at it.

Sitting in my hand is the room key to our honeymoon suite, the one I never got to sleep in. It's the card that proves there is another life, another amazing, glorious dimension of life that I don't have anymore. I'm thrilled that at least I have proof. That I'm not out of my mind. But in the end it doesn't matter. What's it going to do? Gogo already believes me.

But I just keep staring at the card. I can't stop thinking about what it represents, what our life could have been, the life we would have lived, the children we would have created, the love we would have shared.

My doorbell rings as I catch the clock turning from 6:59 to 7:00.

I just can't do it.

I can't be a bitch.

I can't be selfish.

I can't make anyone else's life miserable.

I run toward my bureau and pull out a tank, which just happens to be the same tank top I was wearing that night. I don't do this on purpose. It just happens to be at the top of my drawer. I throw it on and head toward the door and open it.

There's Jonah, standing there in a suit. He's got a smile on his face that's even bigger than the bouquet of two dozen roses he's got in his hand.

"You look stunning," he tells me as I look down at my outfit. "These are for you," he says, presenting the flowers.

"They're lovely." I take them. "Come on in, Jonah," I tell him as I lay the flowers on the dining room table. "Have a seat." I motion him toward the couch.

Jonah sits on the edge of the couch, his back is straight, not like it used to be when he'd park himself on it and throw his feet, shoes and all, on the coffee table.

I take a deep breath and sigh.

"Jonah," I start.

"Yes?" he asks kindly.

"I can't do it."

"Aw, for Christ's sake!" He slaps his hands. "I knew it. I just knew it! This is what I get for getting all nice with some woman. Do you see what happens? Do you see?"

He's angrier than I've ever seen him before.

"Please, Jonah, sit down. Please let me explain."

"I don't need your explanations, lady, I'm through," he says, walking to the door, but he stops short, looks over at the flowers, and grabs them.

"Jonah, would you please sit down for a second!" I tell him.

"I don't have time for this kind of thing, Lily," he tells me, turning back into the old Jonah. "Don't think I don't have something better out there. This is your loss, lady!"

"Jonah, I know. I know that you've got something better out there."

"You better believe it!"

"Jonah, I know that the perfect woman is out there for you. Someone who loves you for who you are and not for who you try to be."

"Oh shut up, don't give me that crap."

"I know it, Jonah, I just know it. I know it because if there was someone out there who was perfect for me, there's someone out there for everyone. It's a big world. There are a lot of people in it. It's just a matter of time."

"Oh really," he says. "And what happened to your dream man? I thought you were married? I thought you were in love."

"I am, and there are reasons, good reasons, that we're not together, why we can't be together, but I make up for that by treating you badly. And it's the same for you. You can't go on being rude to women because you're afraid they might find out what you really think of yourself. You can't be someone you're not, because in the end, if you keep up that facade, no one is going to see it, or if they do, it's going to be that much harder to see you."

"So why did you call me over here? Why did you make me feel like an ass?"

"Because I thought I could go on with my life. I thought I could just be as selfish and pigheaded as I want to be, but the truth is, I can't. I know what it's like to find a soul mate. I know that perfect feeling. I don't want you to miss out on that. I don't want you to live your life without knowing that kind of peace."

"I think you're crazy."

"You'll thank me one of these days. I promise you."

"Hey lady, don't think I ever fell for you. Don't think those three little words you long to hear would have ever come out of my mouth. Don't think I ever *really* loved you or *really* wanted to make you happy. Trust me, I'm not that kind of guy."

I don't say anything as he heads for the door and opens it. As he starts to walk through the door, he turns around one more time.

"You think you're even that hot? Honey, trust me, you're not. I was just bored and you're not worth it. Believe me, you won't be hearing from me ever again." He turns around again and then turns back toward me one more time. "And one more thing. You need a shower!" He slams the door.

In an odd way, I feel relieved for Jonah right now. He never loved me. He'll never be cursed. Though maybe that kind of guy will always be cursed. Maybe not, though. Maybe he'll have learned a lesson. You can't treat people like crap for your own selfish reasons. It gets you nowhere in life.

I take the card out of my pocket again and stare at it.

And then I walk back into my bedroom and open up my jewelry box. I put the card in the box and shut it. Maybe I'll look at it from time to time when I need to, but for now, I'm glad it's there.

22.

Each day gets a little better.

Each morning for the past two weeks I get up and make my bed. I straighten up the house and head over to the Starbucks in Ardmore. I grab a tall latte, find a newspaper, and start looking at the want ads. I circle some ads, call some others; I've even got an interview set up for next week.

By noon I head over to the gym to work out with Selma. By this point, she's usually on the treadmill, shooing off poor Carter, so I get on the one next to her and we talk about what's going on in our lives. Sometimes I go back to her house and Dolly fixes us some lunch and I stay on until after dinner. The neighborhood has gone back to its usual routine, waves to neighbors, arguments between Dolly and Poolson. There's always a time, though, when the subject comes up.

"It will get better, doll," Selma tells me.

"Just know that we're always here for you," Dolly tells me.

And then I'll feel better, but soon something else sets me off. Just today, in fact, as I was leaving Dolly and Selma's, it started to rain. It was one of those heavy downpours that comes out of nowhere and lasts about five minutes. I was standing in the doorway watching the rain as it pelted the neighborhood. It was so peaceful and quiet, no sound except for a tiny rattle to my left. When I looked over, I noticed the rattling was the rain collecting in the gutter. It was working perfectly, no leaks.

And last weekend, Rose asked me to come up to New York and

help her with the final arrangements for the wedding. After all, I am the maid of honor.

"I was going to ask my sister-in-law," she told me, "but then I decided I wanted a relative who was also one of my best friends."

She knows not to set me up with anyone at the wedding. She knows not to sit me at the singles table. Instead, I'm sitting with our family—Selma, Dolly, and her parents.

It's the only positive thing to come out of all this.

I lost one potential family, but I gained another.

At night when I come home, there's no one else there but me. There's no one else to talk with about my day. There's no one I can tell about the funny thing that happened on the way to the Starbucks that morning or celebrate the free shipping I got when I ordered new dishes online. There's no one here to ease my fears about the upcoming trial, which my lawyer tells me will be fine, though I'll probably lose my license. Do you need a license to drive a Vespa? Of course, I'm all alone, so there's no one around to answer this question or any other question.

On the bright side, I've started eating better, just like I did with Gogo. That's one positive thing. Vegetables and fruits and whole grains, enough for one person, fill my fridge.

So today when I leave Selma at the gym, I get in my car and proceed to the market.

I'm thinking of making some chicken for dinner tonight and maybe some spinach with oil and garlic as a side. As I head into the market, I'm thinking about all the ingredients I need and I hope this market has chicken with no hormones or fillers.

And then I walk in and the first thing I see is the frozen food section. This stops me in my tracks. For five minutes, life was fine. I wasn't thinking about Gogo or my perfect life in that other dimension. My heart didn't hurt and I wasn't starting to tear up. All I was thinking about was making some free-range chicken and some spinach and now I'm lost again.

I look up at the sign on top of the frozen foods section and it feels like it's become a place of mourning or remembrance, as if it's been dedicated with a plaque like a park or place of worship. Only Gogo isn't dead, and under the heading Ice Cream and Novelties, the sign doesn't say, "Place where Gogo and Lily used to come and dance."

Still, I stare at those letters as if they mean much more than what they're really saying. The pain returns to my heart once again, and the only thing I can do to make myself feel better is walk into the section and spend a little time.

The air feels good as I stare blankly at the Breyer's fruit pops and Good Humor strawberry shortcake bars. I close my eyes and put my head in my hands.

"They say Philadelphia is a small place," I hear a woman say. I open my eyes and turn around.

It's Rhonda and Gogo standing in front of me with a cart full of items.

"Hi," I say to Gogo, shocked.

"Hi," he answers.

"Hello, Rhonda." I smile.

"Lily." She half smiles back. "I want Ben and Jerry's," she tells Gogo, then turns back to me. "All this baby wants is cookie dough ice cream." She smiles as she pats her flat belly.

"How's Selma? Dolly?" he asks.

"They're great. They love the downspouts," I tell him.

"Well . . ." He leans toward me. I can't believe he wants to kiss me hello, even a peck in front of Rhonda, but I lean in anyway and pucker my lips.

"No," he says, as my lips scrape his face, "I was getting the ice cream. You were in the way, sorry," he explains uncomfortably.

"Oh," I say, feeling flushed and stupid, "simple mistake." I chuckle to Rhonda.

"Well, bye," Rhonda says as Gogo throws the ice cream in their basket.

"See you later," I say, putting my hand up.

Gogo gives me one last smile as they head on their way.

I continue to stand there in the section, but I move away from the Ben and Jerry's and stare at the Häagen-Dazs.

I'm standing there for about five minutes. The music has changed from the Carpenters to Phil Collins as I begin to go on my way.

Hold on! I drop my basket on the ground. Ben and Jerry's Chocolate Chip Cookie Dough Ice Cream? I've got her!

I run down to the end of the aisle and then past each aisle, trying to find them. I don't see them in the condiments aisle or the breakfast cereal aisle. They're not in the soda and water aisle, and they're nowhere to be seen in the toilet paper and tissue section of aisle two.

It's only when I get to the vegetable section that I spot them, right by the brussels sprouts, loading a bag to make Gogo's favorite.

"Can't you just leave us alone?" Rhonda remarks drily as she sees me heading over to them.

"You're not pregnant," I tell her.

"Excuse me?" She laughs.

"You're not pregnant and you need to admit it now before you ruin this man's life even more."

"And what makes you think I'm not?" she asks calmly.

"Lily," Gogo says, trying to calm me down.

"*Gogo, she's not pregnant!*" I shout. I go into their cart and pull out Ben and Jerry's Chocolate Chip Cookie Dough ice cream and hold it up to them. "You're a doctor in another dimension, think about it. She's eating raw chocolate chip cookie dough. A pregnant woman who has tried to have a baby for as long as she has would never want to eat anything that contains raw eggs. No pregnant woman who has gone through as much as she has would even sip a glass of unfiltered water, much less eat raw eggs."

Holding the ice cream container in front of her face, I stare Rhonda down.

"Admit it, Rhonda. You're a fraud!"

Gogo looks at Rhonda, who looks like she's just been found out.

"You let this good man think you were pregnant for your own selfish reasons. You were both unhappy, but you just couldn't let him get on with his life!" I shout.

"Are you pregnant?" he asks her.

"Of course I am," she answers self-consciously.

"Are you?" he asks a little louder.

"Gogo, let me explain!" She begins to cry.

"I knew it!" I shout.

"I can't believe you," he tells her softly. "I just can't believe you would lie to me, after all we've been through."

"I love you, Gogo," she tells him.

"No . . . you don't," he says.

The jig is up for Rhonda and she knows it. I stand there staring at her with this satisfied smile on my face.

"Give me the car keys, Gogo," she says, holding out her hand.

Gogo digs into his pocket, pulls them out, and hands them to her.

"Don't bother coming home."

"Like I want to?" he tells her.

"No, of course you don't, you never did! You've been in love with her all this time! I had to fake a pregnancy for you to stay with me! I'm going to sue you in divorce court for alienation of affection, for adultery, you name it! No wonder I could never get pregnant. You're a shell of a man, Gogo! You're nothing! You're a weak, little man!"

I want to punch this woman. I want to punch her with every little bit of strength I have.

"This is not going to end well," she warns.

"What's not going to end well?" he asks. "All your lies? Are you going to steal all my money? What money? What are you going to take from me that you haven't taken from me in the last fifteen years? And I put up with it. You want me to say it? I'll say it! I'll say the words I've been wanting to say for the last three months!"

"Wait, what are you going to say? Wait, Gogo, what are you going to say?" I plead, knowing exactly what he's going to say. "Don't say it. *Gogo, please, don't say it!*"

"*I'm going to say what I've wanted to say for the last three months! I. LOVE. Li—*"

"*Nooooooo!*" I shout at the top of my lungs.

And instead of using all my strength to hit Rhonda, I tackle Gogo to the ground and put my hand over his mouth.

"You know something?" Rhonda says, looking at us sprawled out on the floor of the fruits and vegetable section of Acme Market. "You two deserve each other." She turns and walks away. "I'll see you in court!"

I take my hand off Gogo's mouth very slowly.

"Gogo, please, do not say those words. For your own good, please, do not say those three words you want to say."

"But I do, Lily," he says, sitting up. "I do . . . you know . . ."

"But you can't have me!" I cry as I get up off him. I realize that all the people in the section are now staring at us. I don't care, though.

"But Lily, maybe . . . if you could just listen to me. Why did you just do what you did to Rhonda if you didn't want us to be together?"

"Because it's like I've said all along. Because even if I can't be with you, I still care about you. That doesn't stop, but Gogo, this pain is just too much. I just, I can't see you right now." I start to walk away. "I have to go; I left my basket in the frozen foods section."

He begins to follow me as I rush ahead of him through the aisles.

"We can still be together, we can—"

"We can't, Gogo, and you know this as well as I do."

We're back in the frozen foods section. I head over to my basket, which is sitting right where I left it.

"So what if a tree falls on me or a bus hits me? What's the point of being alive if I can't be with the person I—"

He stops himself from saying the forbidden words.

I shake my head.

"Gogo, it's just not going to work. I wish and I wish and I wish, but this curse is too powerful and I just can't seem to break the spell. I'm so sorry."

"No, I know, I know." He sighs.

And as we stand there, right in the frozen foods section, Hall and Oates come on the loudspeaker. It's our song.

Because your kiss . . .

I hold out my hands to Gogo. I know that he's not aware of our frozen food ritual, but he nonetheless takes me in his arms. We begin to sway back and forth to the music, even though it's a fast song. I look up at my sweet husband, knowing it can never be like this again. He looks down at me, and before I know it, we kiss.

It is the sweetest kiss I could ever feel. It is home.

"I can't believe this is reality," he tells me.

"But it is," I answer.

"There is no way to break this spell?" he asks.

"I've tried everything. I thought that if I gave you back to Rhonda, that even that would make me feel better. That what happened to Emmalina would never happen to anyone else in this family. It's just this curse. It's unbreakable. No, there is no way."

I take Gogo in my arms once again.

"Gogo, when I think back to that wonderful moment in that hotel room when you were mine and our life together seemed certain . . . How excited I was, how happy and at peace, so at peace I thought I was dreaming. I even asked you to . . ."

And then I realize.

"Gogo, do you love me?"

"Of course, you know I do."

"So pinch me," I tell him.

"What?"

"Pinch me," I repeat.

"Why?"

"Gogo, pinch me right here," I say as I hold out my arm.

"Pinch you?"

"Jesus, Gogo, pinch me already!"

And Gogo takes my arm in his hand as he takes his other hand to the spot I'm pointing to.

Because your kiss . . .

And he pinches my arm. He doesn't pinch hard; it's just a soft pinch as I close my eyes.

And suddenly, we're not in the frozen foods aisle anymore.

We are back.

I open my eyes to find us back in the hotel room, back in that moment. Before me is strong and handsome Gogo. Handsome with a full head of hair, treats me like a queen, summa cum laude Harvard Medical School graduate Gogo.

Gogo.

The good man I'm madly in love with.

"*We're back!*" I shout at the top of my lungs as the tears start to pour from my eyes.

"What are you talking about?" He laughs.

"Gogo, we're back! Don't you remember? Don't you see?" I laugh with tears streaming down my face.

"Lily, what's suddenly gotten into you?"

"Gogo, Gogo!" I smile as I put my arms around him and kiss him madly.

"Are you okay?"

"Gogo, I've broken the curse!"

"What curse?" he asks. "What the hell are you talking about?"

"What curse?" I ask him. "Gogo, don't you remember anything?" I shake my head in amazement as I grab my phone. "I have to call Dolly and Selma," I tell him as I dial their number.

"Lily, would you please tell me what's going on here?"

I look at Gogo. "No, I'll them in person," I explain, though Gogo has no idea what I'm talking about.

"Gogo, we have to go home. We have to go back to Philadelphia right now. I'll explain everything on the plane."

"No, tell me now, I'm worried about you," he says, taking my arms.

"Gogo"—I start to cry—"I love you so much. I love you with every bit of my being. I love every single thing about you. Just . . . please, tell me that you love me too. Tell me over and over and over . . . Just tell me you love me."

"I love you, Lil," he says, taking me in his arms. "I love you more than I've ever loved any woman. I love you, but you've suddenly gone crazy."

"I haven't gone crazy," I tell him, "just the opposite, in fact. Just promise me we'll spend every day for the rest of our lives telling each other those three words every day."

"I love you, Lily Burns Goldblatt," he says, kissing me.

"I love you, Gogo Goldblatt," I tell him.

23.

*M*om!" I shout as I run through the door of my childhood home with Gogo holding my hand. "I've done it! I've broken the curse!"

"What have you done?" Dolly asks, rushing to the door. "Your mom isn't here. She's at the gym!"

"Gram! I've broken the curse!"

"What do you mean, you've broken the curse?"

"I did it! Don't you remember telling me about the curse?"

"Of course I remember telling you. I told you not to marry the man you were in love with! Is this him?" she asks, pointing to him. "Lily! We told you not to get married!"

"But I did! And everything went terrible just like you said, don't you remember? Don't you remember the downspouts?"

"Downspouts?" she asks. "What the heck's a downspout?"

"It doesn't matter!" I laugh. "All I know is that the curse is broken! You can go on with your life!"

"MA!" we suddenly hear from outside the house. It's Selma. "MA! COME QUICK, IT'S RAINING MEN OUT HERE!"

The three of us rush outside to find Selma running up the driveway with six different men.

"*Look, it's Bobby!*" she shouts. "And Ron, and Paul and Carlos, and Larry! Carter!"

Dolly follows Selma, hugging each of her sons-in-law. Then she stands at the end of the line as she looks around.

"But where is my Sherman?" she asks all of us.

We look around as if we are searching for him, but in reality we all know the truth.

"Ma," Selma says sorrowfully, "he was fifteen years older than you. He'd be a hundred by now."

"I know"—Dolly bows her head—"but I just thought maybe one day . . . I guess it was too late." She looks at me. "He'll never know the curse was broken. He'll never know how brave and wonderful his granddaughter really is," she says as I put my arms around her.

"I wish I could have met him," I tell her.

"He was a nice man," she tells me. "He smoked too many cigars though. Maybe he would have been here if he hadn't smoked so many cigars." She shrugs sadly.

"Dolly!" we hear, as Poolson walks out of his house and heads toward us. "What's all this racket going on out here? You're not building another bonfire, I hope."

Her face suddenly brightens.

"POOLSON!" she shouts as she runs toward him. "POOL-SON, I LOVE YOU!" she shouts with her arms open.

Poolson stops in his tracks when they meet in the middle of the street. He looks wary. "What's this, another trick?" he asks angrily.

"It's no trick," she answers him. "I love you, Harvey Poolson. I love you with all my heart."

As we watch, his face slowly changes from angry to overjoyed.

They grab each other and begin to kiss madly. My heart melts.

"Wait, hold on a second," Gogo asks bewildered. "So who are these guys?"

And just as I'm about to answer him, one of the men puts his hand on my shoulder.

"Hello, darling," he says.

I begin to cry as I put my arm around him. Gogo looks bewildered.

"Gogo," I whimper. "I'd like you to meet my father, Bobby. Dad, this is my husband, Gogo."

Gogo, still looking like he's unable to grasp what's going on here, looks at my father and smiles. "It's very nice to meet you," he says.

"Pleasure to meet you, too," Bobby says as he takes both of us in his arms.

As Dolly served the large table of people, she announced, "I am sorry to tell you, but after this, the kitchen is closed." With a flirtatious glance at Poolson, she explained, "I have better things to do now than cook." She winked as Selma and I made sour faces. "So enjoy!"

It was a joyous night, sitting around the table with all these wonderful men. And as I looked around at everyone laughing and eating and each man oddly getting along with the other, I looked over at my darling husband.

"Bizarre," he whispered to me.

"Welcome to the family," I whispered back.

Dolly leaned over me. "Lily," she whispered as Selma who was sitting next to me leaned in, "you haven't told us yet. How did you break the curse?"

"Here's the thing," I explained as Selma, who was siting next to me, leaned in. "The curse wants you to be with a man you don't love. That's what it was trying to do. That's why it didn't kill all the husbands—it just gave them excessive hair or big egos so we wouldn't love our men anymore. In my case, the curse made Gogo a shell of the man he used to be. It gave us every reason to fall out of love with our men. It was all a test."

"So I gave up on my husbands?" Selma asked. She and Dolly look at each other sadly.

"You just thought there was no way out," I explained. "Who could blame you? I thought there was no way out, but then it dawned on me—the curse was testing our love for our husbands, plain and simple."

"But we're all going to be okay now," Selma whispered to us.

"The curse is broken." I smiled.

"And we all have Lily to thank for that," Dolly said as the three of us put our arms around each other.

As we arrive home that night, the home I share with Gogo, there are no pinks or purples to speak of. No unsmiling pictures of Rhonda or any sign of another life.

"You coming to bed?" he asks me.

"Just one second," I tell him. "I have to make one phone call."

I pick up my cell phone and turn it on, only to find I have about fifty emails, including "Subject: Tomorrow's Best Buy Pitch."

Of course, I have my job. Of course nothing has happened. It's the same day it was three months ago. In this life. In this dimension of life.

I open up the email and write, "See you tomorrow. Everyone get a good night sleep. I've got this pitch covered."

I hit send and then go into my phone book and realize the number is not there. Luckily, I already know it by heart.

"Hello?" the voice asks on the phone.

"Hi, is this Rose Golden?"

"Yes," she answers.

"Okay, this is going to sound strange. You don't know me, but I wanted to say hello. I'm a cousin of yours, Lily Burns."

"Okay . . . ?" She asks hesitantly.

"And . . . well, we're actually related, distantly, and I was wondering—I'm going to be in New York this weekend, and I was wondering if we could maybe get a cup of coffee."

24.

I'm not awake.

I'm dreaming.

I'm somewhere up above the clouds. Actually, I'm standing on a cloud. I feel like I'm waiting for something, for someone, but I don't know who or what.

Suddenly an elderly man appears before me. He looks like he's about eighty years old; a little shorter than me, he wears glasses and smokes a cigar.

"Let me tell you something, my dear," he says to me with a thick gruff voice as he pulls the cigar to his lips and breathes in. Oddly, I don't smell the cigar smoke. "It's nice to finally meet you."

"Are you God?" I ask him.

"God?" He chuckles. "Would God look like this?" he asks, presenting himself.

"I don't know." I smile.

"How's your grandmother?" he asks.

"She's fine. She's wonderful, in fact."

"Yeah, she was always a strong one. You've got her eyes. You're pretty like she is."

"Thank you."

"And your mother?"

"They were the best parents a girl could have ever had," I tell him.

"Wonderful," he says with relief, taking another puff of the cigar.

"Grandpa?"

"Yeah, sweetheart?"

"I'm sorry about everything that happened."

"It's not your fault. It was mine. I was warned. The things we do for the women we love, huh?" He laughs again. "But you, of all people, you shouldn't be apologizing. You're the one we should be celebrating. I'm proud of you, kid. Very proud.

"To see your face, it was worth it," he says, beaming at me. "And now, I think you have some place to be." He places my arm in his as I turn around to find a set of white doors at the edge of our cloud.

My grandfather and I walk arm and arm as the doors swing open.

And suddenly I'm in a room decorated in white.

I'm at a wedding, my wedding.

I look down to find that I'm standing at the beginning of the aisle in a beautiful white gown. My grandfather unlocks his arm from mine as Dolly touches his cheek, blows him a kiss, and turns to me. Selma and Dolly, who is now on the other side of me, are dressed in gowns. They look stunning. I take Dolly's arm and then Selma's.

And we begin to walk.

Further along, my great-grandmother Hilde Burnswurst and her husband, J. J. Gainsboro, sit a few rows up. J. J. takes Hilde's hand as they smile to me, loving smiles full of warmth and good cheer.

Next is Poolson, who silently raises his hand in great cheer. Dolly blows him a kiss.

Rose and Leo and Rose's family are next. Rose mouths, "You look absolutely beautiful."

I mouth the words "Thank you."

And then my fathers, Robert and Carlos, Ron, Paul, Larry . . . and there's Carter again. Selma winks at them, to which they all give little waves and winks back.

"I'm so tired." Selma inhales. "But believe me, it's worth it."

"Ma!" I wince.

"Sorry."

"No prob." I chuckle.

And at the front of the aisle, there's Gogo, dressed in a tuxedo, smiling, even more handsome than I've ever seen him before.

I kiss my mother, then Dolly, as I turn away from them and take Gogo's arm. We face forward.

Only there is no one there to marry us.

Because we're already married.

And I begin to laugh. I laugh with such happiness. It is the purest feeling I've ever known. I have never felt so at peace, so euphoric.

And the next thing I know, I'm awake.

I'm in my home, the one I share with Gogo.

In this dark room, it's the middle of the night, but I can't help myself. I lean on my side and look over at my sleeping husband. As usual, he's lying flat on his back with one pillow under his head and the covers pulled all the way up to his chin. Nothing in the world has changed.

"Gogo?" I whisper to him.

"Yeah?" he whispers back immediately, as if he's been up the whole time, but I know he hasn't. For someone who sleeps so peacefully, Gogo is a light sleeper.

"I love you so much," I tell him.

And then he turns toward me and he swallows me in his arms as I rest my back up against him.

"I love you too, Lily," he whispers back.

As I lie in his arms staring out at the darkness, feeling his body against mine, I know for sure: this is the most wonderful place in the world.

Acknowledgments

This story is a love letter to my husband, Jonathan. Four years ago, I promised to love, honor, and protect you all the days of my life. Thanks, Mr. Goldstein, for keeping up your end of the bargain as well. It was the best deal I ever made.

And to the other men in my life: Brian DeFiore, Brian Lipson, and Eric Brooks, because behind every strong woman there should always be a couple of incredibly smart, shrewd, kind, and above all, tolerant guys who let you know when you're being overly dramatic. Special thank you to John Francis Daley, who never fails to save the day when I need a quick quip.

As always, I thank Susan Swimmer, Erin Moore, Allison Dickens, Trish Grader, and Lesley Jane Seymour, and to my family and friends, especially my mother, Arlene, goddess of fabulous.

Finally, with deep gratitude, I thank my most amazing editor, Trish Todd, and everyone at Touchstone involved with the publication of *Pinch Me*. It was the second best deal I ever made.

Pinch Me

From the author of *29* comes a delightful modern fairy tale about Lily Burns, a young career woman with the perfect life—until an ancient family curse threatens to take everything away. Lily has been told all her life not to marry for love. Then she meets the man of her dreams in Gogo, a handsome, successful pediatrician who wants nothing more than to marry her and make her happy for the rest of her life. But accepting his offer sends her to an alternate universe where Gogo is not only a shell of the man she knew— but he's already married! If she's ever going to reunite with her beloved, Lily must first discover how to break her family curse—and learn the true power of love and family bonds along the way.

1. All her life, Selma and Dolly have told Lily to "never marry a man unless he's short, bald, fat, stupid, and treats you badly" (p. 1). Why do you think Lily never questioned this odd advice?

2. Dolly and Selma keep their family curse a secret from Lily until circumstances force them to reveal it. Why do they hide the curse for so long? What are they protecting her from?

3. When Gogo is first described, he has perfect looks (p. 10) and is a perfect fit for Lily (p. 20). His proposal, on the Eiffel Tower in Paris, is incredibly romantic. Did Gogo seem like a realistic character at first? How did that perception change when Lily describes Gogo's not-so-perfect characteristics later in the story?

4. Astrid and Emmalina's parents doted on the spoiled Astrid and, by comparison, treated the quiet, accepting Emmalina poorly. Do you think parental treatment is that unequal between real siblings?

5. *Pinch Me* has been described as a modern-day fairy tale. How does it compare to the classic fairy tales you learned?

6. *Pinch Me* features a curse and alternate realities. What effect does it have on your belief—or suspension of disbelief—in the story?

7. The story's curse—to never be able to marry for love—causes emotional pain for Lily and her family. However, in the alternate reality Lily makes a wonderful friend in her longlost cousin Rose. Could Lily have broken the curse without Rose's help? Are there any other benefits to the curse? What does it teach Lily about her family and the strength of her love?

8. Lily shows incredible tenacity in her efforts to break the curse, even when all hope seems lost. Could you have been as persistent as Lily?

9. Lily's choice to marry Gogo—and go directly against the advice of her mother and grandmother—brings on the curse. In order to break it, she must go further than they, and many generations before her, were able to. What does that say about the importance of following your own heart?

10. Selma and Dolly have suffered heartbreak time and time again because of the curse. As a coping mechanism Dolly cooks up a storm and Selma exercises almost constantly. Yet, despite their loss and struggles, both manage to keep a strong sense of humor. How does that help them? If you were in their situation, what would be your outlet?

11. Lily finds and fights to keep true love. Have you ever struggled to find love? Keep it?

With your own website and a presence on Facebook, Twitter, MySpace, and Goodreads, you are clearly very active online. How does interacting with your fans online compare to meeting them in person at book signings or other events?

I love having an online presence to meet and keep in touch with fans. I have "met" so many amazing people from all over the world who I never would have met at a book signing. In addition, thanks to the Internet, I've received so many kind letters and have corresponded with fans who might otherwise been unable to contact me.

One of my favorite things to do is to go on Skype and speak at book clubs. It's always a blast to hear people's comments about the book, to hear what they liked or wanted to read more about. In fact, the idea for *Pinch Me* actually came partly from talking to fans who wanted to read my take on a fairy-tale romance.

Your first two novels, *The Ten Best Days of My Life* and 29 are scheduled to be adapted into feature films! Have you been involved with the screenplays? What is the most exciting (or nerveracking!) part about this process of turning your novel into a movie?

Honestly, I have been nothing less than ecstatic about the process of my books being adapted into movies. As I am writing this, I know that the screenplay to *The Ten Best Days of My Life* has just been completed. It's *just* completed so I haven't read it yet, but the parts that have been described to me gave me such chills they brought tears to my eyes. A lot of people ask me how I feel giving up my *babies*. I think that's a strange question. I don't feel that I gave up my babies. Yes, I created these characters, and they're a huge part of my life, but coming from a film background, I know it's virtually impossible to adapt a book exactly as it was written and turn it into a movie. It's been really exciting for me to give someone else the creative freedom to explore my characters and come up with ideas I didn't think of. The screenplay of *Ten Best Days* has a component to it that makes me want to kick myself for not thinking of first. I'll also be very curious to see how I visualize heaven corresponds to how it looks in *Ten Best Days*, or if actresses that I thought of when I was writing *29* will see themselves in the parts.

In a way, I think of optioning my books in terms of renting out an apartment. Once I "rent out" a book, I'm not going to walk in at any moment and ask, "What are you going to do with that wall? I don't think you should put that picture there, that's not the way I had it when I was living here." For now, I put my trust in the screenwriters, producers, actors, etc. The people who are involved in these projects have shown me that they have as much passion for them as I do, and they have valued my opinion the whole way through. I couldn't have optioned my work if I hadn't seen their passion for it in the first place. For that reason alone, I can't wait to see how the work will be interpreted.

Your previous books have received warm critical praise. Did you find that to be more inspirational or intimidating as you wrote *Pinch Me?*

Any writer who tells you they don't care what the critics say is probably lying. Obviously, I hope each of my books is well received by the critics. But the most important thing to me is satisfying my readers. The main thing I like to explore in all of my books is the idea of telling a love story of an unsexual nature. If you consider my previous books, *Target Underwear and a Vera Wang Gown* was my own love story about a girl and her closet. *The Ten Best Days of My Life* was a love story between a girl and her parents. *29* was a love story between a family of women: a grandmother, her daughter, her granddaughter, and her best friend. In *Pinch Me*, I wanted to tell a love story about a husband and wife, but I didn't want it to just be about sex and romance. I wanted to explore the idea of soul mates and what that really means. For Lily, it wasn't about claiming her man. Lily would have and did do everything she could so that Gogo would be happy and safe, even if it meant never seeing him again. That's what we do for the people we love most. From what I gather, that's what people want to see in my books. I have no interest in telling a straightforward boy-meets-girl love story. There are so many amazing writers who already do that. At this point, readers expect me to turn the notion of romance on its side and really explore what it means to be in love.

Although you currently live in Los Angeles, you chose to set *Pinch Me* and your other novels in Philadelphia. Why does that city hold such allure for you? What is your favorite part of Philadelphia?

This summer will mark the twentieth anniversary of my move to Los Angeles. I've now lived in Los Angeles longer than in Philly. That's crazy to me, especially since I still have my Philadelphia accent. Philadelphia is where I was born and where I was brought up. The city itself has shaped who I am, just as much as my parents and teachers and childhood friends. There is a bond that we Philadelphians have that can't be broken. We're a club of folks who, no matter how far we stray or how old we get, will never be considered anything else but Philly kids. I love being a part of that club. It's a comforting feeling to know that I will never feel lost in my life because there are people who know me so well and for so long I start to wonder if we came out of the same womb. That's something about Philly that I try to bring out in my books. I am very proud to have been brought up in Philadelphia and to be known forever as a Philly kid. Using that amazing, beautiful city as a backdrop in my books is my way of saying thank you for letting me be a part of the club.

Do you share any characteristics with the main character, Lily? What was your inspiration to create her?

The great dancer, Agnes De Mille, once famously said, "To dance is to be out of yourself. Larger, more beautiful, more powerful . . . This is power, it is glory on earth and it is yours for the taking." I think the same holds true for writing a character in a book. Yes, Lily is a part of me. All of my main characters are some form of me, as much as I try, I just can't help it. But as Ms. De Mille said, they're on a much grander scale.

The idea for Lily Burns came to me as I stood in line at the hot foods bar in Whole Foods one day about two years ago. Five years earlier, I had pretty much frequented that hot foods bar every day of my life from the day it opened some seven years earlier until I moved into my husband's home across town. That particular day I happened to be in my old neighborhood and stopped in for a quick bite to eat. As I was standing there filling up my little cardboard container with whatever was there, I suddenly had this bizarre thought: What if I walked outside and my old crappy car from five years ago with the leaking transmission and dented bumper was parked in the spot where I had just left my brand-new sparkling gorgeous car? What if everything that had happened to me in the past five years—meeting my husband, marrying him, moving in with him, etc.—never happened and I suddenly woke up from a dream? What if I was still living in my dingy studio apartment with that freezer contained in a block of ice? What if all those idiot guys I dated (well, not all of them, but you know who you are) were still in my life? I really freaked myself out. Then I started to think, "What would have happened to my husband? Who would my husband be? What would have become of him in those five years? Who would I be? What have I learned since then that I could now tell those guys I dated who weren't so nice to me?"

Each of your novels features strong elements of magic or the fantastic. How does that help you develop your stories?

I usually start with a question that contains some form of fantasy and go from there. In my worst days of being single, it got to the point where I really had to start to ask myself if there was a curse on me when it came to dating. That question has always stuck in my mind when single girlfriends say the same thing to me about themselves. As I was thinking about the idea for the book, I thought about exploring that idea. What if there had been a curse? What would I have done? That's usually how it goes for me. I could tell a story about a woman who has bad luck with men, but to me it seems much more fun if there's a concrete reason why.

In terms of Lily Burns, I actually went through a couple of drafts where the curse wasn't there. Gogo pinched her and then he just vanished and she was back in her old single life. I really wanted to tell the old fashioned love story of girl meets boy/ girl loses boy/ girl gets boy back in the end, but every time I tried, Lily just seemed pathetic. Then one day I was watching *The Graduate*, one of my all-time favorite movies. If you really think about Dustin Hoffman

(Benjamin Braddock) in that movie, it's kind of creepy the way he goes up to Berkeley and follows Katharine Ross (Elaine Robinson). Then I saw a movie with Sandra Bullock called *All About Steve*. Both movies have that element of chasing their love, but one really, really works and the other just doesn't cut it (even though I love Sandra Bullock, and in my opinion, that woman can seriously do no wrong). What I discovered was that I was writing a girl-meets-boy story and not the other way around, and sadly, there's a big difference in that. If a girl chases a boy, it's really difficult not to make her seem like a stalker to the reader, even if, as in *Pinch Me*, she was married to the guy in a previous life or whatever you want to call it. It sucks, but that's the world we live in.

So I set it in another world.

I thought, what if there was something beyond her control that prevented her from getting the guy she loved? That's when I thought of the curse and I got really excited and it all came together after that. If I couldn't use that element of fantasy, it just wouldn't have worked for me.

Your memoir was based on your series of essays for *Marie Claire*. Do you also incorporate any elements of those essays into your fiction?

Yes, I would say that I incorporate elements of my *Marie Claire* essays into my fiction, but throughout my books, I've created kind of a chain focusing on what readers have told me they've enjoyed most. The *Marie Claire* essays were the basis for my book *Target Underwear and a Vera Wang Gown*. This was about my love for clothing and how it has affected my life. I carried my love of clothing to Alex in *The Ten Best Days of My Life* and to Ellie Jerome in *29*. They were both passionate about clothing and how it spoke to them. In

29, Ellie Jerome was seventy-five years old and her daughter, Barbara, was fifty-five. So many kind people wrote to say how much they loved hearing the voice of people of that age so I created Dolly and Selma Burns in *Pinch Me*. In my next book, I'll probably incorporate something from *Pinch Me*. I know what it is, but I won't give it away yet.

In your author Q&A for 29 you explain that you are very influenced by films, especially the dialogue. You also have a master's degree in screenwriting. What is your all-time favorite movie?

My all-time favorite movie is a lovely, touching, and still really funny movie from 1940 called *Christmas in July*, which was written and directed by Preston Sturges (who, next to my husband, is my favorite screenwriter of all time). I can still remember seeing it for the first time as a teenager, on television at the Jersey Shore in Margate after a hot day at the beach. Dick Powell plays a lowly office worker who dreams of winning a big fortune one day so he can marry his girlfriend. His co-workers decide to send him a phony telegram telling him he's won the latest contest he's entered. I don't want to tell you what happens next because I don't want to spoil it for you, but it's so hilarious and earnest at the same time that I have no idea why this movie hasn't garnered the "classic film" status of *It's a Wonderful Life*. This film has definitely influenced my work in terms of writing something that can be funny but heartwarming at the same time. I can only watch it once a year because I don't want to get sick of it, and when I do, it's always with someone who hasn't seen it before so I can see it through their eyes. It never fails to delight. I know it's on DVD, so if you see it, let me know what you think.

What message do you hope readers will take from *Pinch Me?*

Like I said earlier, I was single for a really long time. I never thought I would find him. Believe me, I looked everywhere. Now that I have found him, I don't even care that it took so long. It was worth every minute of waiting. I want people to know that if you are single, no matter how old you are, and you think all the good ones are taken, trust me, your soul mate is out there. You might even start to think that you've got a curse on you, but I'm telling you: you don't. He/ She is out there for you. Plain and simple.

Are you working on a new novel? Will any of the characters in *Pinch Me* appear in your upcoming work?

Did you catch the cameo made by Barbara and Larry Sustamorn from *29* in the very beginning of *Pinch Me?* I thought it was fun to bring them in. I thought a nice trip to Paris was just what Barbara would have needed after everything she went through.

I am working on something new right now, but I never like to jinx what I'm working on by saying what it's about. So far, none of the characters from *Pinch Me* have popped up, but it's not to say they won't. It's fun for me to add a brief appearance from a character from a previous book just to see what they're up to. I miss them when I'm not with them on a day-to-day basis anymore. Sometimes I think about what it would be like if I could have them all over to my house for dinner. I think about what I would serve and where everyone would sit and if they would get along. Who knows . . . maybe that's a book somewhere down the line.

1. Learn more about Adena Halpern on her website, www.adenahalpern.com. You can link through to her Facebook, Twitter, MySpace, and Goodreads pages. Use her website's comment section to ask Adena a question or to tell her about your meeting.

2. Lily uses ancestry.com to find her relatives, eventually locating her cousin Rose, who becomes a great friend. Log on to see if you have any longlost family members in your lineage. Or, try starting a family tree with the help of family members. Share any interesting discoveries with your group.

3. Central to the curse in *Pinch Me* is the "ill-fated chocolate chip cookie recipe." Bake your own "well-fated chocolate chip cookies" to bring to your next book club meeting!

4. If you enjoyed reading *Pinch Me*, check out Adena Halpern's other novels: *29* and *The Ten Best Days of My Life*. You can also read her memoir *Target Underwear and a Vera Want Gown: Notes from a Single Girl's Closet*.